Best wishes to Jim

Lionel Domreis

HAPPY Birthday ALWAYS

The Missing Gambler

———◆———

Lionel A. W. Domreis

This Novel is dedicated to my fellow Veterans
of World War II and The Korean War
who did not return.
MAY THEY ALWAYS BE REMEMBERED,
NEVER FORGOTTEN.

THE MISSING GAMBLER.

with Barney Lange playing the lead,
as the search moves from Portland, Oregon to Australia.
Two young Infantry Division Veterans, both trying to adjust to
Civilian Life
Get Caught up in an International Search.

RETURN TO THE 1940'S

This Romantic Mystery blends 4 books into one. Mystery, Romance, World War II, and a little of the Author's Biography as he brings in Portland landmarks all Seniors remember well. He adds some World War II references to bring you a story of young men, recently out of Combat and trying to establish themselves in a society they left years ago as kids and returned to as men.

It takes place in 1949 when Dirty Words and Murders every day were not commonplace.

The setting is Portland, Oregon and Sydney and Melbourne, Australia.

Barney Lange, Oregon 41st Infantry Division Veteran, is shocked when fellow salesman Frank Beckman leaves town with no forwarding address. Beckman's girl friend Bobbie is very angry. Barney is further challenged when he hears of a Gambler Missing since early 1941.

By a strange twist of circumstances Frank Beckman is located and then Frank and Barney team up in earnest to search for The Missing Gambler.

CAST OF PRINCIPAL CHARACTERS & KEY SCENES

In the introduction. Ray Pearson escapes from Portland, Oregon on the China Queen, a tramp freighter. He takes on the name Jerry Wasco. He leaves a wife Mabel, daughter Ruth and son Kevin. World War II begins a few months later and Wasco's ship is torpedoed.

INTRODUCTION
WHEN THE MISSING GAMBLER BECAME MISSING

It was October 1941. Less than two months before Pearl Harbor shocked the world. Ray Pearson's family was about to experience their own Pearl Harbor. Ray was in bed with his wife. She was sound asleep. Earlier they had made love, something they did less and less the longer they were married.

In their other two bedrooms their High School daughter and grade school son were asleep. This was a different kind of "D" day for Ray. He was leaving, not making a landing. It was his day of "Departure." He had to escape from Portland, Oregon, the city he was born in and had spent all his life in and he couldn't leave any tracks. He had hinted at this to his wife, but she had never taken him seriously.

As to his two children--well, he hadn't been much of a Father to them. He had stayed out late many nights, not getting home until they were in bed. Last night they had dinner together. He would always take with him the delight in their young faces as the four of them ate together. His daughter Ruth even asked if she could give a short prayer of thanks for their being all together.

It was all Ray could do keep from breaking down. Only the overpowering fear in his gut kept him from crying. It was an all consuming fear. He knew he could commit suicide, but that was a shame he would not inflict on his family.

With those thoughts tearing at his mind he was awake most of the night. As usual he left for work before his family was up. He didn't own a car. Bruce, one of his fellow workers picked him up each morning. Bruce's car headed for Northwest Front and Couch where they both worked at Hirsch-Weis. . Front street was the last street before the

Willamette River, on the Downtown side of Portland. Couch was the first street North of Burnside and the Burnside Bridge. There was also an entrance to Hirsch-Weis and White Stag on the Burnside Bridge.

Before you entered either entrance you might have to step over sleeping drunks in the door ways. This part of town, by the bridge, was a part of skid-row.

As they drove Bruce sensed the desperation of his passenger. "Things getting mighty tough for you Ray?"

"Yes, Bruce, you don't know the half of it and I can't tell you. It's one of those things you wouldn't want to hear."

Bruce knew that most factory workers had some skeleton in their closet they kept to themselves. He changed the subject to the oil blockade the United States was proposing against Japan. He could tell Ray wasn't interested so they drove the rest of the way in silence.

Ray's wife always prepared him a bag lunch and he opened it and looked at it. He didn't comment. He knew it would be a long time before Mabel every prepared another one for him.

Noon came and he headed for the door with his lunch bag in hand. Then he saw a car with two suspicious looking men in it. He quickly retraced his steps and headed for the third floor which opened onto the Burnside Bridge. There was no parking on the Bridge, but there was a trolley stop almost opposite the door he just exited. Large concrete markers were imbedded into the pavement making a kind of safety island.[1]

A streetcar was slowing down for the safety island and Ray leaped across the traffic and made it in time to board the Street car. He only went two blocks from First street to Third where he jumped out, looked around quickly and headed into Erickson's Bar on the Northwest Corner of Third and Burnside. Erickson's Bar claimed they had the longest Bar in the West.

For sure it attracted a lot of drunks. Their goal of course was to attract the would be drunks. A bouncer saw him. Ray was out of breath as he said, "This is it Henry."

Henry replied, "Follow me."

---

1   There was a violent snowstorm in Portland about 1950. Big snow plows were used
     to clear the streets and those big blades also scooped up the safety markers.

Henry went to a door, beyond the end of the main bar, inserted a key and Ray followed him inside and Henry carefully locked and checked the door. It was down another hall, then into another locked room and then down some stairs. Then down a passageway to where it ended and a heavy metal door blocked further progress. Henry pressed a button, put his face to a spot covered with a grill and said, "Ray Pearson is here."

A minute later the door was opened by a Chinese man and Ray slipped inside the underground passageway leading to the entrance to the main Chinese Tong. His heart was pounding and he was so short of breath he could hardly breath. He knew he'd had a close one and now he would soon be on his way.

He was led to a very small room. Once inside it he saw it was sparsely furnished. A cot, one piece of furniture that had some resemblance to a dresser, with a pan and a pitcher of water on it. A single light bulb hung from the ceiling. He still had the bag lunch Mabel had prepared, clutched in his hand. Soon another Chinese entered the room and the two Chinese engaged in rapid conversation. Finally one turned to Ray. "You will sail on the China Queen, maybe in 24 hours."

Ray assured them that would be fine and he bowed in thanks several times. One of them pointed at the bag. Ray opened it and said, "My lunch. My wife prepared for me."

Neither Chinese answered and they left the room. Ray sat down and first took out the letter he had written to his wife. He read it. Then he ate his lunch and read it over a dozen more times as he ate. This is what he had written.

Dear Mabel,

I said I might have to leave town. That time has arrived. My gambling debts are so large I have been given only two alternatives Pay my gambling debts now or participate in a robbery in San Francisco. I can disgrace you by leaving town, but I cannot disgrace myself or my family by being a thief and perhaps getting caught and put in Jail for years or the rest of my life.

The mob that has me in it's foils is headed out here by two thugs known as The Brothers.

From now on I am changing all my identity to the name I once gave you in the event I had to leave town. Tell that name to absolutely no one. Do not send the police to try to find me as I am leaving by my own choice and with the help of others who do not want to be involved.

I don't know when I will be able to write. The Brothers will have some kind of a contract out on me, so I can't leave any kind of a trail. I have been a lousy husband. I don't expect you to forgive me. Try to help Ruth and Kevin. I am crushed to do this to them. My heart is broken. With love to all of you.

Ray Pearson.

The Chinese brought him an early dinner that day and suggested he take a shower and then sleep fully dressed. He followed their instructions and weariness overtook him and he slept.

Sometime during the night he was awakened--told it was time for his departure. He was given a dark rain slicker and a similar cap. One of the Chinese blackened his face with something that smelled a lot like shoe polish. Then he was led through a myriad of tunnels and when they exited to a street it was raining and a non-descript car was waiting for them.

Soon looming out of the darkness of the rain and the night he saw a ship. Only a narrow gang plank still connected it to the dock. A minute later he was on board.

A NEW LIFE AND EXTREME SORROW FOR HIS FAMILY.

Ray Pearson was now Jerry Wasco. He found his sleeping accommodations on the China Queen were rough, dirty and bore absolutely no relationship to what he had been used to.

He was allowed to sleep until 8 A.M. and breakfast was a rough and tumble affair, but the food was adequate and seemed to be well prepared. The men were complimentary toward the Chinese Cooks. It was a relief to find would not starve to death or find the food inedible.

He was assigned to a man whose name Bull fit his appearance. Bull was a rough looking character and looked at Wasco's hands and said, "Take a good last look at your hands, Wasco. They aren't going to look nice and pretty like that very long. You're an apprentice seaman and you'll do as I order you to do. As long as I know you're trying I won't beat the hell out of you."

Wasco looked Bull in the eye and replied, "Thank you sir."

To himself Wasco thought, "Making sleeping bags at Hirsch-Weis got boring at times, but it never wore me out. This job isn't going to be boring and I am going to get worn out."

Then he wondered if gambling was a big part of a Seaman's life. Maybe he'd finally make a few bucks as a gambler. There were a lot of questions he wanted to ask Bull, such as what would his duties actually be and where was the ship headed, but he didn't ask.

———◆———

Back in Portland, Oregon the department manager at Hirsch-Weis was told of Ray Pearson's failure to return from work. That evening Mabel and her children kept waiting for him to return. By morning they were worried, but a couple of times Ray had gambled all night.

By the second evening their worry was running very high. By the next morning they were very panicking When Mabel returned from work that evening Ray's letter had arrived. She read it and reread it. So he hadn't been joking. He actually had to leave town.

Mabel knew she could not show the letter to her children. She hid it carefully and made up a story that Ray had called her at work and said he had to leave town due to some gambling debts. **That way she could amend her story as she felt the need.**

Mabel wanted to immediately go to the police, but decided not to. Two days later there was a front page article in The Oregonian.

Armored Car Hijacked in San Francisco.

San Francisco police apparently suspected an Armored Car robbery might occur. They surprised the hijackers and killed two of them. One was badly injured. Neither the Armored Car driver or the two employees were seriously injured.

Mabel said to herself, "Oh Ray, if this was the crime you were to take part in I am so glad you left town."

As each additional day came and went and Ray did not return Mabel noticed her daughter was not able to handle her Dad's absence. Kevin sensed this too and both he and Mabel both took it upon themselves to work hard at keeping Ruth from completely falling apart.

The China Queen's first stop was San Francisco. Ray was told to stay in his quarters. A newsboy came to the top of the gang plank hawking the San Francisco Chronicle. At dinner a copy was passed around. There Ray Pearson, now Jerry Wasco, saw the article on the Armored Car Attempted Heist. His whole body shook as he read the article. He knew that was the heist he had been selected for. Right now he would be either dead, or wounded and in jail. Now he knew for certain his decision was right.

December 7, 1941. Pearl Harbor Attacked.

It was almost like the cliche that's it's an ill wind that doesn't bring someone some good. The over two thousand deaths at Pearl Harbor and the disaster occurring in the Philippines and elsewhere turned our placid life in the United States upside down. Men were dying, men were dropping out of their jobs and enlisting **and suddenly the disappearance of Ray Pearson almost seemed like an everyday occurrence.**

The war prompted Mabel to go to the police with some of her story. She ended up being assigned to a Lieutenant Morton, whose nickname of course was "Salty."

Salty was in the Naval Reserve and informed Mabel that he expected to be called to active duty any day. That didn't surprise Mabel. He promised to keep her information confidential and after going over her story informed her there was nothing he could do.

"Your husband seems to have left voluntarily due to a predicament he was responsible for getting himself into. People leave town for a variety of reasons most of them being they have problems in Portland and are escaping. Many have debts they cannot pay. Some have wives they want to leave, or girl friends. We'd go nuts trying to track them down."

Then Salty added, "Look at it this way Mrs. Pearson. If we could get those people to come back to Portland most of them would just turn around and leave the next day, unless we put them in jail. That would take trials and our courts already are overburdened. Now we have the War to contend with and our manpower is going to be short. Things don't look good for us in this War. The Japanese with those damn Zero's are shooting down all our aircraft. Maybe your husband will enlist and you'll hear from him. I sure hope so for your sake and your children's."

Mabel looked at Salty and extended her hand. "Thank you Lieutenant Morton for your time. I wish you well when you get called to active duty and thank you for serving our country."

Mabel waited until she was out of the police station before she began to cry. **"Oh, Ray, I wish you well too. I wish you well so very much! I guess I wasn't a good enough wife to keep you interested in a home life. I'm sorry for all of us."**

Mabel walked uptown to her office from the Main Precinct on Fourth Avenue. Ray was probably too old to enlist. Where had he gone to hide?

Christmas without Ray Pearson.

Mabel dreaded the approach of Christmas. It certainly was going to be a blue one. Three days before Christmas one of her fellow workers who made it a practice of getting up early each morning and devouring the Oregonian article by article, along with their breakfast, said, "Mabel, did you read the article on the Letter to Santa Claus Contest."

Mabel replied, "I read about the contest, but not the results."

"Well, it was for ten years olds and younger, but apparently your neighbor Ruth won."

"Oh yes, little Ruth, that is the eight year old next door, is a special pal to my Ruth."

"Maybe you should read little Ruth's letter that won her the contest."

"Oh, is it in the Oregonian?"

"Yes, I brought it to work. Here it is."

Mabel Read:

Dear Santa Claus and God,

I know you are related because you both do so much good. Maybe you live together. I'm not asking for anything for myself. I promise I'll never ask for anything more if you'll just help my neighbor Ruth. Her Father has disappeared and she needs him back. Please bring him back to her by Christmas. With love, Ruth Jackson.

Mabel began to sob. Her co-workers couldn't maintain their composure and cried with her. Mabel stammered, "It's a real tear jerker isn't it. Oh Ray, I hope you're safe someplace."

CHRISTMAS FOR MABEL, RUTH AND KEVIN..

It was a disaster for them. Only the increasing tempo of the War brought a little relief. Horrors such as the over 1000 men entombed in the Battleship Arizona at Pearl Harbor made them realize sorrow was in season for Americans all over the United States.

In Oregon the 41st Infantry Division was spread out endeavoring to cover the Oregon and Washington Coasts. All it's members were on a three hour alert. In the State of California the same fears of a Japanese landing on the West Coast prompted them into emergency measures.

Jerry Wasco was at sea on Christmas Day trying to adjust to the rigors of apprentice seaman. These were tempered by his gratefulness to have escaped being a participant in the Armored Car heist. He had constant nightmares dreaming he was captured.

The China Queen, the tramp freighter he was working on, had previously called regular on the Japanese Mainland. Now the crew wanted to stay as far away as possible. As shipping schedules were arranged and rearranged they settled into a routine of carrying munitions, gasoline and supplies from Southern California ports to Australia. Loaded troop ships were being sent to Australia and these had to be supported by tons of equipment and supplies.

On board the China Queen there was much dissension. Many men deserted every time they made port because they feared the slow moving ship was a sitting duck for either a submarine or a Japanese War ship.

By the time January was almost ended their apprehension was with them 24 hours a day. They knew it was going to happen. And one late afternoon it did!

Wasco was on watch so he was above deck when the torpedo hit mid-ship squarely. Then a second torpedo hit just aft of mid-ship. The China Queen seemed to rise up for a second. Then it burst into flames and sank in minutes. The first torpedo threw Wasco overboard and clear of the ship. He was knocked out completely and as he was going down for the third time the water revived him. He was clear of the fire. Debris was everywhere and only a few men were visible. All were looking for something to hold onto.

The attack had come too suddenly for the men to don life preservers. Wasco looked around for a lifeboat or raft that might of been cut loose. Nothing like that was in sight. A few loose boards floated by and he slipped his belt from around his trousers and belted two boards with it, and held on to the slack in the belt.

He figured they were around 100 miles off the Australian Coast. The weather cycle was reversed there and this was summer and the water was not frigid. As he struggled to stay afloat he thought of the thousands of brave sailors that sailed the Mermask run bringing supplies to the Russians. There the German U-boats were sinking a high percent of our ships, and a man could only last minutes in those terrible cold stormy waters.

Then Wasco thought of the Sharks in these tropical waters and he began to shake. With the China Queen now an unwilling guest of Davy Jones locker at the bottom of the sea Wasco tried to count the men that had survived. He was shocked. All he could see was perhaps a dozen.

Each man was holding on to something. In some cases two men were holding on to just one plank. It had been dusk when the torpedoes struck their ship.

Soon the horror of the sinking would be overtaken by the darkness of the night.

The injured cried for help. Ray was unafraid, "At least this won't shame my family. I died helping the War effort. I'm sure the Chinese will notify Mabel, Ruth and Kevin."

—◆—

CHAPTER 1, World War II is over.
The Missing Gambler is still missing. Now Frank Beckman Disappears

It was a very wet Thursday morning. I held firmly onto my hat with one hand and my brief case with the other as I stood on the corner of Southwest Twelfth and Morrison waiting for the light to change. This was the kind of a day to have an inside office job and not be an outside salesman. Finally the light changed to green and I hurried across the street and into the lobby of the Terminal Sales Building. My coat and hat dripping from the rain.

My office was on the sixth floor of the twelve story building. One of the two elevators soon opened it's doors and I stepped inside letting the waiting female employees enter first. That was something I never could figure out. Letting the gals in first--no matter what floor they were headed for and then squirreling around in the elevator to let the gals out first. Well, at least that was the very least of my problems as I was still getting used to being a civilian again after almost five years in the United States Army Infantry.

There had been no elevators in New Guinea. Just a lot of jungle and misery and thousands of Japanese on that eleven hundred mile long island, second largest in the world. The Japs believed it was glorious to die for the Emperor. Will Rogers once said, "You can't believe or trust our leaders. (Politicians) The Japanese hadn't learned that.

So battling for space and entry and exit rights in an elevator was just a momentary diversion of little consequence to me. As I exited I almost ran down the hall to my office as I was at least five minutes late. With my glasses wet and steamed from the inside heat I almost ran into a young lady. Our elbows bumped and I saw she was dabbing at her eyes with a handkerchief. I was embarrassed and tried to come up with an eloquent apology, "I am sorry I was so clumsy"

1

I had grown up with three brothers and no sisters and in our more youthful days we never passed in our very small hall without a nudge or maybe a fist punching the other. So my growing up roots experiences in apologies was definitely lacking.

"Oh, you didn't hurt me. I was crying before you ran into me!"

Well, that was a relief! So I came up with a brilliant, "Are you all right? Do you need some help?"

While I was trying to get my male-female words into gear I was also getting later for work which made me more nervous. I looked more closely at her. She was at least six inches shorter than my one quarter inch less than six feet, had blonde hair and maybe was about a size eight. As to her face and eyes, she apparently didn't want to entirely remove the handkerchief from her face. She did answer, "It's just personal, thanks."

I knew this wasn't Greta Garbo saying I vant to be alone, but right then I felt like running away, so I apologized again, and headed for my office. I hadn't taken five steps past her when I heard her voice, "You wouldn't happen to work for the Standard Register Co. would you?"

I stopped, turned and walked back toward her, "Does it show?"

That brought a slight pleasant note into her obviously distressed state. "No, but I am very concerned over a friend of mine that did work for them. He seems to have disappeared."

The picture suddenly became clearer and it wasn't an oil painting or watercolor to be admired. This lady must be a friend of Frank Beckman! It was only a couple of days ago that we had learned he had taken off for parts unknown.

In my best diplomatic voice I asked, "Do you mean Frank Beckman?"

"Yes, and I was just in your office talking to your Manager, Mr. Sanders. He kindly took a few minutes to talk to me, but made me promise I would not reveal anything we discussed."

"Sounds like Mr. Sanders. Always the cautious person. Frank and I were slight friends. We both fought the miserable battle of New Guinea.

"That's about the way Frank described it. Do you have any idea what has happened to Frank? I thought we were kind of good friends."

I decided to throw caution to the wind. "I don't mean to be personal, but were you his girl friend?"

"I always hoped I was--I was doing my best to be his best friend, but there was a wall between us I never really understood."

Then she began to cry again.

I responded with. "I'm sorry. I need to get to work. I'm Barney Lange. Here is my card and I'll write my home phone on it. At this point I probably don't know anymore than you do, but you could call me at my apartment most any evening and I'll let you know if I have learned anything. My boss isn't very strong on personal messages at the office.

"Oh, thank you, Barney, I desperately need to talk to someone that knows him. I didn't know a soul that knew him. Could I call you this evening?"

"Sure, that's fine. I expect to be home."

'Oh, and my name is Bobbie Day I work for Precision Oil Co on the eighth floor. Oh I feel so relieved. I wondered if I was going to be so sick I would have to go home. Now, just knowing I can talk to you about Frank makes me feel better. Thank you again Barney."

Bobby put out her right hand and squeezed mine in a kind of desperate handshake. The handkerchief was away from her face and I saw a bewildered look on her face. She was pretty. Fine features, but her tears had stained her mascara giving her complexion kind of a blotchy look. I moved by myself to my office door, still half of the long hallway away. I was now at least ten minutes late, but the thought came to me that because Bobby had just left my office she had left some turmoil and my lateness would be inconsequential. Sure enough, the men seemed to be milling around and they made me think of the fact it was only a hundred years earlier that the main wagon trains had arrived via the Oregon Trail in the early 1840's...

It was unbelievable what had transpired in a century. Instead of horses and wagons we now had offices and cars and a big time war I had somehow survived. My two buddies from the University of Oregon I was sworn in on June 25, 1941, just before Pearl Harbor at the Portland Armory, located on N.W. 11th Avenue, one block North of Burnside, had not survived.

The boss looked at me and said, "Now that Barney has decided to arrive I want to talk to all of you."

I walked down the isle, with desks on either side of it, hung up my wet coat and hat in the small adjoining room which served as a cloak and storage room and moved to my desk. By that time the men had all returned to their desks. Mr. Sanders could stand in the back of the room and talk to all of us, but the men had to swivel their chairs around as the desks faced the front of the office.   .

None of us liked sales meetings except on rainy days. One man remarked, "It's sure raining like hell outside. I hope this is a long announcement."

One of the many wit's in the office quickly responded, "The hell you're going to go to when you die isn't going to have any rain."

The first man's response was, "Look who's talking."

Mr. Sanders was obviously agitated and wasn't in the mood for frivolity or gaiety.

He snapped, "O.K., lets quiet down. This is going to be brief so you men can get your stuff together and get out in your territories. I'm sure you noticed the young lady leave my office. I never met her before today."

One of the old timers chimed in with, "I told you not to run around with those young dolls. Boss, did you get her in trouble?"

"Oh shut up Henry. I just look at them. You're the guy I see out with them."

"Wouldn't I like to be. O.K. Boss, I apologize for my unnecessary roughness. It's just this damn weather. I'd like a little sunshine for a change."

"Well, my message this morning isn't going to bring sunshine. I still don't have the slightest idea what happened to Frank Beckman. The tearful young lady that just left my office claims to be a personal friend of Frank's, but she isn't any more anxious to solve this puzzle than I am."

Sanders continued with, "Let's concentrate on our job and not Frank, but please let me know of any rumors that come your way."

There were two big windows at the end of the office and with everyone facing in the direction of the windows the rain pelting down didn't make anyone anxious to leave the office. One man, obviously desirous of prolonging the discussion said, "I bet every man here has at one time or another had the desire to chuck all this damn rain and get out of town. I think it's great that Frank had the gut's to do it. My wife and I both drank a toast to him at dinner last night.

That broke the ice and most of the men started making outrageous remarks as if they were going to actually do it. "I never got to see gay Paree'. I think it's now or never."

Several chimed in with, " Sunny Southern California here we come. Oranges and grapefruit trees in your back yard. Let's see. I'll take the Newport Beach or Malibu territory."

"Mr. Sanders, let's move the whole damn office. Tell the company we all want a transfer or we quit."

Mr. Sanders was getting so nervous I expected him to bite his finger nails. He was really a rather polished and efficient boss, but not far below his very thin skin was a tempest and a hot fire. Some of the men laughed as they saw how irritated he was becoming.

"O.K. you guys, cut out the comics. Time to hit the road and take care of your customers. That's where you make your money."

We all knew that remark was aimed at getting us to spend a minimum amount of time having coffee across the street at Rigg's Pharmacy on the Southwest corner.

———◆———

Riggs Pharmacy was a long established upscale drug store. The only thing old in it was a beautiful marble topped soda fountain. The fountain sold more coffee than sodas and made a wonderful wait if you suddenly came down with a miserable winter cold and had to wait for a prescription. Also if you had kids or grandchildren with you the fountain made their day. Mr. Riggs was not only a nice pleasant guy he was also an excellent businessman.

This Thursday morning the men laughed and joked as we drank coffee, but our minds were not on business. Our minds were on Frank. He had a hell of a lot more nerve and guts than any of us had. As Frank Sinatra would later sing, "He had done it his way."

CHAPTER 2, Bobbie Day calls me.

The rain continued all day without any indication it was ever going to stop. My sales territory was Northeast Portland. At lunch time I was close to Yaws Top Notch in the Hollywood district. In the 1930's and 1940's there wasn't a soul, living or dead, that did not know about Yaws, one of Portland's best known places for hamburgers.

Yaws had competition if for no other reason Portland was a city of a third of a million folks. Other well known competition was the Tik Tok at the corner of Northeast 12th and Sandy, a few blocks east was Munden's ice cream and not a lot further away was Honey Dew Ice Cream at Northeast 26th and Broadway.

As I ate my hamburger at Yaws I spent some time contemplating Bobbie. I wasn't quite certain what she would look like without tears in her eyes, but she was attractive. My mind asked what kind of a relationship had she really had with Frank?

For the rest of the day my mind would bounce between business, the rain, Frank and Bobbie. I stopped at the Grocery store at 5:30 and was back in my apartment by 6 P.M. I was tired and still fighting the Malaria I had almost died from in the Jungle. I slipped out of my clothes and crawled in bed for an hours nap, hoping I could wake up at 7 P.M. and fix myself my usual healthy, but not too interesting dinner.

At 7 P.M. I was in deep sleep, but my phone awakened me.

"Oh, you are there! I was just going to hang up. This is Bobbie, can you talk? Did I wake you up? You sound kind of spaced out."

My apartment was not only old, poorly furnished, but it was also lonely street. I was pleased to have anyone call me. "I fell asleep and am glad you woke me up. Otherwise I'd of slept all evening and stayed awake all night."

Bobbie answered, "I have the same problem, but I still live with my Mother and we both keep each other from falling into that trap. I wanted to apologize for my tears this morning. I told my Mother about running into you and she insisted I call you."

"Bobbie, no apology is needed. Our office is plenty wound up over Frank."

"Oh, that is interesting. At least I am not alone."

"It was almost funny. One of the men accused the Boss of having an affair with you and causing you to cry."

"Oh, my. I did cause trouble didn't I. Can I ask you to tell your Boss I am sorry?"

"That won't be necessary. They found out you were inquiring about Frank and I'm sorry to say I don't know any more at this time."

"Barney, I understand. Could I give you my phone number and if you come up with any news I'd sure appreciate a call. I think I'm driving my Mother crazy as well as the gals I work with. May I add another comment."

"Sure."

"Right after Pearl Harbor they asked kids to write letters to Santa Claus. A girl wrote asking Santa Claus to bring back her neighbor's missing Father. Her letter just ruined my Christmas. I have worried about her since. I went so far as to pressure my Dad into making inquiries. He did find out the man Gambled a lot, but I didn't care what he did. His daughter was begging for his return."

Bobbie continued with, "Then two years ago my Dad died, and now Frank disappears and I guess I feel like all the men are leaving us."

Whenever anyone started telling me about their losses of loved ones I was severely tempted to tell them about my own experiences--but for now I held off and didn't bring my past into the conversation. Instead I asked, "Any word since about the Missing Gambler?"

"No word, Barney, and so many of our family friends lost men in the war that I guess I felt our war heroes who gave their lives were more important. My Dad was really a war hero. He worked long hours in the shipyards and had a heart attack the day the war finally ended. He rallied for a few years, but finally passed on. He was fifteen years older than my Mother so he did live until he was sixty-three. Mom and I sure do miss him."

'Bobbie, maybe I understand a lot more than I am indicating."

"I'm sure you do, Barney, any overseas Veteran has seen a lot."

"There are however several men from my Infantry Division that are in the Portland Police Department. Maybe I'll stop by and chew the fat with them and see if they have any suggestions."

"Oh, Barney, that would be wonderful. That would help me a lot."

"I'll bring up the subject of the Missing Gambler also. Maybe they have news on him."

"My Mother would appreciate that also. She called a number of times, but never received any news. Finally she had kind of a row with the police and gave up. Afterwards she did call them back and apologize."

"Bobbie, can you give me some names in the case of the Missing Gambler?"

"Oh yes, I know them by heart. Ruth was the neighbor girl that wrote the letter. The missing gambler was Ray Pearson. His wife was Mabel. The actual daughter was also Ruth. The younger brother was Kevin. They lived next door to the girl that wrote the letter.

Right then my head began to ache. I was asking myself if I wasn't just being a damn fool again. Trying to help someone--sure the whole world needed help, and maybe after what I had been through with an unfaithful wife my need for help should get some priority. Well---I felt suddenly very tired. I said to Bobbie, "I'll stop by the police department and call you."

I think she could sense I was tired. She was profound in her thanks.

We hung up, I fixed myself some dinner and read the Oregonian slowly and completely as I ate. I then went over my prospect list and tossed some customer ideas around, but my severe tiredness had not left me. I took a shower and went to bed.

CHAPTER 3, To the Portland Police Main Precinct.

Thursday morning the men laughed and joked after we left the office and had our coffee at Riggs Pharmacy. Frank hadn't given us any indication of his planned disappearance as he didn't want anyone to know he was just marking time---for what--and where?

"He was smart like Truman. He knew the buck stopped with him and he'd make the decision when the time came. We weren't close friends. Whatever he was Frank played his cards close to his vest.

Instead of heading for my territory I headed for the Portland Police Precinct on Southwest Fourth Ave, about eight blocks East of my Terminal Sales office. When I entered the Police Department I said to the duty officer, "I was in the 41st Infantry Division. Some of the Military Police in our outfit went to work for the police department. I heard that Fizz Fitzgibbon and Dud Dudley were two of those."

"I think you have their last names correct, but maybe not their first names, Sir."

I laughed, "I forgot we're back in civilization. That's the way I remember them." [2]

"You may think this is civilization buddy, but by the end of the day we're thinking the City of Portland has gone to hell. That no one is civilized anymore."

"Isn't that the truth, Officer. The War is never over for the police department."

"Right on, buddy. Let's see now. Fitzgibbon and Dudley. One of them is on duty right now! you're lucky, I think Fitzgibbon is on coffee break. What shall I tell him?"

"Tell him there's a guy out front that tracked him down from Biak. He owes me $100.00"

"That'll get him up front here in a hurry."

---

2   Factually many 41st Division Veterans went to work for police departments. One became the Portland Police Chief and another Commanded the Oregon State Police Department for a long and very distinguished career.

When Fizz appeared the duty officer said, "This guy says you owe him money from Biak, wherever that is. Maybe you should just lock him up."

It took Fizz several seconds to recognize me. Then he laughed, "Oh, Yeh, I remember this guy. He spent most of his time in the stockade. I should have memorized his name, but right now I can't recall it."

"It's Barney Lange. I was never in the stockade."

"Sorry, Barney, just kidding. I do recall I almost locked you up for trying to impersonate a soldier. Now I suppose you're trying to impersonate a civilian. Ain't you never going to learn?"

My mind went back to those days overseas when the MP's were always teasing us.

Fizz realized he had non-plussed me. He said, "Now I remember you better, Barney. You weren't one of those guys that lipped off all the time. I think you were trying to impersonate a gentleman. In the Army that only goes so far. How about a cup of coffee?".

I'd just had two cups of coffee at the old marble ice cream counter at Riggs pharmacy and wasn't quite certain if I could hold another cup, but replied, "O.K. and I do have something that I wanted to run past you."

I followed Fizz down a non-descript hall that needed repair and painting. The building wasn't so old, but the doors, their casings and the walls were just made of wood and plaster. I had grown up working on property and noticed the condition of any building I entered. I knew the police operated 24 hour's a day, seven day a week and one days use might equal a whole week for a private business. There were no five day weeks for the police department. Weekends they had to go into overdrive to handle the drinking, partying and various other mischief..

I often thought of my first Christmas back in the United States. I had returned to the States just the month before. I called my wife. She said, "I won't be down to see you I am in love with someone else."

George and Goodwin had died, so I took the Bus to Los Angeles, stayed at the same YMCA George and Goodwin and I had stayed at when we got those two weekend passes from Camp Roberts. I spent that first Christmas eve sitting at the lunch counter of a small cafe drinking coffee. The Los Angeles police department was sending out emergency broadcasts. Twenty five motorists had been killed and 300 were hospitalized. The hospitals were full--please don't drive--please just stay home--so in my first few weeks home I had learned the Police Departments didn't even get Christmas Eve off--instead they got to work overtime handling the dead and injured.

They weren't singing, "Silent Night, Holy Night."

I was tempted to tell Fizz that story, but as he handed me a cup of coffee I got right to the point. I said, "I've got two questions, Fizz. First a guy quit working for us, but he quit so he isn't a missing person. His girl friend is pretty shook up. Any suggestions on how to find him?"

Fizz looked at me, "Barney, you are one of the nicer guys, but don't go around trying to help everybody. You wouldn't believe how many missing person calls we get each day. They drive us nuts. It's usually money, equipment, and all kinds of relatives. Also women calling trying to find men, but some are the reverse, men trying to locate a woman. If it involves wives and kids we do our best, but someone has to file a missing persons report."

"He never told his girl friend he was leaving town."

"So, he's not missing. Maybe he's on a vacation."

"His phone is disconnected."

"So who needs a phone when they are on vacation? You can check where he lived. If he has moved out and paid his rent he can leave. Isn't that what we went through those five years in the service for? The guy wants to leave town!. Maybe someone like his girl friend was putting some pressure on him and so he left."

"So you're suggesting I drop the matter and go about minding my own business."

"Barney, do what you feel you have to, but in this police business we haven't got the time for problems that don't have a sound basis for our involvement."

"You sound like you have that statement down pat."

"Look at the facts, Barney, Hell, we're sympathetic--don't you ever believe we aren't compassionate, but we're here to uphold the law and not mess into matters that don't concern us."

"You're probably right, Fizz. Now, I do have another man to inquire about. His name was Ray Pearson, and it is the case of the Missing Gambler."

I gave Fizz the little information I knew about Ruth and the letter to Santa Clause begging for the return of her Father. As I finished he looked at me and smiled, "Barney, you are a soft touch, but I will inquire around. I was in the National Guard in Pendleton. The Division had just been called to active duty at Camp Murray, September 16, 1940. I wasn't in the Police Department then. We were living in tents in the mud. Remember it was called, "Swamp Murray."

"Go check with his landlord. See if there is any clue there. Give me your home phone number. I'll call if I come up with an idea, but I can't promise anything."

"That makes sense and I know you are busy. Thanks for your time."

———◆———

I walked back to my car. I had never visited Frank at his apartment, but I knew exactly where it was. That was because in my last 3 years of grade school my Journal route had been next to the Church at Southeast corner of Northeast 24th and Broadway.

From the Police Headquarters it was an easy short drive. I went North a couple of blocks to Burnside, crossed the Willamette River on the Burnside Bridge and turned left to the Sears Roebuck store. Then right in front of Sears, following along the North Side of Sullivan's gulch, (where the Lloyd Center is now) to Northeast 15th and Broadway. Then right up Broadway to N.E. 24th and then right to Frank's apartment house..

I rang the landlord's buzzer and told him I worked with Frank and we were told he quit his job and his phone had been disconnected. I was wondering if he knew where Frank had gone.

The landlord was kind of a grizzly looking character in perhaps his fifties. He glared at me and I wasn't surprised when he said, "I don't know if it's any of your business do I?"

I had learned the "Yes, but," theory of selling. It goes this way. First never argue with a customer. Try to agree with him, but after you do so say "but." and then say your piece.

So I fired away with, "I guess you're right, but Frank and I were fellow Army buddies and I mean him no harm. I promise you that. I'm not trying to collect any money from him."

Old grizzly had the door halfway shut on me. My "Yes, but," apparently worked just a little. He didn't shut the door on me and looked me over carefully this time.

Then he said, "On the other hand if you asked me if Frank's old apartment was vacant and for rent I guess the guy that owns this building would raise hell with me if I lied."

Right then I knew it was time to shut up and hope old grizzly would talk a little more.

And he did. Grizzly said, "So I'll tell you. Frank gave me his notice thirty days before he moved out. He told us he could not afford to lose any money and he had been planning a trip for a long time. I asked him if he cared to give me a forwarding address and he gave me a post Office Box number. Then he made me promise I would not give it to anyone."

"Have you rented his apartment?"

This time the old geezer almost smiled. Yes, it's rented. In case you're about to ask if you can snoop around his apartment let me tell you a little old lady retired lady moved into it and don't you try pestering her. I'll call the police on you if you try."

"I don't plan to try."

"My old lady and I carefully cleaned the apartment before she moved in. I can tell you he didn't leave any clues behind as to where he was going.

He was in the Infantry in the South Pacific. Badly wounded he once told me. He earned the right to go where he wanted to go. He paid his rent and was a good tenant. That's all I can say and don't leave me your card. I ain't going to call you."

"That's fair enough. I'm sure you're busy. Thank you for your time."

Grizzly shut the door quickly so I left. I was up to strike two right now and I hadn't the faintest idea if my mind would pitch me any better ideas. Was Frank Beckman, the quiet guy, really a Dr. Jeckle and Mr. Hyde? He didn't seem the kind to lead a double life, but I guess like the guy I actually knew who had been married twelve times the unexpected happened every day.

Then my thoughts went to Ray Pearson, the Missing Gambler. So he took off years ago and left a wife and two kids.

Suddenly I asked myself, "Could Frank Beckman have a much more serious problem than just avoiding Bobbie. Maybe he had several wives, or maybe just one and Bobbie was pressuring him to marry her."

I sat in my car and knew Fizz was probably right. Folks had a myriad of problems and they often hid most of them and only told you what they felt like at the time.

People even lied to their Attorneys. And what about people lying to themselves. Most people knew the difference between right and wrong, but when the when the wrong opportunity presented itself they did not have the decency to decline.

Yes, that was probably it. Like the guy said, "The devil made me do it."

It was almost noon. I had used up the entire morning worrying about other people's business and had not made a single business call in my own territory. "Shame on me."

It hadn't rained for a couple of hours, but the clouds had moved back in place and the rain decided to go all out and not be just a drizzle. Today I had brought my lunch, two peanut butter sandwiches, an apple and a small thermos of coffee. My Newsweek magazine had arrived yesterday. I could relax read it while I ate and this was an opportunity to scan it quickly I did have one very good customer I could call on and maybe get out of the rain.

CHAPTER 4, World Headquarters, Jantzen Knitting Mills

The April showers were getting on my nerves like the rain all winter. I was reminded of the couple of weeks sales training I had received a couple of years ago. It was in Los Angeles and the trainer was an old timer. He was Jewish and sure knew his stuff. I asked him a million questions and he gave me first class answers. One of the things he had stressed was that it was easy to not put in a full day in selling. An outside salesman could think of a hundred things to do rather than call on customers.

The company had put me up in a downtown Los Angeles Hotel, but the timing was terrible. Apparently General Motors and others had convinced the city fathers that streetcars were now obsolete and that GM buses would do the job better. So they were tearing out the streetcar tracks around the hotel during the night, so as to cause minimum traffic problems. Those jack hammers kept me awake most of the night. I sure hoped they would not take out those convenient streetcars out of Portland.

Another thing the Jewish salesman had stressed was that you had to continually call on new customers. It was easier to go back to your regular customers, but many small businesses were growing and you needed to get out there and get started with new accounts.

My best customer was Jantzen Knitting Mills located at Seventeenth and Sandy Boulevard with the huge billboard of the Jantzen Swim girl on top of the one story building.

In the third, fourth and fifth grades I stood outside the employees exit selling the Saturday Evening Post one day a week. Another Day outside Doernbecker Furniture eleven blocks East. (Doernbecker later donated just $50,000 to start the Doernbecker Crippled Children's Hospital. Now it is a giant Hospital at the U of O Health Science Center. The old Doernbecker plant is a multi-level storage locker. Co-incidentally our other big furniture plant, the B.P. Johns, was where Johns Landing is on Southwest Macadam Ave.)

Now twenty years later I was a Systems Consultant to Jantzen Knitting Mills. Part of my job with Standard Register Co.

At that time Standard Register held the exclusive patent rights to the pin feed platen, a device that controlled the passage of paper going through various office machines. Millions would tear off the edges of the paper to get rid of the little pin holes.[3]

Standard Register like Jantzen Knitting Mills would survive to the 21st Century.

One thing about a rainy day like today--folks are a little more receptive to you--almost like they don't want to throw you out on such a miserable day. Especially if you are polite and don't try to cram your product or services down their throat.

In the block just East of Jantzen was a big shoe. The shoe was actually bigger than the Jantzen sign. As a kid in the thirties I watched that shoe being built.

Just twenty blocks further East, at Northeast 37th and Sandy, was a huge milk bottle. In the thirties it was the Stigerwald Dairy. Then if you went four more blocks East, on the very same corner Fred Meyer build his second store. The next store on Sandy found, one couple refused to sell so Freddy built the store around their house with on and off ramps to the roof parking on either side of the house.[4]

The rain never let up all day and it was tough going making cold calls. Trying to make a good first impression and not getting tossed out unceremoniously. I tried to concentrate on what another older salesman had told me. His name was B.M. Mason. He claimed the harder it rains on any one day it was going to rain that much less for the rest of the year. "So rain hard today and get it over with."

---

3   At the time these pages were being written by the Author was playing the part of a snow-bird in Mesa, Arizona The Standard Register-Ping Ladies Golf Tournament was being played in adjacent Phoenix.

4   The house I grew up in at Northeast 28th & Wasco was first moved by Hyster for their world headquarters. Then Fred Meyer took over built a huge store. My home space is now in Freddy's parking lot.

A few blocks North of Jantzen was both the Betsy Ross Bakery and the Davidson's Bakery. As a kid I had sold lots of magazines to the bakers. During the bread rising and baking cycles, they would sit in their own lounges, which were mezzanines, and read.

They pulled the bread out of the deep ovens with big flat wooden ladles. The broken bread was tossed into a wood barrel and sold for one penny a loaf to the employees. They included me and my Dad being out of work a lot of the depression I could buy one loaf of bread from the one penny I made for selling a Saturday Evening Post.

Today I stopped at Davidson's and got some day old bread and some cup cakes. I never saw a cupcake or cinnamon role overseas. It was like returning to my roots to walk into Davidson's or Betty Ross as a 30 year old, some twenty years later. Near the end of the war we got a California Corporation Attorney as a private. His Mother would send him a monthly cake with a pint of bourbon in the center of the cake. The cake was smashed, but the Bourbon survived.

Back in my apartment by 6 P.M. I quickly removed my wet clothes, put on my pajamas and crawled into bed, and fell asleep right away. I woke up five hours later drenched with perspiration and dragged myself into my shower and was eating dinner by 11:30 P.M. I read the Oregonian as I ate, brushed my teeth and went back to bed being grateful that I wasn't buried under one of those little white crosses in a clearing in the Jungle.

CHAPTER 5, Thank God it's Friday.

There was something about Friday that brought great joy to those that got Saturday and Sunday off. Even the businesses you called on seemed to be a little more cordial. Some of the more stupid salesmen had convinced themselves to not even make calls Friday afternoon. I found that rumor was all wrong. I found office people often didn't want to start any new projects on Friday and might be receptive to a pleasant salesman giving them an excuse not to work. .

As I made calls in my territory that morning my travel took me up Broadway and as I passed Northeast 33rd I of course thought of my grade school Fernwood, just two blocks North and Grant High just two more blocks North.

At Grant High school the Law of Diminishing Returns would become fixed in my mind forever. My favorite teacher was my Economics teacher Mr. Horning. I was so impressed that now well over 50 years later I can still quote it word for word. It was, "When in a given state of the arts the addition of productive efforts will result in less than a proportionate return."

I found even in the Infantry in the Jungle that was true. Unfortunately, some of the higher ranking Officers never recognized that. Another thing that helped Mr. Horning to always remain in my memory was: "At the start of the fall term in High School many of the teachers would start the first fall class with complete details of how they went to Europe, or some exotic spot that a young man like myself couldn't relate to. But, Mr. Horning had a different story. He had to work all summer and his job was delivering heavy dirty gunny sacks of Gasco Briquettes.

It was such a dirty oily job he couldn't clean up totally at the end of the day. So his wife would banish him to a tent in the yard for the summer. I thought that was terrible until I spent those years in the New Guinea Jungle. We were filthy, dirty, sick and bedraggled every day, too.

I would have gladly exchanged that for being banished to a tent in the yard and delivering Gasco Briquettes.

While I had been trying to concentrate on work this Friday morning my mind had been telling me I should I go to the Oregonian Newspaper Library and hope the Librarian would dig up some old newspaper clippings on the **Missing Gambler.**. I felt I could get help via George Vanelli, the General Circulation Manager. George was one of those guys everyone liked.

Way back in 1936 the Oregonian was reorganized by a Col. Guy T. Viskniski, an ex-Russian Colonel and then efficiency expert. I was one of two Oregonian Carriers picked to take the Circulation Management Courses and while just a Junior in High School I became Branch Manager of their office at SE 13th and Morrison. Complete with Roll-top desk![5]

So I tried George's office first and he was in. "Nice to see you, Barney. What brings you in this pleasant day?"

"I'm hiding from the weather."

"Think about it when you were a Branch Manager in High School and had to get up at 3:30 A.M. in weather like this."

"You know, George, the Army made that seem like a picnic."

"Are you here on a Mission, or just hello?"

"Both. I explained to George what little I knew about The Missing Gambler. Also that one of our salesmen was missing. George escorted me personally to the Librarian. She quickly responded with, "I can find that in less than five minutes. I remember the name Ruth now that you mention it. Everyone has a Ruth in their family tree and all our sympathies went to Ruth. I do know one thing for certain there never was an article in this newspaper indicating the Father was ever found."

I replied, "I'm sorry to hear that. May I just sit down and wait while you look?"

"Excellent. It won't take long. Then you won't have to come back."

———◆———

In five minutes the Librarian brought back a file. "It is unusual for me to keep a separate file. The man was Ray Pearson. Here is what we have on him."

---

5   True story.

She handed me the file and I carefully went through it. When I finished I was disappointed. The Librarian looked at me, but did not say anything.

I hoped that if I discussed it with her perhaps she had some information missing from the file. I looked her in the eye. "I see he worked near Northwest First Street near where I worked one summer for the Noon Bag Company."

I figured she knew where that was, just one block behind the big White Stag sign. It was just off the Burnside Bridge and the ramp was very high there and you could go just a couple of blocks to Southwest First Avenue. I said to the Librarian. "I recall there were some so called Chinese Gambling Dens only a couple blocks South on First Avenue."

The Librarian just said, "Oh."

I knew that was how it was. Most folks had been to the Chinese Gambling, maybe only once for curiosity.

One of my high school buddies who was a lot more sophisticated than I took me there. I bet one dollar and lost it. It was probably the most illicit thing I had done in my entire life. [6]

Still trying to get the Librarian to speak I said, "When I worked under Mr. Cruickshank and Mr. Dowling, the Manager of the Noon Bag Company the employees got paid in Cash on Friday. Many of them gambled before they went home and their wives were forced to come down Friday at paytime and take the pay and their husbands home.

I thought I wasn't ever going to get a word out of the Librarian, but my personal experiences that summer at the Noon Bag Company finally broke the ice. I wondered afterwards if perhaps the Librarian and her friends hadn't dropped a few bucks in those so called Gambling Dens. Whatever it was the Librarian said, "The newspaper articles don't say he was a gambler. I picked up some unsubstantiated scuttlebutt from our reporters was that he was a gambler and he had to get out of town. He also had an alias he used in gambling circles. Now let me think, our reporters had all kinds of unofficial tipsters working for the police department."

---

6   True story.

23

"Let me look at that file again. No there is nothing there, but I guess it was your comment about the Chinese Gambling. Yes, I recall now! There was a rumor that he was known in Chinese Gambling circles, but he was well liked there. They took a shine to him and tried to help him. Yes, I think that was it. Maybe they helped him get out of town because he owed big dollars to some kind of a mob group that the Chinese didn't like."

I thought to myself that comment was sure interesting. I figured the Chinese were not into big time gambling and they were kind enough to not want to see someone taken to the cleaners. I did not understand anyone stupid enough to gamble and loose their weeks pay of $15.00. For that I worked there from 8 A.M. until 6 P.M. But I kept my job as Branch Manager for the Oregonian so I was up for that at 3:30 A.M. Then in the evening I had to be back at the branch at 6:45 for the evening papers, and to get the carriers out making their collections and soliciting new orders. Additionally I had a route of 125 papers a day of my own.[7]

Then four years later when I got into the Army I got $21.00 a month less $6.60 insurance. Well I was doing better now. The Librarian said, "I've got to get back to my other work, Barney. May I return the file now?

I thanked her, but left a parting shot. "If you think of anything I sure would appreciate a call."

I left my card, but she said nothing. It was time for me to go back to work

My first three calls were on businesses which followed the rule. They didn't want to work the rest of the afternoon, but really didn't want to talk about their business, just about anything else. So I made the calls short.

The fourth call was the way to end the week. Here was a guy that had taken over his Dad's small lumber yard. When I pulled my blue coupe into the parking area I could see into the yard and he was just getting off a Hyster straddle lift truck.

---

7   Again true.

From the third grade until I went into the Army I lived in the next block to the Hyster World Headquarters. In the third, fourth and fifth grades I had gone down the assembly line in the plant selling the Saturday Evening Post.

Mr. Gustav Grab, who invented the Straddle Lift Truck and the Presto Log Machines always bought a Post. When one of the office gals backed over my bike he personally told a welder on one of the Presto Log Machines to weld my bike back in place. Across from Hyster was the Willamette Iron and Steel plant. [8]

When I got in the office of the small firm the driver of the Straddle Lift truck had just entered from the yard entrance. He was perhaps 5'10", muscular with a pleasant smile.

He was obviously the kind of a guy people liked to deal with. He was maybe only 28 years old and his straight brown hair was sticking out of a baseball cap.

He invited me into his tiny office, put his dirty shoes on his desk and I could tell he was ready to call it a day. I knew my time was short so I explained what I did and who I worked for and asked him the key question, "Are you 100% satisfied with your billing, your collections and your inventory records."

He looked at me as if I had kicked him in the teeth. "Very strange you come in here on a Friday afternoon asking such a crazy question. I think it's a set up question and you know damn well a small business like mine goes from one paperwork panic to another."

Then he said, "Tell me about your own business training. Do you know a damn thing about accounting or are you one of those guys that get by bluffing his way through?"

I opened my brief case and took out a sheet of paper upon which was my background including my taking accounting at the University of Oregon through Advanced Cost Accounting.

---

8   True and I thought I was having fun. Everyone was always so nice to me.

He started to just glance at it--then he seemed to start all over and was really scrutinizing it. Finally he said, "So you grew up working on houses besides all this business training. I think you're the kind of a guy I sure could use when I get big enough to pay for a full time man. Right now I have no one really skilled and my Accountant doesn't know a 2 × 4 from a floor joist."

He had introduced himself as Dave Block. I said, "Mr. Block, I would need to look over your present system, along with your comments as to what you think of each part of it. Then I can make some recommendations."

"How long will it take, and how much will it cost."

"Mr. Block, there will come a time when consultants will charge you a lot for this, but for right now part of my job with Standard Register is to do this analysis for nothing."

He took his feet off his desk, stood up and said, "It's a deal, when do you want to start?"

I said, "How about Monday after lunch?"

"Excellent, I will get some of my questions together and meet me here at noon Monday and I'll take you to lunch and we'll get started. I eat on the run, so we'll just get a hamburger.. Let's make it about 12:30 Monday."

We talked for a few minutes and shook hands and it was only a little after 5 P.M. when I left. This guy needed me and I needed more and more business to keep the wheels of Standard Register going so a pay check would come to me twice a month.

What a great way to end Friday afternoon. I felt like celebrating. That's what kept salesmen like myself going-----we had a genuine product and service that helped businessmen and women successful in their business. Hallelujah!

CHAPTER 6, Friday evening. Recalling Homer and Billy

I stopped at the Grocery store and bought some bread, milk, some vegetables and some fresh flounder. I was still running a fever and knew I'd better eat before I fell asleep.

As I fixed and ate my dinner my mind went to a couple of soldiers from Texas. They were cousins, Homer and Billy Barnes. The latter was so short Homer called him Billy the Kid. They were in the 32nd Infantry Division. We met on the troop ship leaving Port Moresby and returning to the States. I was leaning against the rail, thrilled to be escaping from almost three years in the South Pacific. Offsetting that was the letters from my wife had stopped over a year ago and I knew she was involved with one or more men in the States.

The only radio station we could reach from New Guinea was one manned by Tokyo Rose. She played all those tunes we loved and in-between numbers would brain wash us with messages that always said two things;

1. We would never make it back alive.

2. Our wives and Sweethearts were being unfaithful to us.

I knew she was 50% right, and for many she was 100% correct. As I looked at the ship's wash as it zigged and sagged every six minutes, so a Jap sub could not take a good bearing on it Billy looked at me and then at Homer and said, "It looks like this man is out of Aces."

No one returned from New Guinea or the Schouten Islands just north of them, including Bloody Biak, looking healthy. Homer and Billy were no exception. Each day we looked more like Jungle Lizards. Biak was less than 100 miles off the equator. Our skin and hair were as scraggy as our clothes. Our eyes were sunken and I was down from 175 pounds to 110. Lack of water and anything resembling a balanced diet caused our bodies to cannibalize itself.

Right off Homer and Billy asked me where I had grown up. When I said Portland, Oregon they suddenly treated me as some kind of a hero. They said their folks were share croppers. The war had been a bonanza for them. They were able to give up share cropping and come West and go to work for the Kaiser Shipyards in Portland, Oregon. With the gambling money Homer and Billy had sent them, plus their excellent earnings in the shipyards, both families had bought houses in North Portland, making their commute to work minimum.

As to moving from the dry plains of Texas county to soggy Portland--well that was something they weren't quite used to and they might return to Texas after the War. . However, the thrill of building ships, and working with the dedicated ship yard workers made up for the weather a dozen times over. Homer and Billy informed me that during any lull in the fighting they gambled. Homer said, "After gambling with your life for perhaps a month, surely gambling with cards for a couple of days isn't any more sin."

They offered to teach me the gambling tricks they knew. Finally, they got me into one game, which they obviously rigged, and I came out of it over $100.00 ahead. Knowing my wife had deserted me, and had all my savings, made that $100 almost a pot of gold to me, but I still mentally knew I could never become a gambler.

Homer was particularly incensed over Pearl Harbor. "Our damn Navy, Army and Air Force officers were too busy getting dressed up in their fancy uniforms and going to parties and dances in Honolulu to even consider the Japanese would attack. Then they force a bunch of share croppers like Homer and I and guys like you Barney, to bail them out. If we ever got those guys in Texas we'd Tar and Feather them, and then roast them alive. Think of over 1000 poor Navy guys entombed in the Harbor in the Battleship Arizona."

Then he added, "And people bitch because guys play cards."

Somehow I left that trip ship grateful that I had met part of a family of sharecroppers. In my book they made more sense than most politicians and I knew Will Rogers, if he had been still alive would have agreed.

We had kept in touch and after the war Homer and Billy had gotten jobs running Gambling Casinos on Cruise ships. The Cruise ships used play money and every couple of days had real auctions and many of the prizes had substantial value. Homer and Billy had become Actors. They told folks fancy stories of their past gambling days claiming to be ex-big time Las Vegas and Reno gamblers. They dated all kinds of beautiful ladies on board ship and both had almost married a couple of times. They backed out because they loved their work more.

However, it was stories like mine, that kept them from getting married. Homer and Billy both agreed that Gambling for money was one thing, but gambling that you would enjoy spending the rest of your life with a woman was one they weren't ready for.

I had since joined that same club. I had an additional reason. My former wife had in fact spent all my allotment and savings so I didn't have a nest egg like so many service men had. Secondly, I was just leery, and didn't want more responsibility that might turn into another disaster.   In summary I lacked confidence and my common sense said no for the time being.

I recalled that Homer and Billy's folks had indeed moved back to a small town in Texas and they bought two duplexes next to each other. Homer and Billy with their Army savings each bought half of a duplex with their parents. The parents lived in one half and rented out their son's halves. The acquired skills in the shipyards gave them employment in nearby cities and they were doing all right.

Homer had said to me, "Barney, you know how I bitched on that troopship about Pearl Harbor. Look what it did for my folks. No longer beaten and down trod sharecroppers, but now property owners with good jobs."

Then he would become very somber, "Except for the millions killed in the war. Some of my best buddies." I knew what he meant.

I decided to call Homer's folks. Mrs. Barnes answered the phone, and seemed very pleased to hear from me. "Why, Barney Lange, why haven't you all been visitin' us folks. Why we is almost next of kin to you."

I allowed to myself they all wuz pleasant folk, and after making all the inquiries about their health and what they were doing, I asked about Homer and Billy. "They all was jus' fine, thank you--why them guys are havin' the time of their lives. Just eatin', drinkin', gamblin' and letting the prettiest girls chase em. We all is expectin' some kind of call from them soon. They are on their way to Australia if my memory is still good."

I told Mrs. Barnes about the missing Frank Beckman and the Missing Gambler and she said she would pass the word along to Homer and Billy. Also why didn't I call Billy's Mother and Dad. I promised I would, and made the call right after talking to Homer's Mom.

I got the kind the same kind of enthusiastic pleasant response. I had met them after the War in Portland before they moved back to Texas so the parents and I were kind of buddies.

I then took a hot shower, put on clean pajamas and went to bed. Maybe I would dream about Homer and Billy, and not some stupid dream that I had been sent back to New Guinea. That dream was driving me nuts. Certainly that war couldn't ignite again.   Why   did   our subconscious, in our dreams, not let us forget the past. It wasn't fair. It was double jeopardy!

CHAPTER 7, Saturday Morning, I called Bobbie Day.

One of my greatest fears now was that I was dealing with gals that had spent a lot of time entertaining soldiers while I was overseas in the jungle. It was frightening to observe how smooth they could be. They were smart enough to get pregnant on purpose.

For certain I was running scared.

So now I was divorced. Who could I trust. She got $50.00 a month. First I got $1.40 a month. Overseas pay added $6.00 a month. Likewise I bore the stigma of divorce. So who could trust me. Would a parent trust me. Why was I divorced. Mostly I was just angry at myself for getting married the month before I went overseas.

I often picked on myself. Here I was thirty and still single. Obviously I had screwed up and was deathly afraid I would do it again. I said to one nice lady, "You're worried over your daughter dating a divorced man. I'll bet I'm more worried than you are."

I could tell she didn't know what I meant. Was I talking about her daughter?

———

I luxuriated in fixing myself a leisurely breakfast of hot-cakes and an egg and reading the entire Oregonian as well. I thought of Bobbie several times. Finally I picked up the phone and called her. She answered, "What a nice way to start Saturday morning. I have been wondering if you had any news."

I replied, "At what degree is your fretting today."

Her joviality diminished considerably as she answered, "I'm still mad as hell."

Then she added, "I don't think I'm really as bad as I sound."

I replied, "I'm not sure what you mean."

She answered, "I'm not the kind of a girl that goes around swearing, but I guess I'm a perfect example of the statement 'Hell hath no fury like a woman scorned!'"

We spent the next 15 minutes discussing my trip to the Oregonian and my calling Mrs. Barnes last night. Bobbie seemed very excited I was working at it. She said, "My girl friend Sue has been bugging me to go to the Uptown Ballroom tonight and get out and socialize a little. Do you ever go there?"

"Only I had a few times. Never got to know anyone that goes there regularly, but I need to get out and meet a few people that don't lead me astray. I think these gals that danced at the USO during the War are so experienced I feel like a fly running into spiders."

Bobbie really laughed at that remark. "Barney, I was too young for that. I graduated from High School the year the War ended. My Mother never let me go to the USO and I only had a few dates my Senior Year in High School and they were with students at Grant High."

I calculated quickly. She graduated in 1945. I graduated from Grant in 1938. That meant she wasn't running around during the war in the unfaithful crowd my wife was. That relieved me. "I think I'll go tonight. Will you be going to the dance class before the dance?"

"My friend Sue insists on going to it."

"Fine, I'll try to get there a few minutes before the class. Look forward to seeing you."

Bobbie thanked me profusely and we agreed to do the first dance set together when the regular dance started.

After I hung up I thought of Sir Arthur Conan Doyle who wrote the Sherlock Holmes mysteries and spent the last eleven years of his life traveling the world and lecturing on clairvoyance. He stressed his views were in no way opposed to our Christian approach to God. In fact his point was there was a life hereafter and we did get messages from another world while we dwelt on this earth. Doyle was a brilliant person, Physician and Military genius.

Wasn't it so strange I was late for work or I wouldn't of run into Bobbie. If I hadn't run into Homer and Billy on the troop transport of wouldn't have met them or their folks. So what did destiny have in store for me next?

Next on my schedule was to visit my folks. I called them first and they insisted I come for lunch. Like most folks they were overjoyed to see me---and wanted me to tell them in minute detail everything that had happened the past week.

When I brought them up to date on my slight involvement with Frank Beckman and The Missing Gambler they wanted me to forget both and concentrate on my job.

I gratefully collected a loaf of whole wheat bread and six big cinnamon rolls. My Mother was so pleased I still loved her cooking. She did quiz me about women as usual, and gave me a lecture about being careful and not putting some gal in a family way and having to marry her.

CHAPTER 8, Saturday night at the Uptown Ballroom.

Saturday night could be the loneliest night of the week and I was pleased I would not feel entirely alone when I showed up. I arrived promptly fifteen minutes early and after a brief look around I found Bobbie and she introduced me to Sue.

The dance class was on the rumba. I liked the beat and because I was a little musical I had no problems with the timing. I was too timid to do the very pronounced body movement in the rumba box. Moving my left foot and hip to the left, back on my right moving my right hip and then forward with my left foot and hip. The women seemed to enjoy the opportunity to move their hips in a tantalizing manner.

When it came to the forward break, the back break and the open break the hip movement seemed no longer paramount. We danced in a circle changing partners every couple of minutes, a standard way a large dance class is taught. The circle moved completely twice so twice I danced a couple of minutes each with Bobbie and Sue.

Sue was dark haired and about the same size as Bobbie. It was remarkable how their facial features were so similar.

The dance began with a set of three slow fox-trots. That was an easy way to get everyone moving around. I had that set with Bobbie.

I had the second set with Sue. The tempo for those three dances was livelier and I could tell Sue was a peppier person. I had the next set, which were Waltzes, with Bobbie and the next set, which were Latins with Sue. We did all right on the Rumba, not well at all on the Cha-Cha, and gave up on the Tango. I had the next couple of sets with other gals and before I knew it the refreshment intermission had arrived.

During that intermission I also found out that women were adjusting for rides. Some came on the streetcar planning to see a certain guy and get a ride back. Sometimes the guy never showed up. That was the case with one gal who hit Sue up for a ride. So Bobbie asked me if I would take her home. I wished the cards had dealt me Sue instead of Bobbie.

I danced another set with Sue and wished even more I would be paddling Sue home and not Bobbie. Sue wasn't complaining that some guy had done her wrong. I did learn her last name was Gish and she was in the phone book. She worked at Jantzen knitting Mills.

During the set Sue asked, "Twenty five cents for your thoughts."

I said you won't like it, but here they are. "There are so many things in life that can buy and you are not obligated to forever. I don't like my Apartment so I can move. I like my car, but in a couple of years I can change models. In girl friends and marriage it isn't so easy."

"So Bobbie is driving you nuts about Frank Beckman. She is doing the same thing to all of her friends, but you're right dating and marriage is not easy. Remember, I'm single too."   When the dance ended I left with Bobbie and asked her if she was hungry. "No need to spend any money. There is pie in our refrigerator and I can make some coffee to go with it."

This time we took the Broadway Bridge and in no time were at 24th. Bobbie's house was only a couple of blocks North. We walked to her door and she said, "Mother and I both sleep upstairs, but let's be kind of quiet."

As we sat in her dining room having delicious apple pie and excellent coffee Bobbie said, "Mother made me promise to ask you over for dinner tomorrow. Roast Beef is on the menu. I would enjoy your company too, but wanted to let you know how it all came about."

I hardly had a chance to answer before she continued with, "My Mother grieved terribly for my Dad. Over a year later a couple of married men in her Church congregation paid unexpected calls on her and explained very carefully how they were married only in name and they were attracted to her and wanted to be a part of her life."

"Of course that made her exceedingly angry and she threw them out of our house. Then a single older man invited her to some shows. She decided he was too old for her. I think she has decided to look for a man much younger than her. Mother is fifty. "What do you think of her going out with men younger than fifty?"

I knew only a fool would get caught in that trap. I replied, "A woman fifty could be actually younger in agility and health than some women who were forty. Also common interests play a big part in a relationship. If two people are enthusiastic about the same things that makes a big difference. I think you have to treat everyone on an individual basis."

Bobbie looked at me and her eyes widened. "My that was a clearly defined and sensible answer. If I tell Mother that she will really like you. It's obvious she is looking for reassurance. Are you accepting our invitation for dinner tomorrow?"

I replied, "Yes, I would be pleased to accept. What time shall I be here?"

"Mother suggested about one. Will that be all right?"

I assured her that would be fine. The dance had ended at midnight and it was now one A.M. I said, "I'll be seeing you tomorrow, so perhaps I should take off?"

Bobbie replied, "It is late, but I don't mind talking a little longer. Why don't we sit on the sofa for five or ten minutes?"

She didn't wait for a reply, but took my hand and led me to the sofa. She sat down. I sat down next to her. I put my arm around her as we had been dancing arm in arm. She lifted her lips to mine and I accepted the invitation to kiss. I barely touched her lips, but she immediately presented her lips to me again. This time our lips meshed firmly. A third kiss brought some passion into our embrace and by the fourth kiss both our arms were around each other and our lips were parting further with each kiss. She broke the spell with, "Oh this is so nice, but I'm not trying to vamp you. Maybe my Mother and myself are both kind of mixed up. I can tell you are a nice guy. You were willing to go home without trying to overwhelm me. A girl likes that in a man.

Well, as I drove away from her house I thought about her bitching about Frank and here she was necking up a storm of passion with me and I hardly knew her. If I had a real date with her would she invite me to lay alongside her on the sofa instead of sitting up.

CHAPTER 9, SUNDAY AFTERNOON

Bobbie's Mother. -----A Very Nifty Fifty

I slept until 10 A.M. and had a light breakfast and read the Sunday paper completely. I then took a shower and put on a clean shirt and my suit pants. At 12:45 I pulled away from my apartment, in my little blue coupe. I was apprehensive, but tried to concentrate on the fact I needed to add to my social graces and a nice home cooked Pot Roast dinner with a middle aged lady and here daughter was something I would of given a million dollars for when I was playing Big Time War in the Jungles of New Guinea.

As I neared Northeast 24th and Broadway I always felt a special roots thrill. Through the eighth grade I had gotten my Oregon Journals on the Southeast Corner where a Church stood. Across the street was a drug store owned by the Father of a girl in my same grade in school. Bobbie and her Mother lived just a couple of blocks North of the Church."

Bobbie's home, on Northeast Handcock, was typical of hundreds of Portland homes in that area.. Wide front porches with the gabled roof extending over the Porch. Also the side gables were huge and extended at least two feet from the house. The siding was lap with at least eight inches to the weather. The parking strip was lined with large horse chestnut trees that spread their messy fruit all over the sidewalks and streets. No one ate the chestnuts and their spiny covers were like tiny porcupines. So why did folks plant them---apparently the shade they afforded was worth it, but the mess they created was sure a negative.

One couldn't help, but occasionally think of perhaps Longfellow's poem, "Under a Spreading Chestnut Tree the Village Smithy--did he stand, or sit?" Obviously during my five years in the Service, most of it overseas, my literary skills--never very high--had degenerated. .

The weather had actually turned sunny. I parked on the street, walked up steps and Bobbie opened the door. She was dressed in a rather classy beige skirt and matching jacked with a white blouse. She was friendly and proper as she invited me in.

Then she looked toward a doorway and called, "Mother, Barney is here."

Well--I was about to meet what I had learned was so often a girl's guiding light--her Mother. Bobbie had told me the night before her first name was Elaine. Just then Elaine came through the doorway wearing a rather short apron over a knit dress that was molded to her figure. . Elaine was Blonde like Bobby and they looked like Mother and daughter. Elaine didn't look like she was 25 years older than Bobbie. She looked fifteen older at the most.

Elaine had Bobbie by twenty pounds for sure. That twenty accented her hips and her bosom. Elaine had genuine cleavage and the V-cut knit barely covered half.

"Mother, this is Barney."

Elaine extended her hand to mine in such a gracious manner I wished a little of my small French Heritage would of permitted me to raise her hand an kiss it. I thought to myself many a man, bolder than I was, had done just that looking at her cleavage instead of her hand. I immediately understood why the Devil had easy prey when he urged some men from her congregation to call upon her and console her in whatever ways they had in mind.

I was about as far as humanly possible from being a Connoisseur of women, but to me Elaine was a knockout.

Elaine said, "It is a pleasure, Barney. You look like such a nice young man."

Elaine kept looking at me and Bobbie picked up on it and asked, "Do you recognize Barney from some place?"

Elaine seemed at a loss for words. Then she slowly said, "Many years ago I knew a young man that looked so much like Barney! It's almost like---well, it's--well, I don't know what to say. Please excuse me Barney. Dinner will be ready in about fifteen minutes. Would you like a glass of wine and Bobby will entertain you while I get things ready."

I had noticed in the adjacent dining room the table was set.

As to the wine I said, "Yes, that would be great."

Bobbie said, "Please sit on the sofa, Barney. I'll get the wine."

I knew the first thing Bobbie was going to do when she got into the kitchen with her Mom would be to ask her who I reminded her of and when and how.

As I sat on the sofa I hoped whoever I reminded Elaine of was a nice guy. I didn't want to be the reincarnation of some monster in her life.

Bobbie was a little tardy in getting the wine, which turned out to be a Gallo Rhine. I surmised I was right and a fast quiz program had taken place in the kitchen. Bobbie raised her glass and said, "Here's to Barney, Bobbie, Elaine and Sammy?"

"Who is Sammy? I asked."

"Sammy is was apparently a dead ringer for you--maybe 20 years ago. He was a next door neighbor. I wonder if my Mother had a crush on him. Dad was a lot older. It could be?"

Bobbie sat on the arm of the chair I was in and reached over and gave me a kiss on my cheek and then one on my lips. Then she said, "Better wipe off the lipstick."

I asked her why and she moved away from me and onto the sofa. After a few minutes of chit-chat Bobbie said, "I think I had better help Mother serve the dinner. She took her half full glass with her. It was only a few minutes later and we were all seated at the table. Elaine asked me to say grace and I pretty much bungled it. She had served the salad with the main course, which was all right and more efficient.

The salad was loaded with shrimp on lettuce with some slices of Avocado and Tomato.

The Pot Roast was served with sliced red potatoes, white corn and peas. A plate of sliced fresh carrots and celery was passed around. Midway through our dinner Elaine got up and brought the bottle of Rhine wine to the table. Her glass was empty. I had a half glass more as did Bobbie, but Elaine took a full glass more.

Needless to say the dinner was fantastic. With my income barely covering my living expenses I could not help but look at the financial aspect of Elaine's situation. If she really was hell-bent on teaming up with a younger man here she had a nice house, nice furniture, her own car, a super figure and was obviously a marvelous cook. If her bank account was relative she would have no trouble finding all kinds of young men.

My revere was interrupted by Elaine, who said, "We have rhubarb pie for dessert!"

Both women looked at me. I said, "Could I wait maybe a half hour?"

Bobbie replied, "I'm sure we can all wait. If you are still full when you leave you can take your piece of pie with you. I think I'll eat the rest."

We all laughed. "Coffee now?" Elaine asked.

We all agreed and soon the dishes were removed from the table, the rest of the pot roast probably went into the refrigerator and we were seated in the living room having coffee. Elaine raised the subject I would just as soon stay off. "Could you tell me what your thoughts are about Frank Beckman and the Missing Gambler?"

We discussed briefly what I had investigated so far and then I suddenly thought of something. "I wonder if we should check where Frank Beckman parked his car? I think he told me he parked it in the garage of a retired couple. Maybe they would know something."

Bobbie and Elaine responded simultaneously to that. They both exclaimed that was one place that should be checked. Then all of a sudden Bobbie seemed to get super-charged., "Barney, let's you and me drive over there right now. It'll give Mother a chance to relax for a few minutes while we're gone. I know where he parked it. He rented from a little old man and a little old lady."

In five minutes we were on our way. As we pulled away from the curb Bobbie said, "Drive almost to the apartment Frank lived in, but as you reach the corner turn left and go to the middle of the block."

Bobbie seemed so steamed up I wouldn't of been surprised if she was hyperventilating. We reached the corner, then turned and just as we reached the middle of the block Bobbie said, "Stop here, Barney."

She pointed to an open garage and we both saw it at once. For a second it was almost like I was back overseas in the jungle and someone had just said, "Look."

But this was no cautious exclamation from the deadly jungle. Bobbie screamed, "Oh, my God, Barney, there is Frank's car. Maybe he's back."

We had sort of halfway learned to deal with the unexpected in the Jungle, but dealing right now with Bobbie Day was something I was unprepared for. She was becoming hysterical. .

I quickly said, "Hold on now, Bobbie. He could have sold the car to someone else."

"I know! I know!. Just stop your car! I want to get out and find out!"

Then suddenly her voice dropped and she started to cry as she said, "Oh, Frank, why did you do this to me?"

I thought to myself, "She's got that handkerchief in front of her face again"

I was getting panicky myself. I said, "Bobbie, maybe I should just go check by myself?"

She didn't look at me and shouted, "No, Barney, no. I want to talk to whoever has that car. If Frank is back, why that dirty rat I'll need you to keep me from killing him! Why, I'll give that Frank Beckman a piece of my mind. Just give me a couple of minutes to wipe my tears and powder my face."

Then she turned her head and looked at me and said, "It isn't every guy that would help a girl find her boy friend."

I thought that over as she powdered her face. **Maybe I was some kind of a freak.**

In a few minutes Bobbie looked a little more presentable. She opened her door and said, "O.K. Barney, let's go!"

Right now I was realizing being a civilian again was plenty complicated. I was sure Frank had not returned, but I was plenty curious why he left his car. That indicated something. Maybe in the next few minutes we might find out. Just then a kindly looking older man with white hair and slight of build stepped from inside the garage and started to close the door. The garage had a double door on hinges with a big clasp that took a hasp lock. He snapped the lock shut, turned and was about to head for a side door which looked like the typical Northeast Portland side door.

The door would open and there would be a landing and from that landing stairs would go up to the house and down to the basement. I had been seriously injured during the construction of such a set of stairs. They fell and a nail ripped open my hand.

Bobbie didn't wait for the old gent to talk. She said, "I was a good friend of Frank Beckman, we're looking for him and I noticed his car is in your garage."

The little old man had glasses with rather thick lenses and he looked first at Bobbie and then at me. I thought it might ease the old fellow's mind if I chimed in with, "I worked with Frank out of the Terminal Sales Building."

The older gent was wearing old gray corduroy pants, a blue denim shirt and battered loafers on his feet. For sure he hadn't just returned from Church.

He looked back at Bobbie and said, "You must know him to recognize his car. I'm sorry, but Frank has left town and I promised to not give out any information. Anyhow, he didn't give me any."

Bobbie came right back with, "When is he coming for his car?"

"Well, that is another subject. I don't know what can I say without misleading you and getting you to think I'm not telling the truth?"

He replied in almost a solemn voice, "I'm retired and have such a small Pension for my wife and I to live on that we had to sell our car. So we had our garage for rent and Frank rented it. When he moved he said he wouldn't need his car for awhile and he paid us rent in advance to keep the car.."

Bobbie almost snapped back in a voice that didn't have any hint of graciousness in it. In fact the tone of her voice made me a little angry. "How long did he pay you in advance?"

I knew what was going to happen. The old gent was going to clam up. Instead the old man showed his true colors--that he was a genial kindly sort.

"Now there is a funny thing. My wife thinks he said to her he might be back in less than a year or he might stay away for a long time. Don't count on that because he never said that to me."

I reached over with my right foot and gave her left foot a not too gentle kick. I whispered, "Take it a little easy, Bobbie."

"Are you sure. Maybe your wife does. I'd like to speak to her."

Right then I sure was curious what this approach was going to bring.

He looked at Bobbie, "Miss, I know you would like to know. My wife sort of Mothered him. She made him cookies, and maybe she gave him some advice and he confided in her."

"But my wife is not well and both of us did promise we would not discuss where he might go with anyone else. Please let us keep that promise. **If Frank wanted you to know don't you feel he would of told you?"**

I smiled to myself. The little old kindly gray haired man had delivered the knockout punch to Bobbie. Obviously Frank would of told Bobbie if he wanted her to know. I knew it was time to cut off the conversation. I had learned in my sales life when to back off. I had seen too many salesmen challenge prospects. I knew that was stupid.

So I piped up with, "My name is Barney Lange and this is Bobbie Day. Here is my card and tell your wife I wish her a speedy recovery. She will recognize I work for the same company as Frank did. I also spent three years in the Infantry in the South Pacific. If you think of anything you care to pass on to us please give me a call. Bobbie will be grateful and so will the other men Frank and I worked with. We're all curious what made him take off so suddenly."

The old gent stuck out his hand and I gripped it lightly knowing he could easily have arthritis and a strong handshake could make his hand ache. Then I couldn't hold back and stuck out my chin. I said, "Some of the men sort of admire him for having the guts to do it his way."

Bobbie gave me a look that could kill and snapped, "Admire him? Why, that was a stupid thing he did?"

The old gray haired gent came back in rather a kind voice considering the vindictive attitude Bobbie had taken, "Miss, I don't know this for certain, but I have this feeling Frank and my wife anguished over what he should do. I'm sure she didn't tell him what to do, but she probably also did not tell him not to. I wouldn't stand for anyone picking on my wife."

I quickly said thank you, grasped Bobbie's arm and turned us both around and we left the porch and soon were back in my car. I was also learning how important it was to be up front with everyone and particularly not to mislead a woman you were dating. Make certain she understood where you were. And of course don't marry her when you knew damn well you shouldn't.

Bobbie was crying and I put my arm around her. "I wish I could say something funny, like the song---and he did her wrong."

"I know he did me wrong! The lunkhead could have at least been up front and told me where he was going. . You know Frank reminds me of the Missing Gambler. If he did something so wrong he had to go out of town why didn't he at least tell where he was going and why?"

All I could answer was, "I don't know the circumstances, Bobbie."

I did know it was time to start my engine. I didn't say a word more until we reached her house. Bobbie regaled me with occasional remarks such as, I'm going to take Frank's picture off my dresser and throw it in the ash can. I'm going to--I'm going to wash my hands of him--you miserable Frank Beckman. She was doing a first class job of cussing out Frank as she cried.

I didn't pull into her driveway. I parked in front under a huge horse chestnut tree. I said, "Under the spreading chestnut tree the Village Smithy stands."

I knew that was rather a stupid thing for me to say, but frankly I was getting a little fed up with Bobbie. Afterall she had been very kissy to me last night. Now Bobbie was bitching and crying about Frank Beckman and last night pitching woo at me.

We went in the door and her Mother came in from the kitchen. "Why, Bobbie, you're crying. Whatever happened?"

"Frank's car is still here!"

"I do declare! Is Frank back?"

"I don't know where that dirty rat is. He could be back. Why he could be living in another apartment nearby and still using his car. Maybe he got married. You know, that might be it. He might of gotten married and right now be on his honeymoon."

"Bobbie, please settle down. Please sit down, and let Barney tell me what happened."

"O.K. let Barney tell you. I don't want to. I'm going upstairs to my bathroom and bedroom and try to settle down. Please excuse me for a few minutes."

Bobbie took off for upstairs and it was obvious Elaine's composure was shaken considerably. She was flustered and nervous. "Barney, I'm so sorry."

Elaine sat down on the sofa and patted the cushion next to her. Sit down Barney."

I did and Elaine took one of my hands as I gazed at her attractive face and the fullness of her breasts. I replied, "Well, it isn't your fault, Elaine. I presented the idea to Bobbie about checking where Frank parked his car. Likely it was just lucky I was with Bobbie. If I had found out on my own and just told Bobbie over the telephone I think she would of gone there on her own and it might of been a mess. She might of demanded to see the sick wife and created a scene."

"That darn, Bobbie. My husband and I spoiled her, but basically she is a very nice lady. She has had everything and hasn't learned to handle adversity and you're so nice to not blame me You are a very nice young man."

She patted my thigh and reached over and gave me a firm kiss on my right cheek.

As she moved back her breasts seemed to be struggling to not pop out. I continued with, "Adversity is something I have experienced a lot of. It started when I was in the third grade. The depression began and my Dad did not have a job for four years."

"Then right in the middle of the depression, in 1932, my 18 year old Brother drowned at a Church picnic on the Clackamas River at Carver. Those were terrible days."

I guess Elaine was so embarrassed over Bobbie's shall we inappropriately call them antics and now was suddenly shaken at my revelation of my own terrible family tragedy.

She put her arms around me and held me tightly. After a few seconds she moved her head and kissed me again on my cheek and then moved her lips to mine and kissed me fully and forcefully on my lips. She held that kiss for a few seconds--then moved her lips away from mine and then suddenly she moved her slightly open mouth back to my lips.

This time she kissed me passionately and afterwards I wondered and wondered.

Elaine looked at me. "You are a sweet guy, Barney. I've had a few men call on me since my husband died and received a few kisses. I didn't like any of the men as much as I suddenly find I like you. Maybe you have a charm for older ladies you had better watch out for. You might have them lined up for a little bit of affection from you. I am going to guess you didn't have any sisters."

"You are right. I had 3 brothers until one died and then I was the oldest."

Elaine replied, "That figures! You don't know how to stand up to girls. That's why you got married just before you went overseas even though you knew it was a mistake."

Then Elaine changed the conversation to Bobbie. "I told her to bug off Frank, but she wouldn't listen. I could tell he wasn't that interested in her, but she insisted that he just wasn't very talkative. She claimed she was certain he was very interested in her. Perhaps most of her problem is she is really mad at herself."

I was finding this afternoon a pretty dramatic occasion in my life and those words from Elaine were exactly what I needed. I looked at her face maybe only 8 inches from mine and she winked at me and kind of wrinkled her lips. Boy, she had that down pat, and did she ever look cute and inviting to me. That wink of hers seemed to say, "I'm waiting to have fun with you!"

She had crossed her legs and made no effort to pull down her skirt which had now risen on her thighs enough to reveal just the tip of the snap of a garter belt.

My heart was pounding as I said, "Thanks for those comments, Elaine. It was nice to receive them from a beautiful lady like yourself."

Elaine looked at me and seemed in considerable thought. Neither of us spoke for almost a minute. Then Elaine said, "I think there are some things I could help you with, Barney, and maybe help myself at the same time. Does that sound reasonable to you?"

She paused for just a second and then added, "Barney, dear. I want you to feel free to call me at any time. I've learned and observed quite a bit in my time. You don't have a sister to ask questions of. Ask me anything you want to at any time."

JUST THEN THE TELEPHONE RANG. IT WAS FOR BOBBY.

Elaine went to the bottom of the stairs and called, "Bobbie, it's for you. It's Betsy. A couple of minutes later Bobbie came downstairs, looked at her Mother and said, "I completely forgot I was to help on a

Church sewing project at Betsy's house. It will take a couple of hours. I need to get away right now. Could I be excused?"

Elaine took over with, "I'm sure Barney understands."

I replied, "I can leave any time if I can take that piece of Rhubarb pie with me."

Elaine then said, "I'll try to get Barney to stay for a few more minutes. He's nice to talk to and we can get better acquainted."

Bobbie seemed relieved I wasn't running off angry. "Fine, Mother. You take over. I'll need your car."

Her Mother nodded. Bobbie got her coat and went out through the kitchen door, which I assumed was the short route to their garage.

Her Mother stood by a window watching Bobbie back out. She shook her head and said, "Bobbie, Oh. Bobbie dear, how can I help you?"

Elaine sounded so sincere I was deeply touched. There was not a bit of hostility in her voice indicating her daughter was a burden to her. There was just concern.

CHAPTER 10, Elaine and I get a lot better acquainted

Elaine turned away from the window and looked at me. "All any Mother wants is for her daughter to marry a nice guy, be very healthy and happy and have lovely grandchildren. That's really a tall order."

Elaine looked kind of forlorn as she said it. Almost as if she was asking Bobbie to climb a mountain that would be very difficult for her. I looked at the somber Elaine and said, "I'm sure she will accomplish all of those things."

Elaine seemed to perk up. Then she said, "Let's have a little more wine. Please stay for awhile."

My generally dull life wasn't awash with invitations like that. I looked at Elaine and she could have read my mind if I hadn't answered. My honest reply was, "I'd like to."

For that reply Elaine winked at me and wrinkled her lips.

Soon she was back, handed me a glass, sat down on the sofa and patted a spot right next to her and said, "Please sit next to me, Barney.

We talked about simple things in our lives. Elaine turned to me. "I need to perk up my life a little, Barney. I've been tempted to try going out dancing some night, Barney. Maybe I'll just go to the Uptown ballroom. Could you give me a little dancing practice now?"

That seemed like a very reasonable request to me. I said, That is fine. I'm not a dance teacher, but I might be good at basics. Where shall we practice?"

"The entrance hall is large. If you rolled up the entrance rug would that be enough?"

I took a quick look and while it would be small it would be very adequate. Often on the dance floor you had less than half that space to move around in."

I went ahead and rolled up the rug and while doing so Elaine asked, "If I came to the Uptown and you were there would you dance with me?"

I quickly answered, "It would be my pleasure."

Elaine put on a record, started the music and reached for my hand and we moved the few feet to the uncarpeted floor. Then I faced her and she winked at me again and wrinkled her lips. She was really getting to me with those two gestures. I took her right hand in my left hand and put my right hand on her back.

In ballroom styling the lady is to put her left hand on the man's right shoulder. It was always interesting to me to observe the variety of places individual ladies actually placed them.

Some women put their left hands almost around the neck of their partner and that was what Elaine did to me. I was tempted to correct her, but thought, "Oh well, the music has started. Let's just concentrate on staying in time.."

She had put on a Glenn Miller record and the first song was Moonlight Serenade. I began leading her and I could tell she had no problem with staying in time. Her footwork was pretty clumsy at first, but by the end of the first song we were doing better. "We're doing all right, Elaine, I said.

Whether it was the compliment, or what, she moved closer to me and I felt the pressure of her bosom against my chest. Then she laid her head on my shoulder causing her to move even closer to me. Now I felt all her body against me. At first it was difficult for me to lead her, but I found if I moved forward her body had to move forward too. Factually I had danced with at least a dozen gals at the Uptown Ballroom who sort of threw their bodies into you like they were tackling you. I did know on some dances the lady is supposed to dance very close to the man.
She whispered to me, "You can tell I haven't danced much. Just hold me tight and lead me, Barney, I'll try to follow."

Holding Elaine close was a nice sensation and I kept thinking about Bobbie's comments that her Mother wanted to date a younger man. I seemed less worried about Elaine dancing close to me than if it had been a younger gal--with perhaps going steady ideas.

The next song was not romantic and slow so she suggested we sit it out. Finally the record came to Stardust and she wanted to dance to it.

This time she began the dance by moving just as firmly against me. Her lower torso was firmly pressed against me. Then she put her head on my shoulder again and a couple of times murmured, "In Church we hug our friends, but dancing is one nice long hug."

After a few more numbers the record ended. Lot's of question marks were running through my mind--maybe even a few red flags. Elaine only partially broke our embrace and she reached her lips to mine and then wrapped both arms tightly around my neck and kissed me firmly. It was one firm kiss! Then she kissed me again. This time her lips parted mine. Her lips were warm and sensuous and I found myself no hurry to break apart.

We were kissing slowly and more passionately with each kiss. The warmth of her body against mine was intoxicating. Then she slowly unwound herself from around me, took my hand and led me back to the sofa.

"That was wonderful, Barney. Do I ever love dancing with you! Let's rest for a few minutes and dance a couple of more dances."

We both leaned back on the sofa. Then she put her head on my shoulder and continued with, "I'm enjoying this so much, Barney. I hope you are too!"

I noticed the way she phrased her comments left me with only the opportunity to agree. I was really struggling for a remark. I knew I had to say something, but just couldn't come up with a response I felt comfortable with. Finally, in kind of desperation, and not wanting to be a cad to such a nice lady I replied, "If you're enjoying it and have the time I have the time and there is something about you that is very special and I'm enjoying sharing it with you."

As I tacked on that last part I wondered if I hadn't blown the whole sentence. Then I felt better as I thought this was a very gracious lady and as long as I wasn't being pushy she would be satisfied with whatever I said.

She looked at me, winked at me again and wrinkled her lips. "I'm putting you on the spot, Barney. I am being very affectionate and then asking you leading questions. This is a real thrill for me this afternoon. You are such a sweet young man."

Then she continued with, "Will you go for another round of dances?"

I answered quickly, "You bet, Elaine."

This time we danced to True Love and Love is a Many-Splendored Thing and two other numbers and I could tell she was getting a little tired. . She held me so closely I could hardly move with the music and she again moved her head on my shoulder as we danced.

When the music ended, and her head still on my shoulder, she said, "I guess I am a little tired. I went to Church, fixed dinner and I need to sit for a little while."

She didn't move her body from mine, just her head from my shoulder. She again took her right hand from mine and wrapped it around my neck. This time her lips were parted on the first kiss and it was sensuous. We kissed a couple of times more and I was realizing that this fifty year old lady knew a lot more about kissing that any younger gal I ever kissed. She was sensational. Then she took my hand and led me back to the sofa and took my right hand in hers. .

She said, "You have strong hands, but you have a very gentle touch. I understand you are born with your touch and as you grow up you just develop that touch. 'Do you know anything about massage?"

I replied with, "I've always wanted to go to Harrison Hot Springs where they include with the package a back massage each day. I have never gone. I have read several articles on massage and last year had a couple."

She said, "Could I lay down on the sofa and you rub my back with your nice hands?"

I answered, "You'll need to instruct me."

Turn your back to me for a moment and I will give you a couple of basic instructions. First dig your thumbs into my shoulders. Don't touch my spinal chord. Then use the palm of your hand and thumb and rub. Just do that for starters.

"Now I'll flat on my stomach and you will have more leverage."

I seemed to have had kind of the hang of it and she would occasionally say I was doing great. I could feel Elaine relaxing and after about five minutes I heard he breath heavily and I realized she had fallen asleep. At first I was shocked, but then I realized she had a busy and unnerving day, plus three glasses of wine at least, which would of put me to sleep.

I stopped touching her and moved to a nearby chair and watched her. Her breathing was regular and sounded good to me. I had put my first patient to sleep.

So now the question was 'What To Do?"

I had already read the Sunday paper and looked around for a magazine. I found a Newsweek and for the next 30 minutes read it, never concentrating too much on the magazine as my eyes were continually diverting toward Elaine.

Then I thought I heard a car come up the driveway. I quickly got up and looked out catching a glimpse of Bobbie just as her Mother's car passed the window.

I quickly went through the kitchen and out the back door and Bobbie said, "Oh, you're still here. This is a surprise. I replied, "Your Mother asked me to dance a couple of dances and then she seemed to get tired. She decided to lay down on the sofa and asked me to rub her shoulders a little."

Bobbie seemed to be amazed as she listened to me.

I continued with, "She fell asleep within a couple of minutes and I have just been sitting reading a magazine."

Bobbie still looked startled. Then she said, "Dad worked so hard and such long hours in the shipyards he got some massages to help some of the pain at the end of the day. You know there is a ladies fitness center just up the street on Broadway. Mom went there and cajoled them into giving her a few instructions and then she bought a massage table and gave Dad a daily massage. He loved it, but was too tired to massage Mom. She taught me a little, however.

She does relax and falls asleep almost immediately. So I understand."

I replied, "I'll not go back into the house. I'll just walk down the driveway. My car is on the street and I'll head for my place. Thanks again for the nice dinner."

I was halfway home when I remembered, "I had forgotten my piece of Rhubarb Pie."

———◄►———

Back in my apartment the power of suggestion was too much. I took off my good clothes and lay down on my bed. I fell asleep immediately and was awakened by my phone. I heard a lovely modulated cultured telephone voice. It reminded me of how some movie stars spoke.

"Barney, dear, sounds like I woke you up. It's me, Elaine, can you talk?

I smiled to myself as I wondered what her reaction would be when she awakened and found I had left. Now, maybe I would know--then again, a lady like Elaine might never tell. I answered, "I'm pleased to hear from you, Elaine. I came home and fell asleep, too. I wish you had been massaging my back.

Elaine responded with, "You were so sweet, Barney, to let me sleep after your nice soft but firm hands worked on my shoulders. I slept like a baby. I may have trouble going to sleep tonight, but I'll just lay awake thinking of the wonderful time we had together. You know I could teach you how to give me a full massage. If you gave me one I would be in heaven."

She continued with, "I do flatter a lot of people, Barney, but in your case it isn't flattery."

I had already told her once I wished she had massaged me and her desire for me to give her a full body massage was kind of spacing me out just thinking about it. All I answered was, "How is Bobbie?"

"First, Barney, Betsy picked her up a few minutes ago for a Church meeting on the project they are working on. I was glad to see her go. She is very angry with me. She was mad at Frank this afternoon and me this evening."

I boldly asked, "Why is she mad at you?"

"Well, Barney dear, first you have to understand Bobbie and then you have to understand women. I don't think you understand either."

Well, I could think of a humble reply to that without straining my mind, "You're right."

I also knew that even in the sales field dealing with men or women whenever you can say, "You're right," you kind of pick up a Gold Star with that person.

Then Elaine continued with, "Of course I never gave Bobbie any idea I was so affectionate toward you, nor would I ever tell her or tell anyone else. That's between you and I. Promise, Barney, dear?"

That was an easy commitment so I replied, "For sure, Elaine."

Between you and I, Barney dear, I don't fully understand why I was, except I want to get out and taste a little more of life and you are so nice. I have absolutely no regrets. Do you?"

I had to answer, of course. "I said--and I said it very slowly and I knew Elaine would understand I was searching for the right words. I really kind of stammered, "Elaine, I'm not sorry in the least. I am very flattered that a very beautiful gracious lady you would care to be affectionate toward me."

"Barney, those are very sweet words. Life isn't always easy to define and we turn corners that are lovely and all we can do is be thankful for those that are very special. I do want to see you when you feel you would like to see me. Do you have any time this week."

"Elaine, I'm sure I have some time. Let me know."

"Why don't we set a time and you call me if something in your business calls makes you change it. How about Thursday for lunch at my house about 12 noon. I'll fix us a light lunch.

We could dance for perhaps a half hour and then I'll show you how to do an upper back massage. I think we could get through all of that by 2 P.M. So many men think all there is to a relationship is kissing and sex. Tenderness includes massage and touching."

"My husband never would of made it through the war working in the shipyards if I hadn't given him a full back massage after he got back from his shift at the shipyards. I bought a massage table and it is folded up in my bedroom. Luxury resorts offer massage. Old cultures have made it a part of their lives for centuries. It helps blood circulation and is the best relaxer in the world. People smoke and take drugs--they want to do everything in five minutes or less. It might help you get the right girl some day."

I knew Elaine was right. My Dad had studied Nutrition a lot so I was perhaps more receptive to things that helped a person live a healthier life. I was still greatly underweight from when I had entered the Jungle. I knew I was a long way to full recovery--maybe I never would. I was eating very carefully. Lots of vegetables and lots of fresh fish. I would of had lots of massages, but they cost from $5.00 to $10.00 each.

A massage partner would be a lucky break, especially an experienced older lady without the worry of a commitment after the first massage. ,

So I enthusiastically replied, "You sold me Elaine. I'll plan to be at your place Thursday at 12 noon."

Then Elaine replied, "Barney, you sound like you are really looking forward to it. I know I am. Is there anything I can do for you?'

"Elaine, I'll toss two things at you. First, should I ask Bobbie out, or what?"

"Good question. Don't ask her out this week. If you feel like going to the Uptown Saturday maybe she will be there. Thursday I'll try to bring you up to date on her."

"My second question is, "Could you track down the former Mrs. Ray Pearson, the wife or ex-wife of the Missing Gambler."

"Sure, Barney dear. I will be pleased to do so. It'll give me a little extra excitement."

I always loved the way Agatha Christie said someone 'Rang Off." when they hung up. So a few minutes later Elaine and I, 'Rang Off."

And I suppose both of us spent the rest of the evening wondering and thinking. I couldn't help but think that Elaine held all the cards. She would deal them as she saw fit. And she was fit enough to deal them very well.

As I crawled in bed that night I hoped I would dream about Elaine. And I did. It was a very exciting dream. I woke up during the dream and was very sorry it was only a dream.

CHAPTER 11, I hear from Homer and Billy in Melbourne, Australia.

Monday I had my luncheon appointment with Mr. Block and after lunch I did a several hour survey of all his paperwork. I worked on that Monday evening and Tuesday morning went through all the company files on Lumber Yards and picked up every form and idea I could find. Then Tuesday evening I went to work in earnest trying to put together the ideas that had been running around in my mind.

I was having a very difficult problem concentrating on anything but Elaine. Wednesday morning I called Mr. Block and while he was busy he wanted to meet with me at 5 P.M. I agreed. Right after lunch I called Elaine from a private phone booth. She was in.

She assured me she was looking forward to Thursday at 12 noon. I assured her I was too and she thanked me profusely for calling.

My appointment with Mr. Block went very smoothly and he said, "I want you to go ahead with it. I'll give you a purchase order now. Then I spent an extra hour going over things.

I was home by 6 P.M. and my phone rang.   It was the overseas Cable Operator. I almost went numb with surprise. It was the first cable I had ever received in my almost thirty years on this planet. The cable operator read as follows:

BARNEY LANGE. DELIGHTED TO HEAR YOU CALLED OUR MOTHERS. STOP. WE ARE IN MELBOURNE, AUSTRALIA FOR A WEEK. STOP SHIP UNDERGOING REPAIRS. STOP. YOU CALLING MY FOLKS WAS PSYCHIC. STOP. READ IN PAPER A YOUNG AMERICAN WITH SHRAPNEL SCARS ON HIS CHEST WAS IN AUTO ACCIDENT. STOP. THEY THINK HIS NAME IS FRANK BECKMAN AND THEY ARE LOOKING

FOR WHOEVER HE MIGHT BE VISITING. STOP. HE IS UNCONSCIOUS. I CALLED HOSPITAL STOP. APPARENTLY GOT MIXED UP MAKING RIGHT TURN FROM LEFT LANE. STOP. BILLY AND I HAVE SOME LEAVE. STOP. LEAVING TODAY FOR SIDNEY GENERAL. STOP. SEND ANY WIRES TO US AT S.S. MONTE, MELBOURNE.

I became so unnerved I fixed myself a drink. Something I seldom did as it usually made me fall asleep and ruined my evening of study and reading. I fixed myself some dinner and a couple of times I talked out loud to myself. It was so fantastic that I wanted to discuss it with someone. Who did I know that could keep it secret?

On the other hand suppose Frank died. Suddenly I felt tears trickle down my cheek.

What had ever made him do this--leave the U.S. And now fate had got him in an accident and his folks had been killed in a hit and run as pedestrians while he was overseas. But like my brother drowning when he was 18. Fate dealt those cards and you didn't know when one would have your name on it.

Suppose Frank did not regain consciousness. I suddenly hoped it wasn't our Frank Beckman. Oh, I hoped it was someone else, but who was I to wish that fate on someone else.

Before I went to bed I wrote a reply. I was up early and was at the cable office at 8 A.M. I sent the following:

HOMER AND BILLY BARNES. C/O S.S. MONTE, MELBOURNE, AUSTRALIA. STOP. FRANK WORKED OUT OF MY OFFICE. STOP. SO SORRY HE IS SERIOUSLY INJURED. STOP HE QUIT ABOUT 10 DAYS AGO AND LEFT NO DETAILS. STOP. HE'S KIND OF HERO TO US FOR HAVING GUTS TO QUIT STOP AND DO WHAT HE WANTS TO DO. STOP. BARNEY LANGE.

From the cable office I drove straight to my office. Boy, when I thought of how I could liven up that office and the morning coffee session at Riggs Pharmacy by showing the boss and the men that cable I could scarcely bite my tongue enough to hold back. At coffee a couple of guys asked me what was on my mind. I looked different and hadn't said a word.

Even the genial Mr. Riggs would of liked to hear that Frank may of been found, but everyone would be very sad to hear that he might be fighting for his life. Whatever caused Frank to leave might become his last tragedy of life. I knew I had to wait first to make certain if it was Frank before I told anyone. Then I needed to find out more about his physical condition.

Hopefully he would come out of it without serious injuries. The poor guy almost lost his life in the Battle of Buna in New Guinea helping save Australia and maybe now he loses his life in Australia. What a mess!

Here I was to spend two hours with Elaine and suddenly all my enthusiasm and light-heartedness had big black clouds settle over them.

CHAPTER 12, My Thursday lunch with Elaine.

I rang her door bell at exactly two minutes before twelve. I didn't want to seem too eager and be early, but I didn't want to be late either. She opened her door with the comment, "How lovely to see you, Barney. I have been looking forward to this."

She ushered me in--kind of quickly which made me wonder if she was a little afraid of some of the neighbors seeing me enter-and they might watch how long I stayed.

As soon as I was in she shut the door and kind of looked me over. In those couple of seconds I looked at her. I had wondered what she might be wearing or not wearing.. She had on a light fairly short blue skirt. Her lightly flowered blouse was almost transparent and it was cut so low at least half of her breasts were visible. We'd all heard that phrase if you have it flaunt it. I knew that many paintings by the old masters showed more bare body than covered. .

I could tell the next two hours were going to keep my blood pressure at an all time high.

She kind of wiggled her body and said, "Am I dressed all right?"

She looked like halfway between stunning and maybe even ravishing, but I hadn't gotten to the stage in life where I could feel comfortable using either of those words, so I kind of stammered out, "You look beautiful."

She looked a me--her eyes seemed to twinkle and her lips had that cute little wrinkle. She said, "I do declare, Barney, that was a wise reply. Let me hang up your coat."

As soon as she had done that she turned to me, stepped close to me and put both of her arms around my neck. Her lips sought mine immediately and I felt her body press tightly against mine. I was just overcome! A guy is just human afterall.

A mature lady like Elaine had to know what she was doing to me. I wrapped my arms around her and we kissed each other almost frantically. Maybe it was because we had set our time at just two hours. Finally Elaine broke her clutch around me. "I hate to break us apart, Barney, darling, but "Lunch is all ready. Would you like to wash? The bathroom is down the hall."

That made good sense and as I used the bathroom and washed my hands I seemed exhilarated and a little troubled at the same time I had advanced from Dear to Darling. Then I made it O.K. in my own mind by thinking that by a classy lady like Elaine that was a real compliment.

Lunch was in the dining room table. I offered to seat her first but she declined. I saw before me a lettuce and cottage cheese salad topped with some mixed fruit and a roast beef sandwich. It looked mighty tasty and as I looked across at Elaine I realized she looked equally tasty. I said, "This looks delicious."

"Thank you. I'm going to have wine to drink. What would you like, Barney?"

"I promised myself not to drink during the day, but I'd go for a half glass if I could have some coffee later."

We ate and when we were finished Elaine said, "Barney dear, I don't want to pry, but maybe you have something on your mind. I hope you're not worried about us."

I answered, "Elaine, what is there about us men that makes it so easy for a lady to read our minds?"

She replied, "We women have to develop that knack because so many men don't communicate very well. It get's plenty tough at times. I know my husband would shut up like a clam at times and I would have to pull out of him what was bothering him. Mostly it was just a problem at work. Are you having a problem at work?"

I was on the spot. Should I tell Elaine Frank had been located in Sydney? "There is a secret that I didn't realized was showing."

She replied, "Is it about us?"

"No. I'd like to tell you if you promise to not tell anyone."

"Barney, we already share some secrets I don't want anyone to know about." This lunch included."

"I got a cable from an Army pal of mine. It might of located Frank. I should know in a couple of days."

"Where do you think he is?"

"Maybe Sydney, Australia. Unconscious in a hospital. So I have to know for sure."

"Oh, my God. How awful. Now, I understand. You do have something on your mind. You must of been working on locating him. How did you do it, Barney, Darling."

"I did nothing special. Just put out some feelers."

"You're being very modest. You must be a super sleuth. Beneath that sweet demeanor of yours is a pretty intelligent guy, who isn't pushy."

She got up from her chair, stepped a couple of steps, put her arms around me and kissed me. "I like you because you are a special kind of a guy. Good-looking, sweet and not pretentious. The world has too many self-righteous overbearing people."

Elaine then went to the kitchen and came back with a piece of Rhubarb pie for me. Then she said, 'You may take the rest of it with you. I just made it this morning."

When she sat down she was a little solemn. "What do you think of older men dating young women?"

I thought of that for a few seconds. "I know a nice guy who married a 30 year old gal when he was fifty."

"My husband was 15 years older than I was. It worked out fine. He was devoted to me and he already had a house and furniture so I never had to struggle and do without."

I finished my pie. Elaine did not have any. She had another glass of wine and I was drinking the coffee she had fixed. She winked at me, wrinkled her lips and said, "Help me carry the dishes into the kitchen and then I'll put some music on."

When this was accomplished I rolled up the small entrance rug and Elaine put on some Bing Crosby records. Then she took my hand and we moved to our small dance floor. She molded her body into my arms as if we had danced that way for years Bing started his crooning with Blue Skies and the second number was Where the Blue of the Night meets the gold of the day?"

Before the third song started she moved her left hand from my right hand and joined it with her right hand, tightly around my neck. Her lips were immediately on mine forcefully and deep. I had to respond or run and had no idea about running. Each kiss seemed to increase in passion, but finally she said, "I better let my dance instructor show me a few more steps."

Well, we did that, but the pressure of her body against mine was so strong our bodies became virtually one as we moved very slowly with very short steps. The record ended and there was kind of a scratchy noise and Elaine moved quickly to stop the player. Then she came back and put her arms around my neck again and said, "Time for me to give you a short massage lesson. The sofa isn't suitable as you cannot go easily from one side of the body to another. The same problem exists with using a bed for massage, although if you don't have a massage table that is all you can do."

"My husband and I finally bought a regulation massage table. We used to leave it set up in our bedroom, which is spacious. Since his death I folded it up and put it in my closet. I'll let you set it up. I don't think I ever did.

She took my hand and led me into her bedroom which was upstairs and in the right rear of the house. The room was furnished with elegance. We men don't notice every flower on a bedspread or every pleat in a drape, or exactly the pattern of wallpaper. Women do with ease!.

I saw the beautiful matching Cherry Wood furniture. A man can easily recognize beauty in wood. I thought how lousy my furniture was in comparison to this. Boy, I would be ashamed to have Elaine every see the junk I had in my apartment. It came with it. Even I would never buy it. Elaine asked, "Do you like my Bedroom, Barney Darling?"

Well, it seemed like maybe I had graduated to the top of the class. Darling was pretty hard to beat. I just answered simply, "It is beautiful. Mine is terrible in comparison."

It took me a little fussing around to open up the table and figure out where braces fit in and get the wing nuts on and tightened.

Elaine attached a head rest and put a flannel sheet on the table. Then Elaine turned to me, "Barney, times a wasting. I'd like you to spend all afternoon, but you said 2 P.M. was the limit. So off with your shirt and those gun boats you call shoes."

I short of hesitated and she started unbuttoning my shirt. Then she said, "You are thin!":

I replied, 'Thanks for not calling me skinny."

"Get on the table, face down, but unbutton your belt first. I'll pull down your pants a few inches so I can get to all of your back."

With that accomplished she said, "First I warm my hands by rubbing them together. Then I place them gently on your back. That is called "Getting in touch with you."

Now I remove one of my hands and put some coconut oil on it keeping my other hand partially on your back so we don't lose contact. Now I move my hand with the oil onto your back and I am going to do some long strokes called Effleurage. I am using the flat of my hands, going up and down, crossing from side to side.

Now I am going to use some Compression; The first is called Petrissasge: I will do kneading squeezing, rolling and pinching with firm pressure. I have this all detailed out in writing. I will just do these few at this time, but do them over and over and try to explain them. I think I will work on your shoulders a little more. Remember to stay off the spine."

As Elaine kept working me rolling, pushing and stretching I felt really good. I couldn't help but think how nice a massage would be after an evening's dancing.

Elaine said, "It would take me two hours to explain a full body massage to you."

That thought absolutely intrigued me, but I said nothing. I was half asleep. Elaine kept working on my back and explaining and re-explained. Finally I said, "I think I am going to pull an Elaine and fall asleep."

She replied, "If you do I will wake you at ten to two and you can do my back another time. Right now I'll take a towel and wipe off any oil that hasn't soaked in. Coconut Oil should not stain your clothes however, unless it is in gobs."

Somehow I managed to stay awake. I knew it was the thought I was going to give my first bare upper back massage--and on Elaine's back. Soon Elaine said, "I'm done with this short lesson. You get ten minutes rest and then experiment on me."

While I was getting off the table she added, "Leave your shirt off, so you don't get any oil on it. It's my turn now. Don't be afraid or embarrassed, Barney, Darling.

Elaine began taking off her blouse and said, "If my breasts weren't so large I could leave my Bra on, get on the table and you could unsnap it and work on my back. I have to wear kind of a shoulder harness support so I'll have to take it all off now."

She put a pillow on the table and said, "This is a midriff pillow for buxom ladies."

As she slipped out of her Bra she said, "Shorter ladies like me need some help to get up on the table."

I had seen lots of Native women bare breasted, and a few women without any clothes, but had never helped a lady onto a Massage table. Elaine put her hands on the front of the table and I picked up her lower body and hoisted it onto the table. Soon she was settled. I warmed my hands, put oil on one and began the massage. At first she offered helpful hints, but soon she just relaxed and sighed with pleasure. I can feel the strength in your hands, but it's your gentle touch that makes them feel so good. Don't ever stop, Barney."

I relaxed too, and moved my hands slowly. I reflected about the fact that I was only five years old when my Dad let me put on wood lathe. I lathed as far up as I could reach. I kept the nails in my mouth as lather's did and chopped the ends frequently for you could only lathe about 10 rows before you had to move over one 16" joist. This prevented the plaster from cracking.

I sort of laughed to myself as I thought how difficult it was to describe lathing. Anyhow, now my hands were 25 years older and had been through a lot. My lighter touch must come about because I was an excellent typist, a rather poor piano player and equally bad at the art work I attempted. I had never thought those endeavors would affect my overall touch--but it sure made sense. So that gave my self-esteem a needed boost.

Finally I said, "Elaine, my dear, I think dast ist alles. (That is all) I can see do a person's entire body would take over an hour."

Elaine responded with, "Keep in mind you'd be giving a person an hour of heaven. That's what my dear husband would say as I massaged him. We decided it sure must be hard on a person's hand and back to be in the profession and do it all day."

Then she added, "Darling, please wipe off my back with the towel and I will get up."

I carefully went over her back with the towel and she swung around and sat up she said, . "I can slide off by myself."

As she sat up her breasts were completely bare. She said, "Barney hand me the towel, I will cover up a little."

I handed her the towel and she covered the lower part of her breasts. In process she pushed them up. Two thirds remained uncovered. She slid off the table and walked the step or two we were apart. Then she tossed the towel back on the table and put her arms around my back and squeezed me to her. She kissed me forcefully as he nipples pressed into my chest. My arms were around her bare back and likewise her arms were around mine. I knew this kind of touching I could enjoy forever.

Elaine whispered, "Time to break apart or we'll be on overtime."

I managed a faint laugh, "It's better than time and a half."

Somehow that remark tickled her funny bone and she began laughing. Her breasts bounced as she laughed and she noticed what was happening. She got a little embarrassed, reached over and got her Bra and blouse, turned toward the bathroom. Then she must of gotten a little braver and wanted to flaunt her female seductiveness because she wiggled her hips as she walked away. She was having fun, or maybe the devil made her do it.

I took down the massage table, folded it up, and tucked it back in the closet. I thought to myself, "This is likely where her husband's clothes used to be. Maybe that's why widows who had a loving marriage likely wait a year before getting involved with another man. It's too incriminating mentally to live with a man say 30 years, have him die, and then invite someone else into the same bedroom you shared with him. It must seem strange even five years later."

When Elaine came out I used the bathroom and we walked down the stairs and she gave me the rest of the rhubarb pie. Just before she handed me the pie she put her arms around me once again. Our kisses were sure getting passionate and I was excited, bewildered and whatever else goes through the mind of a naive young man dealing with a sweet older lady. If all the men in her Church knew how loving she was there would be a two block line leading to her front door.

Before I left we tentatively set the following Thursday, same time as a date. Elaine suggested I try to stretch it to 2:30 and this time we would go for an entire back massage both upper and lower. I knew the thought of that would keep my mind humming at high speed.

As I turned down 24th street and was one block from Broadway I was reminded of something slightly related that had happened when I was in the 8th grade. The apartment house at the corner of 24th and Schuyler was on my route. One evening I was collecting from my Journal customers. The apartment had a courtyard and the tenants front doors opened onto it. There was a statute in the center. . I had just collected from a customer on the opposite side and down several doors and was about to head for the courtyard when the door of my next customer opened. Three men came out and hung a Bra on the statute. They were laughing like crazy. I stopped dead in my tracts.

That was the third year I had that route. In all my young life that was the first Bra hanging I had ever viewed. The door to the apartment shut after the three men re-entered and even at my tender age I knew it was not time to ring her doorbell.

As I was wondering if I should run from the whole scene her door opened and she came out wearing a bathrobe and strode quickly to the statue and retrieved the Bra. That then became my first Bra unhanging. [9]

———•———

I knew being new in the singles field, whether divorced or widowed, was a very difficult experience to go through. What was right or wrong or just timely was nerve-wracking at best. It seemed to me that at age 50 Elaine had the right to sow some wild oats, and if she choose to horse

---

9   That is a true story from my tender youth. As to my story about Elaine I had no close experiences with any Elaine when I was 30. On the other hand when I was much older, and single, I did meet a lady just slightly over 50 with similarities to Elaine.

around with me while she was sowing them--well, lucky me. I needed some enchanting luck. I needed it badly.

I wondered if I was starting to fall in love with her. Then I thought, "That might be the best thing I had ever done in my life. If my 50 year old male relative could marry a 30 year old gal why couldn't I do likewise. Yet, I knew Elaine would never go that far. If she felt like doing the unusual she would do it in the secrecy of her home. I was lucky to be her wild oats for now..

CHAPTER 13, I stop to see Charlie Sing.

I made calls the rest of the day and couldn't get my mind off Elaine. I had planned to stop at Helen Bernhard's Bakery, at Northeast 17th and Broadway, across from my old Accounting buddy, Charlie Sing. With almost a whole pie from Elaine I wouldn't be tempted to visit the bakery. At 5 P.M. I tried Charlie's door. It was locked, but sleuth that I was trying to be I had noticed his car around the corner.

I rapped on the door and Charlie unlocked it. "By old Accounting buddy, Barney. I am working on a major Tax Problem. Maybe you would like to help me."

"I have bigger fish to fry right now, Charlie."

So I gave Charlie a brief sketch about Frank Beckman and Ray Pearson, the Missing Gambler. He said, "Life is just like Accounting Problems. Always having to account for someone. Have you any new girl friends?"

I answered, "I've met a rather fascinating lady. Twenty years older than I am."

Charlie looked at me and surprised me with, "Does she have any Tax problems. Think I'd better audit her for you. Tell me more about her."

I changed the subject to, "Charlie, "You and I have argued over the gambling dens not far from N.W. lst and Couch. I picked up a rumor that maybe the Chinese knew a little about Ray. Could you get your curious wife to check into the matter."

Charlie came back with, "I must call Ming and tell her when I will leave here. I'll let you talk to her and she will drop everything and work on your case. I think she likes you a little more than she should."

"I'm sure that's not the case. She is just angry with you because you work so late and teases you that as soon as you die from a heart attack she is going to marry me. She just does it for fun."

Well, soon I was on the phone with Ming, that is after she got through with telling Charlie off for being late again. She told me once again, "Barney, I think Charlie will die of a heart attack most any day now, so don't get tangled up with any females. We'll have a big Chinese wedding. Chinese weddings are the very best."

I skipped Frank and Bobbie and just told her about Ray Pearson. I reminded her that in my early grades in the summer I used to go all the way down to the Portland waterfront and sell the Saturday Evening Post on board the tramp ships. In High School after one boy friend of mine took me to one of the Chinese Gambling Dens, where I lost one dollar.

Now I asked Ming if she could check around and see if anyone seemed to know anything about Ray Pearson, the Missing Gambler. I told Ming that it probably wasn't any big deal and that Ray Pearson likely had disappeared from this globe. On the other hand if the Chinese were involved it was possible there was an ending, good or bad, that they might not care to reveal.

It was always refreshing to talk to Charlie and Ming. Down deep in the recesses of my mind I often fantasized that if something did happen to Charlie would his widow actually want to marry me as she was always throwing at Charlie. Well, as a youth, I was always fascinated with those stories in the Saturday Evening Post about the Dragon Lady. Now with Ming I had gone from being fascinated to fantasizing. She was one gorgeous Chinese beauty and a nice person..

Maybe it was the better weather, or maybe it was just Elaine, but I felt like kicking up my heels, but there were none of my occasional girl friends I wanted a repeat date with.

I toyed with the idea of seeing a rerun of 'Casablanca' with Humphrey Bogart. I would never have the strong personality Bogart had. His first wife was from Portland. I stopped at the grocery store and drove home. I didn't cook any fish for dinner that evening as I limited my meat input to once a day.

I had a quarterly bulletin from the 41st infantry Division, some newspapers and a news magazine I hadn't finished. My mind went back to all those great stories in the Saturday Evening Post and Colliers. Getting the cable reminded me of the Earthworm Tractor Stories in the Post. Alexander Botts always ended up with the sale when he was on the verge of being fired. In 1930 the Post even had a story of him selling tractors to collective farms in Russia.

My Malaria was absent with my thanks. I felt sort of peaceful in my little cocoon until my mind went to Elaine. I wished I could call her, but her daughter Bobbie would be home. I had taken Criminal Law from Wayne Morse, Dean of the Law School, the winter before I went in the service. A favorite expression of his was that 'Life hopefully had it's checks and balances.'

He was really talking about politics, but right now Bobbie's presence was creating a check on Elaine and I. As I was getting ready for bed I fantasized how it might be between us if Elaine lived alone. Life always seemed to have a monkey wrench it threw into relationships. Elaine had suggested I leave the massage oil on my back overnight so I didn't take a shower.

I went to bed and lay on my stomach and tried to imagine Elaine was massaging my back.

CHAPTER 14, Friday morning, another cable from Homer

My phone rang at 7 A.M. It was the cable office. The message read.

> *BARNEY LANGE. STOP. WE OLD VETERANS REALLY GET AROUND DON'T WE. STOP. SENDING THIS FROM SYDNEY. STOP. IT WAS FRANK. STOP. HE IS ABLE TO TALK A LITTLE. STOP. WOULDN'T SAY WHY HE WAS HERE STOP I RECALL HE HAD A BIG CRUSH ON AUSSIE NURSE WHEN IN BRISBANE HOSPITAL STOP. I WILL TRY TO REACH HER. STOP. BILLY AND I WILL STAY IN TOWN FOR SEVERAL MORE DAYS. STOP. SHIP REPAIRS FURTHER DELAYED. STOP. HOMER AND BILLY.*

I became wider and wider awake as the cable operator read Homer's wire. I wanted to have that piece of paper in my hands and know it wasn't a dream. The cable operator said their office would be open until 6 P.M. and I asked them to hold the cable for me and not mail it out.

I hung up my phone and sat on the edge of my bed. Did he have a score to settle there. Just why did he leave and not tell anyone. And how did he get there so fast? He must of gone by Pan-American Clipper and that cost a few bucks.

I wished I knew the answer. Then I asked myself, "Maybe I don't want to know the answer? I thought Frank was a nice uncommunicative guy. He apparently had something knawing at him. Was it possible he might even be a fugitive?"

As I arrived at the office the boss seemed to be really agitated. The men cleared out of the office as quick as possible and at the coffee shop a couple of the older men stated the home office was giving the boss a bad time. I was practically a nervous wreck knowing where Frank was--wanting to tell my salesmen friends--but, knowing darn well I had to remain mum.

SECTION TWO. WE GO TO AUSTRALIA

HISTORICAL NOTES

Special Note from the Author. When the Allies won their major first victory in World War II it was at Buna, New Guinea. The 32nd Division in two months suffered 9965 casualties out of 10,000. It had embarked from Brisbane. Perhaps it was just fate-they were nearer Brisbane. My Division, the 41st, was in the bush outside Rockhampton, which is North of Brisbane. I would never know if a coin had been tossed, or what. Things had become desperate. The Japanese had reached the outskirts of Port Moresby, and that would of given them the entire island of New Guinea, over 1100 miles long and the second largest island in the world.

AND AUSTRALIA WOULD OF BEEN INVADED WITHIN DAYS.

My Division, the 41st, went all the way. The 24th was the other major division. General MacArthur, the much maligned General made some right moves and some wrong ones. In my humble opinion it was our lack of men, lack of a supporting firepower that made MacArthur move carefully. After the battle of Buna with virtually 100% casualties in two months he knew all his forces could again be wiped out as they were in the Philippines. Without the fifth Air Force we of course would of not made it. We almost didn't anyway. The most severe casualties were flown back to Brisbane and so it is now roughly six years later, the spring of 1949 our story returns to Brisbane, Australia.

CHAPTER 15, BRISBANE, AUSTRALIA, *Nurse Frances Burriss*

There were two newspapers in Brisbane then. The Telegraph and the Courier-Mail. In a small cottage in the outskirts of Brisbane a couple, about 30, sat in their living room reading the newspaper. Scotty McGregor had been born in Troon, Scotland. a small city that 50 years later would still have less than 10,000 people, but have almost 10 golf courses. He had volunteered for service and also served in North Africa. Now he was a no- nonsense longshoreman. His wife of two years, Frances, was nearby.

Scotty turned to his wife and said, "Love, did you read about the American Bloke who drove bloody Onkus (All wrong or incorrect) and ended up in the hospital in Sydney?"

"Yes, I did Scotty."

"You were on duty when the bloody yanks saved our necks at Buna and they filled your hospital with the blokes.

Frances was a blonde about 5'6". Still lithe and beautiful she had learned to swim in the ocean at an early age and still had that youthful energetic look. Tonight, however, her hands were shaking as she held them firmly so her husband would not realize her emotions were running so high. She had taken a sedative to keep from completely breaking down in tears.

She had read the newspaper description of the unconscious man named Frank Beckman. and those war years came flooding back. She was overwhelmed and almost crazy with memories. Those war years were flooding her mind. The wards were filled with wounded men and in a way her love went out to all of them. Frank Beckman was in her ward for almost three months. It was only after he had been transferred south to Melbourne for rehabilitation that she realized she could never forget him. As the months continued, and she was busy treating hundreds of other wounded, she finally realized she must be in love with him, but she had never heard from him again.

Right now she said to herself, "Oh, I waited for two years after the war hoping he would write to me. I just wanted to hear from him. It would of meant so much."

"Then I met Scotty. He was so persistent. He wanted to marry me. My sister Katie's husband had been so seriously wounded in North Africa fighting Rommel that he died soon after the war. Men were scarce and I married Scotty."

"Now my Frank Beckman is in the hospital in Sydney. Could he finally have come here because he could not forget me. Oh, I must find out! Maybe he is going to die for sure now. When he was in my Ward in Brisbane he had severe shrapnel wounds from a grenade and two bullet holes in him. I prayed and prayed he would recover! I prayed for all the soldiers. They were so brave. They saved Australia. I never really knew what made Frank so special."

"I felt he recovered because I prayed more for him than anyone else. He didn't have any relatives. His parents had died in 1942 while he was overseas."

"He didn't hardly want to live. He would reach for my hand. I wanted to hold him in my arms, but I couldn't. I knew he would write me after the war if he survived the war, but he didn't. My heart is pounding so I feel faint, like I might collapse. I'm very happy with Scotty--but I guess my first real love was Frank."

———◆———

Meanwhile the tall genial Homer Barnes and his peppy, happy half pint cousin Billy Barnes had arrived at Sydney General Hospital.

When their visit with Frank Beckman was over Homer immediately went to the Staff nurse office. How could I check on a nurse that treated Frank and I in Brisbane during the war."

"Oh, were you one of the Infantrymen that fell in New Guinea. "

"I guess so."

"Thanks so much, thank you forever! Now what nurse are you trying to locate?"

"Her name was Frances Burris."

"I don't know her, but we have a Katie Burris and I know she has a sister who is a nurse. I don't recall her name. She's not on duty now, but I'll see if she is home."

The nurse called and Katie was home. She passed the phone to Homer and he said, "Do you have a sister that was a nurse in Brisbane during the war?"

Katie answered pleasantly, "Yes, I do."

"Well, I was in a ward she worked in. Wondered if I could call her?"

"What is your name?"

"It's Homer Barnes."

"Oh, did you know a young man by the name of Frank Beckman?"

"Why do you ask."

"Well, my sister Frances liked him real well."

"Would she like to see him now?"

Homer, explained and Katie gasped as he talked. "Please call. Oh, I'll call her now myself. She's married now, but I'll give you her phone number."

Homer knew Frank had been wounded again if Frank had come to look her up and now found out she was married. Fate had dealt the poor guy another losing hand.

Homer called the number and Frances answered. She remembered the tall outspoken Homer right away--she laughed and tried to reply with a Texas accent of her own, mixed in with her Aussie way of speaking.

Homer laughed and laughed. "Ma'am you got pretty good at that."

Frances laughed and said, "So many of you Texans got shot during the War we picked up your accent."

Homer said, with no attempt at modesty, "Well, you all know Frances Ma'am, we Texans pretty much won the war by ourselves. There wuz a few guys from other states did a little work, but it mostly wuz us guys."

Frances laughed, and then became very serious. "Did you ever hear from Frank Beckman?"

"Sure did, Frances Ma'am. Matter of fact I just happened to talk to him recently."

"Where is he, how is he?"

"Matter of fact he's in a ward here at Sydney general. He's the guy that rented a car in Sydney and never learned how to make a right U-turn from the left corners of the streets."

"Oh, my God. It is Frank."

And Francis began to cry. She was trying to control her emotions and finally said, "Has he regained consciousness?"

"Just barely. I don't know any more details except it is Frank Beckman from my outfit."   "I'll call my sister Katie, who is also a nurse and ask her to look in on him."

"I just talked to her. She's at home and said she would call you."

Francis and Homer talked for a few minutes more and then they rang off.

———◆———

Frances immediately called Katie. Katie was besides herself as she said, "This is the guy you waited and waited for and never heard from and now that you're married he shows up."

Frances didn't answer to that statement.

Katie remembered all the times and things Frances had told her. Now Frances must be going through Hell. What would this do to her poor sister?

Finally Katie said, "Frances, you've got to take the train down, or fly down. Otherwise you will go crazy just thinking about it. Come down and say hello to him and try to bring some closure to both of you."

"I'll talk to Scotty and see what he thinks."

Scotty couldn't help but hear part of the conversation. As Katie and Frances rang off Frances turned to Scotty. "The Yank that is in the hospital in Sydney was one of my patients for three months. He barely survived."

Then Frances broke down, "Oh, Scotty, the war was so terrible. So many wounded men. I could never live through it again. I hope we never have to! "

She cried and cried and Scotty came over and put his arms around her. She buried her head on his strong shoulders, but her crying did not lessen.

Finally she sobbed, "Katie says I should come down to Sydney and say hello. The first call I got was from another man who was in my Ward. It would be nice to see both of them."

Scotty was giving the matter great consideration. Finally he spoke. "Frances, my love, you haven't seen your sister and parents for several months. It's fine with me for you to take a trip to Sydney. Your visit will show him we Aussies, Scottish and British haven't forgotten the bloody Yanks that put their lives on the line for us."

He paused and became very solemn. "What more can a man do than offer his life for Australia when he probably didn't even know where Australia was."

Frances looked at Scotty. "I guess that's why I agreed to marry you, Scotty. You're a fine looking man, but it's your heart that is made of pure gold. I'll call sis back right now and also ask her to go over to the hospital maybe yet this evening."

"Folks always say Katie and I look like twins. She's three years younger than I am. Maybe Frank will recognize her as me. Might be kind of fun."

———◆———

Frances ended up flying in a DC-3, actually a C-47 left over from the war, to Sydney. Katie had visited Frank and right off he thought it was Frances. His disappointment showed. The following evening Frances and Katie walked into his room. For a moment Frank thought he was seeing double.

Frances could not hold back. Her tears flowed and she ran to Frank and gently put her arms around him. Oh, Frank. It's been so long."

The nurse said, "I can give you folks about an hour to bring each other up to date. You two ladies are both nurses. Here is Frank's chart. Make sure he doesn't overdo, but I think your visit is better than any medicine we can give him."

As the nurse walked away she pondered the situation. She asked herself just what is going on here and what had gone on before to get to this.

Frances finally said to Frank, "Frank dear, I hoped so much you would write and perhaps we'd see each other at least for a visit after the war. There was a man, Scotty McGregor is his name, and he begged me to marry him. I still wanted to see you first, but finally time marched on and I thought if I turned down Scotty I would lose him too. I would of lost the two finest men I ever knew."

With those words Frank knew that Frances must of fallen in love with him and he had just put it off and didn't try to reach her. For a few seconds his mind almost snapped at the cards life had dealt him once again. Then his common sense took over and reminded him he had procrastinated. It was his own fault he had lost Frances. She had waited for him.

He looked at Frances and said, "I will always feel proud that someone as nice as you really cared for me and actually waited for me. Perhaps it was lack of esteem for myself that made me feel you just treated all the wounded so wonderfully. At least I have that to prop me up. Finally I could not stand life without trying to see you at least once more. So I quit my job and flew to Sydney."

Frances looked at Frank and said, "Frank, I will always cherish that you admired and thought of me for so long. It will always mean a lot to me."

"I did come to Australia to see you, but I guessed you might be married. I'd like to stay in Australia for awhile and work."

Frances replied, "My sis Katie lost her husband in the war and works in this hospital so she will keep me posted on you. That would be better than my calling you or your calling me. My husband might object. I will stay over tonight and visit you one more time."

In the doorway Frances turned around, "Maybe my sister will instruct you how to make a right U-turn."

After the two ladies left Frank thought of how Katie looked just like the Frances he knew a half dozen years ago. She was single and also a nurse. She could at least be a friend. All his life he had wished for a Brother or a Sister and then he had even lost his parents. Maybe there was a God up there that was giving him a half a loaf.

———•———

As the two ladies left the hospital Katie had her arm around Frances. "I'll bet you're hurting pretty badly right now, aren't you."

"I am. I'm sure glad you are here so I don't fall completely apart. This is something I must handle between you and I. I can never tell Scotty. It would devastate him."

Are you ready to face Mom and Dad?

"No, let's have a bite of something and talk for a spell."

As they sat having some tea and scones Katie said, "Almost everyone has some kind of a secret love buried in their heart. Those that do have more to remember--life is that way."

Frances replied very seriously, "Soldiers and civilians often change, but if Frank is as nice as I once thought he is perhaps you and he might make a nice couple."

"And have my husband carrying a torch for my sister? No way, Sis. I couldn't handle that."

"Katie, you're a smart lass. Look after Frank at least for a couple of weeks. If he truly fell in love with you and you with him you that might bring a great peace into my life also. The most I ever had with Frank were hugs and an occasional sisterly kiss. I swear that was all that ever happened between us. I wouldn't mind if he loved you. I love you so much, Katie."

"I'll always love you Frances. I can tell right now you are counting on me to bridge a gap in your life. Maybe I can and maybe I can't. At least I'll try. I'll bring him out to meet Mom and Dad. Shall I tell them he your long lost love?"

"You think it over Katie and do what seems best to you and for Mom and Dad. It's in your hands now. May God be with all of us!"

CHAPTER 16, Ming, Charlie's Wife Calls Me.

While all that activity in Australia was occurring things had simmered down as far as Bobbie and Elaine were concerned. I told Bobbie I was going fishing the next weekend at Diamond Lake. She acted as if I was going to create some act of terrorism. Actually, for the fish, that was exactly what our plans were. Not that dealing with Bobbie and Elaine wasn't some kind of a major fishing expedition and at times plain undiluted terror did come over me. In the case of those two ladies I figured I was the bait and which one wanted to land me perplexed me. Then after they landed me what kind of a fish fry was I slated for.

As to Diamond Lake I asked my Army buddies if they were going to camp out and they said yes. I said no to that, but being practical I called the Lodge and while it was full that very weekend they were going to open up their first cabins complete with beds, sheets, lights and a kitchen. I reserved a cabin for the three of us.

It turned out the weather was lousy, but the cabin was dry. In fact I was a hero for demanding it. The fishing was good. We were overwhelmed with genuine trout, big and fat and not those tiny 8 inchers you would have gotten from some stream fishing.

Saturday evening, in the cabin and out of the rain we indulged ourselves in reliving some of our life in the Jungle. The really serious deadly stuff we didn't go into.

We talked of things like the beetle nut chewing Natives. We wondered if any of the reports the Natives resorted to cannibalism really were true.

Our minds always went to Tokyo Rose. In addition to daily trying to demoralize us she frequently called us the 41st Division 'Butchers.'

No matter how much Australian bully beef and hardtack that came in cans also and looked and tasted like dog biscuits one thing we knew for certain was we would not chop up or eat Japanese. We discussed the dog biscuit tins we used during the rainy season to try to boil our mildewed filthy clothes. We needed gasoline to start the fire.

Then after a couple of months an edict from Major General Fuller came out, no more use of gasoline. Too many men were getting burned from the gasoline flashback as they carelessly tossed more gasoline on the fire.

I must have had a bit of senility in those days because I left my dollar Pocket Ben watch in my pants and boiled it. One of my Army buddies said, "Barney, your real senility was before you went overseas, when you married that lying dame."

That was a below the belt punch, but I guessed I deserved it and I said nothing.

Well, the weekend was a huge success. I'm not able to describe it. English Literature Majors felt major eloquence was essential, but we ex-infantrymen knew better. Muck and filth and disease and death was never eloquent. You didn't notice any falling leaves when you were hit by rifle or machine gun fire. You looked for a way you might survive, maybe for another day.

So driving back to Portland, late Sunday afternoon, with a mess of trout, left us a little speechless, perhaps because so many memories kept flooding our minds.

Monday evening Bobbie called and said her Mother had some news for me. It was about Mabel Pearson. She had remarried a little before the seven year period to wait for a missing person and have him declared legally dead. She married a Byron Jensen.

That marriage was rocky enough to end in separation in six months and a divorce soon afterwards.

Mabel lived in a 4-Plex on Northeast Eleventh Avenue, across from the park in the area where Lloyd dug the basement for his Hotel. The October 1929 Stock Market Crash made Lloyd put his Hotel project on hold. In fact he never built the Hotel. (The Lloyd Center was built much later by his family)

Daughter Ruth lived a few blocks away, and son Kevin was a Junior at Oregon State. Well, I didn't have any reason to contact Mabel right now, but at least I knew where she was in case I did. Elaine also told me she was going to the beach for a week with another widow that owned a home at Seaside. She whispered softly over the phone she wished she was going with me instead of the widow and maybe we could some day.

Did that thought ever grab me. I didn't know what to say, but I said, "Thanks."

Elaine also said that Bobbie was pining for the opportunity to go to the Golden Canopied Ballroom at Jantzen Beach and dance to one of the big name bands that regularly came to town. If Bobbie asked me it would be O.K. for me to go, if I felt like it. Then I blew my caution and said, "I'd rather go to the beach with you."

I could sure tell my answer delighted Elaine. She replied, "Barney, we must do it for sure."

Well, I did not say more, but thanked her and we rang off.

———◆———

A couple of days later my phone rang and it was Ming, Her peppy enthusiastic voice was always a joy to hear. "Barney," she said, Glad to find you are not out on a big date. Remember, you're saving yourself for me when my husband drops dead from big time heart attack."

I laughed. What big news do you have for me?"

"Big news is right. You maybe are psychic. Maybe your admiration of Sir Arthur Conan Doyle bring you great results. You have chance to have dinner tomorrow at 5 P.M. with a very distinguished man, Ah Wing. I happen to tell his beautiful assistant, Delores Lee, about you selling the Saturday Evening Post and he wants to meet you."

"Who is he?"

"Good question. He is big time stuff in the Chinese World. He is too big time to live in swampy Portland. He works from San Francisco and is our top diplomat."

I asked Ming, "You mean as in arguments and stuff."

"You accountants. Where are your worldly phrases? It's always one and one make two."

I knew the word Diplomat meant between other governments, but I wasn't going to be a smart alec and point that out to the charming and beautiful Ming. Instead I answered, "I would consider it a privilege to have dinner with Ah Wing at 5 P.M. tomorrow Where shall I be?"

"Be at the Sing Say Restaurant next to our Chinese Benevolent Society Headquarters. I will meet you there. O.K."

I wanted to ask more questions, but figured Ming would tell me more if she felt like it. Instead all she said before she rang off was, "See you later, Alligator."

The next day I arrived at the Sing Say restaurant five minutes early, but Ming was waiting in the restaurant lobby. She bowed to me and said, "Please follow me."

We went through several doors and at first I thought to myself this is sure one heck of a big restaurant. We came to the end of a hall and Ming stopped and spoke loudly. I could not understand a word of her Chinese, which distressed me, but didn't surprise me in the least.

CHAPTER 17, Ah Wing and Delores Lee. (The Dragon Lady ?)

The door opened and we went inside and were greeted by a bowing Chinese, who ushered us through the door and then checked it to make certain it was locked securely.

Ming laughed and said, "If you're frightened and want to run Barney, it is too late."

We obviously had entered the Chinese Tong. Soon we reached a draped doorway and the male Chinese held the curtain aside and we entered. He bowed and asked us to be seated.

I looked at Ming and said, "In the Saturday Evening Post Stories, which I sold and read completely each week there was always a gong heard. Do you folks have gongs."

"Sorry, Barney, no gongs. They are passé."

I tossed in a little levity with, "The gongs are gone, or do I say gone gongs. Boy those stories of The Dragon Lady and Dr. Fu Man Chu really were a big part of my life. And now am I finally in a genuine Chinese Tong."

Ming looked at me and laughed, "Never knew you were going to get in the big time did you.?"

"You're right Ming, but you're as beautiful as the Dragon lady was. I think you probably are sweeter."

Ming looked at me and said, "Too late to be nice. Don't butter me up now! You'll just have to take whatever the Tong decides to do to you today."

Just then the drape was held back by the same Chinese and an older Chinese entered. He bowed. Ming got up and bowed so I figured if two out of three bowed I might as well make it unanimous so I got up and bowed.

Ming introduced him as the very Honorable Ah Wing. Then she was gone, but the Chinese usher stayed. I figured he was the bodyguard and probably had two or three stilettos hidden on him in addition to years of training where he could pick up a person with one finger and throw him fifty feet. Ah Wing was very short, his skin was wrinkled, his white hair was thin and partly covered by a skull cap, small features and a multi-colored cape that someone had spent a lot of time making.

He said, "Please be at ease and be seated. . This is a very important question for me and my mind is going back many years. Tell me did you ever sell The Saturday Evening Post on board The China Queen and what might be the years?"

"That is an easy question. Yes, I recall the China Queen and I went on board a few times and sold the Post. It would be in the summer and I was in the third, fourth and fifth grades at the time. That would be 1930 to 1932."

Ah Wing stood up, walked a couple of steps to where I was sitting and extended both his hands to my shoulders and looked intently at me. Then he seemed to bow his head and said perhaps a dozen words in Chinese. Then he looked at me and said, "First I gave thanks to my Honorable Ancestors for leading you to me. Then I ask them to give us both good health and great happiness for many years to come. I am the Chinese Cook you sold the Post to. I learned to read English from that first magazine you sold me and I remember buying just one more from you."

I was absolutely speechless. "I am so pleased that it worked out so well for you."

Then he said, "Our dinner is waiting. It was so important that we meet privately first.

The Chinese guard led the way. Soon we entered what appeared to be a small dining room and already seated was a dead ringer for the Dragon lady. I was introduced to Delores Lee, several other Chinese and was asked to be seated.

By then I was aware Ah Wing had an aura about him that made me feel it was a privilege to speak to him. I was informed Delores Lee was Ah Wing's assistant. I was struck by her beauty and she made me think of the Dragon Lady. Her features were exquisite. Her skin appeared to be radiant. Her hair, beautifully coiffured. Her gown looked like silk and then I noticed tiny Golden Dragons had been embroidered onto the fabric. If there ever was a China Doll she was it!.

Ah Wing spoke again. His voice was soft, almost like a gentle breeze, but it did have some kind of a sing song cadence to it. My childhood seemed to be rushing back to me. It was almost as if I was a 3rd, 4th or 5th grader again reading a Chinese Story about the Dragon Lady. So many things had happened to me in the past 20 years. Perhaps the only simple part of my life was my youth. Ah Wing asked me to tell those assembled of those days.

I started with, "In the summer I would fill two bags with magazines. I would strap one on each shoulder. Then I would start from Northeast 28th and Wasco and work down either Sandy Boulevard or Northeast Broadway to the Willamette River. There I would try to board whatever ships were moored in that immediate area. It was such a thrill to me and made me want to be a cabin boy and sail around the world. Then when I got older I wanted to be a major league baseball player."

Then I added my home was only a few doors from the Hyster Plant and only a few hundred yards from the smokestack of the Doernbecher Furniture Plant.

As we talked our dinner was being served and Ah Wing said, if you do not like any of the dishes we will understand. Cook fixes what Delores and I like and likely will serve something you will like.

I assured Ah Wing I was not fussy. I liked fried rice, shrimp, the bigger the better. I particularly enjoyed Chow Yuk. To me all Chinese food was delicious.

There was hardly any conversation as we ate and most of that was in Chinese. I wished I knew what they were saying. At times I thought Delores might be looking directly into my eyes, but I dismissed that as fancy on my part. She was likely just being sociable and attentive and looking at me while I talked.

When the waiter had taken away the empty dishes and brought us some more tea he did not bring us fortune cookies. Ah Wing asked me a number of additional questions covering times up to my present life. In a nice way I was really getting the third degree.

Then Delores and Ah Wing spoke rapidly to each other in Chinese and each was nodding to the other. I wondered what that meant and soon I perhaps found out. Ah Wing looked at me intently as he started to speak. I couldn't believe that I saw a couple of tears in his eyes and Delores seemed to have become somber and happy, both at the same time.

Ah Wing said, "As you speak my mind also goes back to twenty years ago. And then back to the start of the War. My ship was sunk by a Japanese torpedo not long after Pearl Harbor and I lost all my possessions including my treasured Saturday Evening Posts. You must have done well as a young salesman."

I replied, "I achieved the rank of Senior Salesmen, Curtis Publishing Co., with my own cards, letterheads and envelopes.[10] I am so pleased to find out you used the Post to learn to read. Actually the same thing happened to me. I read it from cover to cover each week. They had all those continued stories from week to week and I could hardly wait until the next week."

Ah Wing replied, "Yes, I never did find out how those continued stories ended."

Ah Wing now said, "At first I could hardly read at all, but some of the crew helped me. "Ming said you were inquiring about a Ray Pearson. He was the crewman that helped me the most. Why are you inquiring about him?"

I told the Chinese what little I knew. Ah Wing and Delores spoke Chinese to each other at some length. Then Ah Wing said, " "Hasty decision often is mistake. I must think about this matter. Delores is my secretary. We go to Seattle tomorrow and will be back in a few days. Delores will call you and let you know if we should speak further about this matter."

I wondered if I dared ask a question. Ah Wing could tell I was struggling, but he let me struggle. Finally I asked, "Was he on board the China Queen when it was sunk?"

"A very good question, Mr. Lange. Yes, he was on board and he did survive. He saved my life and he went back to sea and served again. I

---

10 I still have several of those envelopes in 1996.

also went back to sea and survived another sinking. I heard he survived another sinking too. That is the last I heard of him. He changed his name on board our ship to Jerry Wasco."

It was now 6:30 and Ah Wing and Delores both rose. They bowed to me and I returned their courtesy and Delores extended her hand to me.

She told me later that early in our dinner she had said to Ah Wing, "Look at Lange's eyes. When my husband, who was killed fighting the Japanese, would get a few days leave he had that same look in his eyes. It's almost like my husband's eyes have returned to life in the eyes of Barney Lange. I must talk to Barney again. I hope you won't mind, Ah Wing."

I wasn't back at my apartment a half hour when my phone rang. It was Ming. She was obviously excited. "Please excuse my female curiosity. Would you care to tell me how your dinner turned out?".

First I said, "That was one of the most wonderful conversations I ever had in my life. It was unbelievable."

"Great, Barney. Fire away!"

So I fired away and gave her the major parts of our dinner conversation almost word for word. I was pleased to be able to share such an experience with someone Chinese.

Ming's response was simple. She said, "You are now in big time Chinese circles, Barney. Only other big chief you might meet someday is Dr. Fu."

I laughed and said, "You mean like a Dr. Fu Man Chu."

"Barney, that is exactly right, but he's a nice guy. When he looks you over you have been looked over. My guess is if they ever talk to you about Ray Pearson in detail you will meet Dr. Fu. Don't ask me why. Maybe Chinese woman's intuition."

Ming's words went to my Remember Forever File. Dr. Fu must be a power. I thought it best to not ask Ming to elaborate. In her own way, in time, Ming would tell me more, if she could and not betray the Chinese family secrets.

CHAPTER 18, I MEET MABEL JENSEN

Former wife of Ray Pearson, The Missing Gambler.

It was still early in the evening and. My mind was doing mental flip flops and the question was should I try to reach Mabel Jensen. I looked up her phone number, dialed and was lucky that she was in. I identified myself and was having some trouble explaining why I called. She said, "Are you sure you aren't a newspaper reporter?"

It was touch and go for a few minutes and I was expecting her to hang up any second.

When I told her who I worked for and what building I worked out of that seemed to make the difference. For some reason or another she knew my boss, Mr. Sanders, and my company.

When I told her that was my paper route in high school and who my one customer was she said, "Why, when Mr. Dowling and his wife left this apartment I rented it and have lived in it ever since."

Then I told her a little about how I got onto the subject of Ray Pearson-- because of the disappearance of a salesman in my office. She thought that rather amazing. I then said, "May I ask if the Ray Pearson that disappeared was your husband at one time?"

She replied, "I guess that's not a secret. Do you know something about him?"

I answered, "Not of recent, but perhaps around the time of Pearl Harbor."

"Oh my, God. Am I hearing you right! You sound like a nice person and I think I am a good judge of even people behind their telephone voice, but please don't make me have a nervous breakdown. Please say that again!".

I repeated myself and added a couple additional comments. She replied almost shouting at me. I have to talk to you right away. I would ask you to my apartment, but I really don't know you. Could I meet you at Munden's Ice Cream for a good cup of coffee. My coffee is lousy. Their's is great."

"What time would be convenient for you?"

"How about thirty minutes from now? How will I recognize you?"

"I am six feet tall. Weigh 140 pounds."

"Maybe I don't want to meet you. I am 5'6" and have graying hair. I also weigh 140."

"Don't feel bad. I went down from 175 to 110 when the Jungle hit me."

"That's too much of a diet for me to take. See you in 30 minutes."

———◆———

She sounded like a business lady, particularly because she knew the company I worked for and my boss, so I was greatly relieved. When I saw her I wondered if she hadn't fudged a little and weighed more than 140 pounds. She was dressed like a business lady with a gray skirt, light blouse and dark coat. Her graying hair obviously had regular care. Her round face showed she appreciated good food in ample portions. I didn't guess women's ages, but maybe forty. .

When she ordered coconut cream pie in addition to coffee my limited knowledge of diplomacy led me to order the same thing. When the waitress left us to place the order I told her how during my last summer in High School I worked at the Noon Bag Company I used to walk to the Multnomah Hotel and across the street have coconut cream pie for five cents.

She looked a little dubious and I had to explain. "I didn't get the pie at the Multnomah. There was a restaurant across the street. Out of the back of that restaurant went the food to serve the prisoners at the main police precinct. Hopefully, minus the Coconut cream pie. [11]

Then I told her about my meeting with Ah Wing and she wanted to meet him right away.

I quickly replied, "For now, Mabel, that would be a big mistake. Let this matter ride with the Chinese for awhile. The Chinese will have to be approached carefully. I will try to accomplish this. If I fail then you can take over."

---

11   Another true story from the Author's youth. Please believe it!

She agreed to that and then said, "Ray and I got married right after graduating from Washington High School. He went to work for Hirsch-Weiss, also later known as White Stag, which as you know is just the block behind the Noon Bag Co.

She stopped and was very thoughtful. "My husband didn't make much money and several successful businessmen made a play for me. I guess I was fairly attractive then--at least I was trim. They dazzled me and made me feel like a queen. My husband and I were living on the other side of the tracks with no view of success on the horizon. He was going out more often and staying out later and later. That gave me the opportunity to play around more. "

"Then he started making hints that he was in over his head. "

Mabel continued with, "I told him to just quit gambling. I noticed he seemed to draw into a shell, but occasionally he would say he was in trouble. One day he commented he might have to disappear. I thought he was kidding. One evening when he was really down he said, "If I ever have to leave town I'll change my name to something like Wasco, but never tell anyone."

"We had lived on Wasco Street the first year we were married. Those were really the only happy days of our marriage. Now his comments about leaving and using the name Wasco did come as a surprise. To go along with him I asked him what he would use as a first name. He answered, "Jerry, Jerry Wasco.""

"Less than a month later he went to work one morning and never returned. Finally I went to the police, but they just told me lots of guys left to avoid gambling debts. Maybe he was safer out of town if he owed a lot of money. I was sure mad at the police."

"Later in the year the war started. We all got swept up in that. Millions of men went overseas so Ray being gone didn't seem so strange. While you guys were dying in the South Pacific and in Europe I worked as a Secretary. I also danced at the USO with the soldiers and sailors and had a great time. Now here is a secret."

"I worked as a secretary for several lumber brokers. They gave me some lumber stock shares as Christmas bonus, and for working overtime. "And sometimes for doing favors for them. You know how some businessmen are. There were no promotions and few raises for secretaries. Unless, well--you know what I mean!. After Ray left I was lonesome and they knew it."

"So I'm not poor. If you get any leads on my ex-husband, and need a little money up front to get more information let me know. I'm a tough bargainer, but if I see merit in it I might advance the money."

She continued with, "It's been tough on my kids. Real tough. The letter Ruth wrote to Santa Claus was not singular. She writes and prays and cries. She dates a little, but has no trust in men."

I replied, "That is tough. Can you say anything to her without her getting up her hopes too high."

"Barney, I promise you I will think that over very seriously. I know if she knew her Dad had served on a Chinese Tramp vessel, got torpedoed and had the guts to go back and help the war effort by serving again and getting sunk again it would change her life. He would be her hero! So I must tell her right away. She lives in an apartment not far from mine."

Well, that cleared the decks and Mabel insisted she pay the bill. I walked her to her car. She shook my hand and then reached over and gave me a little hug. "You're a nice guy, Barney. Don't let this rotten world spoil you."

Then I thought of my Brother who drowned at a Church Picnic when he was eighteen and I was thirteen. It devastated all of us. Our lives were changed forever. We would have done anything to bring him back. [12] It was almost 11 P.M. when I got back to my apartment that Sunday evening My head was buzzing and my directional signals were running amok.

---

12 Unfortunately a true story from the Author's background.

CHAPTER 19, 11 P.M. FRIDAY EVENING.
I send Homer a cable, and write Frank a long letter.

My mind was in a whirl. My thoughts were going up and down like the ride on the Roller Coaster at Jantzen Beach. I was also like the crazy mixed up guy that goes to a performance and at the end sees a half dozen exits and can't figure out which one to take.

My mind told me to do the easiest thing first. That was send a cable to Homer. So I wrote and rewrote and ended up with the following:

HOMER AND BILLY BARNS C/O S.S. MONTE. MELBOURNE, AUSTRALIA.

WHAT A COINCIDENCE. STOP. BEST WISHES TO FRANK. STOP. WRITING HIM LONG LETTER. STOP. HAVE FRIENDS LOOKING FOR MISSING GAMBLER. STOP. GONE ABOUT EIGHT YEARS. STOP. WAS MERCHANT MARINER. STOP. SHIP SUNK TWICE DURING WAR. STOP. NAME RAY PEARSON OR JERRY WASCO. STOP. BARNEY LANGE.

I liked the quiet of the evening and getting things out of the way so I could relax and sleep. I decided to write Frank Beckman right then. I had attained a speed of 100 words per minute in High School typing class mostly because I also sold Remington #5 Portable Typewriters.

I still had my demo #5, so I put two sheets of paper in it and one carbon. It only took me a half hour to write the following:
Dear Hero Frank,

In the battle of Buna you were one of 9965 casualties out of 10,000 men. Here you are the only guy in the Terminal Sales Building who choose to leave town and leave everyone wondering where in hell you went. Mr. Sanders is not happy, but at our morning coffee sessions you are the number one subject. Several other guys are threatening Sanders they are going to do likewise. We all wanted, at one time or another, to go AWOL in the Army so you went AWOL and Sanders can't do a damn thing about it. Congratulations!

If I hadn't called Homer's folks I might not have known for months where you were, but in time you would have let us know, wouldn't you? I'm not going to ask you why you went. Figure that is your business-- but we're sure curious!

You may recall our Division, the 41st, was the first sent over. We arrived at Sydney right after the War started. We stood on the docks and were loaded into small Dutch boats and went through the most violent storm I would ever be in, in the Tasman Sea. We arrived in Melbourne and boarded a 1900 version of a train and headed for Camp Seymour, some 60 miles away

In basic training in the Field Artillery I got an Army drivers license entitling me to drive those big trucks with air brakes we used to pull 155 mm Howitzers. At Camp Seymour they made available to the Colonels some tiny Austin Coupes. As I had an Army Drivers License the Colonel asked me to drive him to Melbourne. I tried a U turn that day in downtown Melbourne forgetting you go from left to right. The Colonel was so frightened he never let me touch his car again. So I am one guy that understands the perils of driving on the other side of the street.

Please get well fast, and I'll be glad to take care of getting your medical application filled out. You are entitled to 30 days medical after you left Standard Register.

Almost three years in an Infantry Division and I got one short leave.

I got to spend five days in Sydney. Ray and I took the train from Rockhampton to Brisbane and then onto Sydney. We of course sat up in the train and it's wartime vintage was at least third class. When we checked into the hotel and saw sheets on the bed it was a grim reminder that we hadn't seen a sheet for almost two years. And only God knew if we would ever see one again. We didn't stay in the room long, but headed out the door not having any idea where to go.

We stopped in a pub and there was a guy that Ray knew from Los Angeles. Unbelievable. We found out he was stationed in Sydney and he was the one that took us out to Angelo's.. More unbelievable, and I still have the pictures to prove it, this man whose name was Tony had high class Aussie Civilian friends. They offered to let us take a short Sunday cruise on their Yacht, the Kyema, which had won the yacht races up and down the Australian Coast.

We moored in the bay for a light Sunday afternoon lunch and again also unbelievable was that the Aussie Navy located a midget Jap Sub that had slipped through the net at the entrance to the Sydney Harbor. They found the sub a few hundred feet from where we had moored. In later years when they coined the word sub-sandwich I immediately thought of how we had sandwiches not far from a Jap sub.[13]

Now as to my wire to Homer I mentioned the Missing Gambler. A Ray Pearson left town early in 1941. His neighbor later entered a Santa Claus letter writing contest and achieved some notoriety by begging Santa Clause to bring her Father home for Christmas. Mrs. Pearson remarried, now divorced again and her name is Mabel Jensen. She has never heard of Ray since.

I told you one day about my selling the Post. Well, a remarkable coincidence took place this week. I met an Ah Wing, now a Chinese Diplomat, who was a cook on the China Queen, in the early 1930's and to whom I sold a Post. Ah Wing told me this week that Ray left Portland on his ship, and saved his life when the ship was sunk by a Japanese Torpedo. Ah Wing says Ray changed his name to Jerry Wasco, and Ah Wing would love to know if Wasco is still alive.

---

13 The Author's stories about the Dutch ship, Camp Seymour, The Austin Car and Ray and Tony in Sydney, the Kyema and Angelo's are all true. Very fascinating was the Author's experience over 40 years later. I had taken a number of the U.S. Navy's Rose Festival trips to and from Portland to the mouth of the Columbia River. One day I was on the Bridge of a Destroyer, making conversation with the Captain. I decided to ask him if he had ever sailed in the Tasman Sea during a storm. The Destroyer Captain looked at me and said, "This destroyer came within one degree of capsizing in a storm in the Tasman sea off the Coast of Australia."

Then he asked me why I had asked him and I told him my story. So there we were, an Annapolis graduate and a former 41st Infantryman, sailing down the Columbia River toward Astoria on a pleasant summer day. discussing our storm experiences off the Coast of Australia.

Frank, old boy, I guess that's it. I have done a lousy job of correcting some typing errors, but it's late and time to sign off. Guess my writing skills, like Cinderella, at mid-night go down the tube.[14]

---

14 I kept that typewriter until I was seventy and moved into a small condo requiring me to get rid of a lot of things. It was manufactured in the thirties and there were clips instead of rollers to hold the paper against the platen. The platen solidified and became hard as a rock and the clips not having any spring to them would no longer hold the paper in place. In the 1950's I bought the first Smith-Corona Electric Portable that came on the market so that obsoleted the Remington immediately except for a keepsake.

For a little history let me add that in 1950 a 9 column credit balance electric adding machine sold for $310.00 plus $20.15 Federal Excise Tax. The next year I bought a new green coupe, replacing my blue coupe.

The new coupe cost $1950.00 and I purchased it from a car dealer in Lebanon, Oregon. So a new car could be purchased for six times the price of a deluxe credit electric adding machine in 1951.

Now 45 years later you can purchase a small one memory tape adding machine-calculator for one tenth the price of the adding machine 45 years ago.

But, you pay 10 times as much for a car than you did 45 years ago.

So what went wrong---well, you figure it out. I am busy writing this book !

CHAPTER 20, Barney tells Bobbie & Elaine.

It was hard on me mentally dealing with my office and Bobbie and Elaine and not bringing the saga of one Frank Beckman into the open. So I decided to go for it, but knew darn well I better get the word to Bobbie before I told my boss and he let the Cat, namely one Frank Beckman, out of the bag. I called Elaine at 5:30 and Bobbie wasn't home yet. Elaine decided that anytime after 7 P.M. would be great. "Call just before you come over."

Elaine then said, "Barney, my daughter is still kind of angry with me and she was very disappointed you went fishing and were not at the Uptown."

"She really likes the Phil Harris band and he is playing this weekend at Jantzen. She is trying to get up enough nerve to ask you to take her. When you get here this evening if I bring up the subject of Phil Harris would you take her to the dance. It's kind of crazy--sort of like something you would read in true confessions--Mother and daughter dating the same guy."

That thought shook me up no little bit. I didn't answer. Had I done it again. Screwed up my life and this time someone else's as well..

Just before we rang off Elaine said, "Remember, Bobbie could be an interlude for you, but I hope you never get serious about her. She's too bossy for you."

Wasn't that interesting! I was also sure I was just an interlude for Elaine. Lucky guy that married her. At least neither was a Japanese sniper so maybe I wasn't so bad off. Two lovely ladies, but then either or both might break my heart again. I fixed myself some dinner and tried to relax while I ate. I wasn't sure it was my lousy cooking or my nerves, but I could hear my stomach growling. I knew for sure I wanted to see more of Elaine. Elaine was at least a 10 and Bobbie was down the scale a ways.

I called at five to seven. Bobbie answered and said, "Please get here as fast as you can!" I arrived a few minutes after seven. Elaine answered the door, and said, Bobbie is upstairs doing a last minute 'Vamp session on her face.' Reminds me, she's never on time, except for work, and that is only because I make her go out the door, ready or not."

Elaine gave me a big hug and a light kiss and quickly wiped my lips with the tissue she had ready in one hand.

Just then Bobbie came bounding down the stairs and actually rushed toward me. She gave me a better hug than Elaine had and gave me a smack on my lips. Then both ladies took me by the hand and led me to the sofa where some wine, crackers and cheese were laid out in beautiful dishes accompanied by fancy napkins. Each time I was more ashamed of my apartment.

I looked at them both and in a solemn voice said, "Unaccustomed as I am to sitting on a sofa with two beautiful ladies I will probably have a sore neck and burned out eyes trying to look at each of you at the same time."

Bobbie laughed, but only for a second. "Come on Barney, give us the news about that dirty Rat, also known as Frank Beckman."

Well, that sounded like Bobbie Day all right. So I looked her squarely in the eyes and said, "I have been in contact with my network of spies over the world. They tell me that Dirty Rat is in Sydney, Australia."

Bobbie's eyes opened wide. "Are you kidding me, Barney?'

"No, Bobbie, I guess that is the fact of life!"

"So tell me Big time world wide super sleuth, yes, tell this fair damsel in distress what in hell he is doing there."

Bobbie's Mother quickly interrupted, "Bobbie, we do not swear in my house."

I found that very amusing considering what Bobbie would have said if she ever saw Elaine and I dancing in the hallway, squashed together like two sardines in a can.

I kept my eyes pointed in the direction of Bobbie, but I felt Elaine's foot nudging me and one of her hands scratch my back, which was now turned to her.

I responded to Bobbie with a tone of voice that might of sounded a bit like a Shakespearean Player, "Fair damsel, Bobbie Day, I cannot reply to that portion of your interrogation because quite simply I do not know."

Elaine was laughing, but Bobbie was just GETTING more angry by the second. "I'll bet I know the answer to that question. He went over to see some Aussie Gal he met and has been carrying a torch for."

I paused for air, and advice from the heavens, but none was forthcoming. So I unwisely blurted out, "There were some gals there worth carrying a torch for."

Bobbie came back with, "So I understand from the number that married Yanks and came to the U.S. with their babies the stork brought them."

Elaine was laughing hard now. "You kids are something!" Maybe I should get out my movie camera and film. I might be able to get big bucks for this scene."

About then I knew I had to make a quick switch of the topic matter so I said, "I have additional news on another subject."

Bobbie replied, "Pray tell very angry damsel your news!"

"Well, it's about the Missing Gambler."

"Come on, Barney, you aren't going to tell me you found him, too."

"No, beautiful damsel, I pray that I could, but I have found out the following."

———◆———

As I related the story I dropped my dumb impersonation of a Shakespearean player and Bobbie stopped me at mid-point and said, "Let's have some more wine. It was only then I noticed both her and her Mother had drained their glasses and mine was half full--or was mine half empty. That always bothered me--sometimes at Riggs Pharmacy while we were drinking coffee all the men got on that subject. The language the men used was not for the Day household.

Anyhow, by the time I had drank, or was it drunk, or was it drained my first glass the two women had emptied their second. Finally I said, "Das ist alles."

Bobbie said, "What does that mean?"

Elaine promptly replied, "He means that is all, that is the end of the story."

Then she added, "Bobbie, sprechen de deautch, nicht." (Bobbie doesn't speak German)

Then Elaine said, "Bobbie is kind of angry over the fact that she likes Phil Harris and he is playing at Jantzen this weekend and while a guy asked her she is holding out for a nice guy, who has not made his presence known on her horizon."

Elaine continued with, "Barney, you can be Sir Lancelot, or some other gallant warrior, by offering to escort the fair Bobbie to Jantzen Beach's Golden Canopied Ballroom."

I feigned surprise as I said, "I could be the gallant knight, Sir Dance-a-lot, by just escorting Bobbie to Jantzen for one night?"

I noticed Bobbie sitting with her eyes open wide and not saying a word. So I replied, "May I have the honor of escorting the sweet beautiful lady by the name of Bobbie Day to the dance at Jantzen this Saturday night?"

"Do I have to be sweet?"

I was thinking of several smart alec remarks I could answer to that, but my thoughts were altered when I felt Elaine kick my foot rather hard.

So all I replied was, "Definitely!"

I could tell Bobbie was fighting a variety of emotions and her Mother quickly said, "Excuse me kids, I am going to the bathroom."

I was glad she didn't add something like, "To throw up."

As soon as her Mother was out of the living room Bobbie reached up to me and gave me one really big kiss right on my lips. She was on my right and she put her right arm around my neck and gave me a second very warm kiss. Her lips were apart this time demanding a strong response. I put my left arm around her and kissed her several times. For a couple of seconds I thought she was going to move onto my lap.

Then she broke apart from me and said, "Thank you, Barney, I will be sweet and you'll have a good time. I promise you!"

After the wine and cheese she just had, she likely didn't have any lipstick left, but she took no chances and wiped my lips with a napkin---and relaxed with her back against the sofa. She said, "I wanted to hear the band and see Alice Faye, who is supposed to be there too. Oh, it will be wonderful! Oh, it will be nice!"

I noticed the emphasis was on how much she would enjoy seeing Phil Harris and his wife Alice Faye and not a great time with Barney Lange.

Just then Elaine came back into the room. She said, "Isn't it marvelous how Barney has located Frank and the good news on The Missing Gambler. And it is so fascinating that a Chinese Diplomat emerges that you met twenty years ago. You must be all wound up mentally, Barney. I envy you."

Just then Bobbie said, "The power of suggestion was too much. I need to use the bathroom. Please excuse me."

As soon as Bobbie headed up the stairs to her bathroom Elaine said, "You did good, Barney, Darling. I sure wish I was going to that dance with you. Would you take me to a dance sometime?"

There I was stuck again, but I quickly responded, "You bet, you set the time?"

Elaine reached over and kissed me and snuggled against me. I knew I had thrown the ball back into her court. She would have to set the time and place and keeping it from Bobbie was likely impossible. So it wouldn't happen soon.

Elaine heard the toilet flush, "Bobbie will be down soon."

As Bobbie came down the stairs I stood up. "Bobbie and Elaine. I think it is time I vamoosed. I'm not sure where that crazy word came from."

Bobbie said, "Let's get to the dance early. How about Sir Dance-a-lot, the Gallant Knight picking me up at 7:30."

I replied, "Fair Damsel, my carriage and I will try to be prompt."

Bobbie hugged me, and gave me a slight kiss on the lips. Then her Mother hugged me and gave me a slight kiss on my right cheek. I did feel rather princely as I departed. My cup was surely running over. The liquid in it was pretty warm. Would I get burned?

As I drove away I remembered how Bobbie never said anything nice about Frank and never inquired how he was. I had not said he was in the hospital. One thing I knew for certain--Ruth Pearson would be so thrilled to hear her Dad was alive. The strange circumstances of his departure were forgiven. Was he alive? If so it might take a miracle to find him.

CHAPTER 21, I meet Ruth Pearson

I wasn't home a half hour and my phone rang. It was Mabel Jensen. Could I please come by and meet her daughter Ruth, and personally tell Ruth what I had learned. Otherwise Ruth was going to have a serious nervous breakdown--she just had to talk to me.

It wasn't more than a hop-skip-and a jump from my apartment at Southeast thirteenth and Morrison Street to the four-plex across from the park.

Near the Southeast corner of the Park was still the basement hole that Mr. Lloyd, wealthy California businessman had dug to build a grandiose Hotel just before the 1929 "Stock Market Crash. Now an exit from the Banfield Freeway which in turn was formerly known as Sullivan's gulch. Only traffic through the gulch was freight and passenger trains.

As far as I knew Sullivan was a legendary hobo.

Mabel answered the door and introduced me to Ruth. She looked at me with awe. She put out her hand for friendship and as soon as she touched me she began to cry. Mabel had shut the door and she put her arm around Ruth, who looked at me between sobs. "Oh, thank you Mr. Lange, for bringing some good news about my Dad. At least we now know he was a hero."

Then she added, "He has always been my hero."

I knew we were treading on dangerous ground. Mabel said, "I told Ruth what you told me. It would be nice if you have the time to tell Ruth. I would like to hear it again."

Ruth's features and color of hair had a remarkable similarity to Bobbie's. But, there the similarity ended. I could see the strain, pain and suffering in her face as I had seen in my own families face. I guessed with Mabel working Ruth had not been able to come home after school to a loving Mother and certainly not to a devoted Father.

I felt crushed for her sake too. I almost broke down and cried. I wanted to get out of there as soon as possible. I talked for maybe an hour.

When I got up to leave they both put their arms around me and hugged me. As soon as I heard the door shut I began crying. By the time I got in my car the tears were pouring down my cheek. I knew I was crying for all the parents, the brothers and sisters and everyone else who had lost someone whether it was during the war or before or after. Why did this have to happen?

The tears hadn't stopped when I re-entered my apartment, but I knew for Ruth the pain would now be a little less for her for the rest of her life. I was thankful for that.

It had been an emotional evening for me. First my meeting with Bobbie and now my meeting with Ruth and her Mother Mabel.

CHAPTER 22, I tell my Boss and Fellow Salesmen

It wasn't raining the next morning, but we counted on some nice days in May. So spirits were up as I entered my office in The Terminal Sales Building and my face had a cheery smile. Right away I asked the Boss's secretary if I could speak with him about Frank Beckman. As soon as she heard those two words she jumped from her chair and knocked loudly on Mr. Sanders door. His answer was, "Now, what do you want?"

That sounded a lot like he was not at peace with the world this morning. Likely some big order that some salesman had promised him had gone to one of our competitors. Ouch!

A minute later I was in his office. Mr. Sanders powers of observation were excellent and he could tell I had something of importance to say. "Sit down, Barney. Do you have word about our AWOL salesman?"

Sanders had not served in the Military, but everyone used those four letters a lot. I kind of resented his applying them to Frank this morning.

"Yes," I replied. "I know where Frank is!"

Mr. Sanders looked at me incredulously with some anger mixed in. "O.K. Barney, spit it out."

That remark didn't win any gold stars with me, and when the Boss was intimidating I didn't like it. When he turned his wrath toward me I liked it a lot less.

All of a sudden I got really bold. I had occasional spells of bravery and defiance. I answered, "Mr. Sanders, aren't you going to say please?"

He looked at me and I could see for a second his face was contorted and if he had some murderous weapon in his hands it might have been my final time on this planet. All of a sudden he seemed to relax, and he said, 'You're right, Barney, I've no right to take out my anger toward Frank on you. Please tell me where he is?"

He even tried a half-hearted smile, but it was Ichabod Craneish at best.

"Well, I heard from an old Army buddy of mine and of Frank's. Frank is in Sydney, Australia."

"I'll be damned. Are you sure?"

"Well, Mr. Sanders, nothing is for sure in this world."

"Don't I know that. Got word this morning our big order from Apex went to Moore. So what's Frank doing in Sydney? He didn't take a slow boat. He got there fast."

"Yes, he did Mr. Sanders. No, Mr. Sanders, I don't know why he went there."

"That puts us back to square one with the guy. When I tell the Home Office where he is that isn't going to solve anything."

I replied, "I don't know anything about the Home Office so I can't comment. As my folks would say, Das ist alles " (That is all)

"Thank you, Barney, keep me posted and Thank You Very Much!"

Mr. Sanders seemed sincere as he spoke those words.

I had hardly gotten back to my desk when he came out of his office. Men, I have a brief announcement to make. I'll let Barney Lange make it."

Well, that caused a few backs to straighten up from the slouch position at their desks. What had happened to designate low on the Totem Pole, Barney Lange, to speak for the Boss.

I stood up straight, and in my best straight face said, "Unaccustomed as I am to addressing all of you men my news is simple, Frank Beckman is in Sydney, Australia and the nature of his business there has not been ascertained."

I thereupon sat down and received absolutely no applause. I immediately stood up and said, "As you men offered no applause, do not expect me to return soon for another speaking engagement. Thank you!"

Everyone thereupon clapped, and a couple of guys kept clapping so loud Mr. Sanders had to yell, "Shut it off you guys."

Obviously there were just doing it to harass Sanders. I was besieged with questions and I successfully irritated the men by saying, "No comment."

I put on my hat and coat, grabbed my briefcase, and headed out the door for a cup of Coffee at Riggs Pharmacy across the street. Now Frank had become even more of a celebrity.

He had not just taken off on a minor trip. He had gone all the way to Australia.

As the men came into Riggs to have coffee I switched the subject to the first murder in Portland in my youth. Some gal lived in an apartment furnished by her Boss and one day she shot him. Well, everyone in Portland could not believe an actual murder had been committed, and by a gorgeous secretary. I remember how my three brothers and I bugged my Dad until he finally drove us by the Courtyard type of apartments. Just driving by was awesome--my first introduction to the word.

For certain, Frank Beckman, was famous at least in the Terminal Sales Building. At coffee we all wished him well, and wanted to read the next chapter. **"Why did he do it?"**

Well, the men were more curious than ever. I did not tell them Frank was in the hospital.

CHAPTER 23, SYDNEY, AUSTRALIA, Frank Beckman moves to Katie's folks home.

It was about noon Sunday in Sydney and the setting was the home small modest home of Katie's parents. Her Dad, another Scotsman, one McIntyre Burris had been the scene of some thunder and lightening. The subject of the bloody Yank, Frank Beckman, and his stupid driving had been constantly discussed. His loving wife Irene had been born in Australia. Her 55 years in Australia had started in a rugged manner growing up in the outback. Small in stature she was still a bundle of energy and while she deftly deferred to her husband, a warehouse man, she had her lines in the sand and when she kindly said yes or no---you looked at her eyes--and knew how determined she was at that moment.

First she had privately explained to the rugged Mac that Frank had no one to look after him and when he was released from the hospital it would be a genuine act of appreciation for his bravery in defending Australia to permit him to complete his recuperation at their home.

Mac's reaction was as expected. He blew up. "That bloody Yank that ditched my lovely daughter Frances is not stepping a foot in my house. His wife Irene let him sputter and swear and then calmly came back with, "My love, remember it was my suggestion that Frances try to contact Frank Beckman in the U.S. and it was you that made her promise she would not. He was almost killed in his first battle for us in New Guinea."

On occasion some of Irene's friends would ask her privately how she put up with him. She would smile and say, "Mac would give his life for any of his daughters or myself. Mac's younger brother called him 'McLoud,' and he bitterly resented that name. If things did get too rough Irene was known to use that word on occasion, but she had a clever and sweeter way to put it to him. **She would say, "Love, I know you're not a McLoud so don't try to prove you are."**

So the smoke settled a little and it was agreed that Frank would stay with them for a few days. Mac had the last word however and said, "That bloody Yank better not cause my daughter Katie any trouble."

Irene was no dummy, having to deal for thirty five years with Mac. She countered with, If Frank was good enough for Frances why shouldn't he be good enough for Katie? Remember it was wartime and Frances did not know she had fallen in love with Frank. It was only later as she kept thinking about him, and comparing him with others she realized she liked him more than any other man. He was the one that finally quit his job and flew to Australia because he could not go on without seeing her face to face again. Frances married, but Frank did not."

Mac knew once again that when it came to the serious aspects of life, such as romance, that his dear wife could be depended on to sort through the sand and come up with the right answer. He knew it was time to agree. He replied, "You are very right my love. I give you my solemn oath, I will be both kind and gentle to the lad."

With that Irene walked over to her husband and put both her arms around him and said, "Your two daughters will now love you even more."

Finally he returned the hug and said, "With three lovely ladies to boss me around a man hasn't a chance."

Irene gave him a kind, but dirty look. He quickly added, "Mac knows he is a lucky man to have three such fine ladies to spoil."

———◆———

Mac had never met Frank, and beneath Mac's blustering he would never admit he was actually anxious to meet the man who had captured the heart of his oldest daughter, and who almost lost his life in the Battle of Buna.

Mac held to his promise. When Frank arrived the burly looking Mac smiled and put out his hand, "Welcome aboard, Matey. Please be feeling at home. The orders will come from the two ladies."

Frances's old bedroom had been kept for a guest room when Frances, or anyone guest appeared on the horizon. Mac and Katie carried Frank's suitcase and hand baggage into Frances' room. Frank was shocked when he realized he would sleeping in Frances' girlhood room--actually sleeping in her old bed. Katie insisted Frank take a nap and she held his hand as they talked for a few minutes before they left the room.

As Frank lay back on Frances old bed a flood of emotions overtook him. He had actually found Frances, but she was married. She hadn't forgotten him--maybe she still loved him, but the nearest and closest he would ever get to the great love of his life was right now--laying on her bed. He felt tears rolling down his cheek and he cried almost out loud, "Oh, Frances, we both blew it!"

He could not sleep. Instead his life played itself out in his mind, but finally exhaustion took over and slept fitfully as his dreams were haunted by nightmares. He was back fighting at Buna. His outfit was being slaughtered by the Japs. Those little concrete pillboxes were virtually impregnable. In desperation his outfit could only hope flame throwers might drive out the Japanese. The men carrying them were mowed down one after another from the Japanese inside the pill boxes. His squad had assaulted one pill box until they were all killed or wounded.

This afternoon, as he had many times before, he dreamed he was killed in the Battle for Buna. He lay there and that evening after dark his body was carried to a prep station and the next morning he was buried in the maggot infested soil in a clearing in the tall Kunai grass. A little white cross was placed over his grave. He wondered who was sleeping next to him and who would join him the next day, and the next day. He tried to inquire as to how the battle was going, but no one seemed to hear him. He shouted out loud in desperation, "Come on you guys, say something. I'm awake so you must be too."

His shouting was heard by Katie and she rushed into Frances' room. She immediately knew he was having a nightmare. She threw her arms around him and said, "There, there Frank, dear, you're in good hands. You're safe."

Then she kissed him on his forehead as he awoke. He put his arms around her saying,

"Oh Katie, I was back at Buna and I was dead. I watched them bury me! I wonder how many years it will be before I get over these terrible nightmares?"

The Author had nightmares about New Guinea for over thirty years after the war.

Katie looked at Frank and could see the exhaustion and fear his nightmare had created. She kept her arms around him and he finally said, "Katie, I've dreamed these dreams a thousand times. If I could only shake them. Are they going to haunt me for the rest of my life?'

She was overwhelmed as she looked at him. It just wasn't fair. She kissed him on his forehead again and then kissed him several times on his cheek.

He turned his head and looked directly at her. Their lips were only inches apart and afterwards Frances wasn't sure who closed the distance between their lips, or if they both met halfway. Their lips met and for a few seconds their lips held together. Then she laid her cheek against his, "Frank, dear, maybe the right lady, someday, will erase those dreams for you."

Then suddenly she realized how she had said the wrong thing. That likely the frustration he had suffered from missing Frances had been a contributor to the nightmares, and now that he had lost Frances forever maybe the dreams would never cease.

Finally Katie went back to the living room where her Mother was. She was in kind of a daze. Since Katie's husband had died from his war injuries, she had been terribly lonely. Watching him die had not made her anxious to start another relationship for life seemed to have no guarantees of longevity. Many of her nursing associates at the Hospital where she worked were not truly happy in their marriages. So being single had some advantages.

Katie said to her Mother, "Frank was having a nightmare. I suppose he will be haunted by them for years, but we nurses have plenty of nightmares so we understand."

Just then the phone rang. It was Homer Barns inquiring if Frank was there. They did not have a telephone connection in Frank's bedroom so Frank got up and came to the living room where the phone was located.

Homer said, "Our ship, the S.S. MONTE which was undergoing repairs in Melbourne had sailed into Sydney for a trial run up the coast and they had the evening off. Could Frank and Katie join them for dinner at Angelo's. Katie was absolutely delighted. Frank went back to his nap so he would have the stamina to go out for dinner.

Frances and Katie, and everyone else in Australia would often comment about Texans. While a soldier from the Bronx was just as distinctive they didn't seem to take the same pride in their state as the Texans did. Some would claim Texas was an independent nation and had become so as part of the settlement of the Civil War. They had volunteered to help the U.S. fight World War II and were really running the war. That is they were responsible for the Victories. The losses were only because their advice had not been taken. It was the only way the United States could hope to beat the Japanese--by learning to fight Texas style.

Katie's frugal Dad and Mom gave them a ride to Angelo's and Homer and Billy had a table waiting for them. The bigger, and louder, Homer said, "I do declare if you ain't the twin of your sister Frances."

Katie replied, "I'm three years younger than she is so I'm close to the age she was when you knew her in the hospital in Brisbane."

Katie immediately grasped the depth of friendship between Homer and Frank. She knew it was a friendship in combat that would last forever. Billy looked at Katie and said, "You must have wonderful parents."

"I do, but Dad gets a little gruff at times. Mom sure knows how to handle him!"

Katie was seated next to Frank. She took his hand. Homer and Billy gave Katie and Frank a complete run down on their job of running a Gambling Casino on their cruise ship. It was all fun money, but each night there was an auction for prizes and your bogus dollars bought you all kinds of prizes. It was a great way to keep folks entertained. Billy commented, "We all tell those great passengers the damnest stories. I bin' telling Homer all us guys in the service liked to lie a little, but we all have become the damnest liars. At times I do get a little ashamed of myself. I went to Church when I was a kid in Texas. My folks were sharecroppers and we didn't have --I can't use that expression in front of a lady."

Katie came back with, "Oh you mean the pot to----."

"Yeh, sorry Katie. We try to adjust our stories to the gamblers. Some times when there are just men at the table the conversation gets as bad as it was in the Army."

To that Frank laughed and said, "I guess I came from a Puritan family. My Army lingo never got too vile."

Homer cut in, "No excuses, old buddy, when the going got tough at Buna there wasn't any man there that was braver than you. More than once I was so shaken up I wanted to turn tail and run and hide. I looked at you trying to knock out that pill box with almost all your squad dead or wounded and I said to myself, 'We Texans have got to be as brave as Frank. To hell with being scared."

Katie patted Frank's hand. "Frances told me she learned from several other men in the hospital what a hero you were. Apparently you were the quietest man in the outfit, but day after day you were an inspiration to the men. Your General was removed from Command and General MacArthur sent in the I Corp Commander, General Eichelberger.

MacArthur's parting words to Eichelberger were, "Come back with a win, or don't come back alive."[15]

Homer said, "Talk about gambling. Men all around Eichelberger were hit, but not Eichelberger. It was hard to believe."

Homer continued, " This is another one of those strange occurrences. Barney Lange called our folks. I guess partly to say hello and partly to let Billy and me know Frank was missing."

Frank, who had been doing practically none of the talking spoke up, "You know that Barney helped solve a mystery in Santa Barbara and

---

15   All reports I have read confirm this.

Los Angeles. He's methodical. He even knew that my medical coverage was good for a month after I quit working. I didn't know that. Of course I never expected to end up in the hospital either."

CHAPTER 24, Frank raises the point of The Missing Gambler

They all went for seafood and the variety was extensive. All three men teased Katie about mutton. They added, almost as bad as the Japanese bullets was the Bully Beef and hard-tack they had to subsist on, day after day.

Frank said, "I got an Air Mail letter from Barney Lange today. He told me now that's he found me he still has someone to look for--a Missing Gambler, by the name of Ray Pearson, who might have changed his name to Jerry Wasco."

Homer came back quickly with, "His cable mentioned that!"

Billy quickly came back with, "That should be right down our bowling alley. You know we gambled our way through the South Pacific and still are."

Katie chimed in with, "And you almost lost!"

Billy replied, "Katie, that was for sure, but Homer is talking about our non-fighting moments. We played every kind of cards that was ever invented and rolled dice in-between. I always carried at least a couple of dice in my pocket. One of us carried a deck of cards in our pack. Why Katie, we couldn't have won the war otherwise!"

Homer nodded and said, "Billy is right. We polished them dice almost night and day."

Then he went on with, "So Barney is looking for a missing gambler. Now that sure does sound interesting."

The service at Angelo's was out of this world. Frank whispered to Katie, "That waiter must be a magician. He fills my water glass and I don't actually see him."[16]

Katie replied, "This place is the top of the line, Frank."

As Katie listened to the stories about gambling both on the S.S. MONTE and the men in Homer's and Billy's outfit mixed in with much comment and

---

16   I experienced this on my 5 day R & R.

conjecture over the missing gambler from Portland, Oregon she suddenly stopped and her eyes grew wide. She put her hand to her mouth. She looked at all three men. Sort of stared at them. "What is it Katie," Homer, asked.

"I recall another patient, besides Homer, that always had a deck of cards in his hands. It was in Melbourne where I did my Nurses training. I was working as an aide to help pay my way through nursing school. There is no way I could remember his name."

None of the three men said a word. It was almost like the three of them were back in the Jungle--listening--just listening, for a sound--for a clue. Katie was trying to pull it up from her mind. They knew it was time to be silent and give her a chance. Here they were three guys that fought the misery and danger of New Guinea sitting in perhaps the finest restaurant and night club in Sydney. Time to pause and reflect, and give Katie time to think.

Homer and Billy minds had often thought what their lives might be if they became professional big stakes gamblers. They had discussed and cussed the idea hundreds of times. Finally Homer said, "Katie, I have an idea. I insist-- take this five pound note and use it to make a few phone calls to the hospital in Melbourne. We should give it a go, Mates."

Homer continued with, "I'd like to send Barney a cable. Let's see I'll say;

Homer wrote out a wire, took everyone's suggestions, and ended up with.

BARNEY LANGE. STOP HAVING DINNER WITH KATIE, FRANK AND BILLY. STOP. FRANK IS RECOVERING STOP STAYING AT KATIE'S FOLKS HOME STOP. KATIE RECALLS A MERCHANT SEAMAN PATIENT, STOP. IN MELBOURNE HOSPITAL STOP. EARLY PART OF THE WAR. STOP ALWAYS HAD A DECK OF CARDS IN HAND. STOP. SEND FRANK A PICTURE IF YOU CAN GET ONE. STOP. LEAVING AUSTRALIA SOON. STOP. SEND ALL CABLES TO FRANK AT KATIE'S HOUSE STOP AND ALSO TO ME C/O S.S. MONTE STOP. HOMER AND BILLY.

Katie declined the five pound note saying the dinner was such a thrill that more than paid for any calls she would make. And if you have time I want you to stop by my folks house. I would like you to meet them. After dinner they took a Taxi to Katie's parents home.

CHAPTER 25, Frank's first home in many, many years.

Her folks became fascinated with these two characters. Just before Homer and Billy left her Mom said, "Homer and Billy, we had a lovely time. Call us any time and do come by and visit us whenever you can. We owe you Yanks a lot--and even if we didn't we like you two men."

After they left Katie said, "It's time for Frank to get some rest,"

Frank replied, "Thank you so much for your hospitality. Because my parents died when I was overseas this is the first home I've enjoyed since the war started.

Frank turned and headed for his room. He had scarcely left the room before Katie and her Mother began to cry, and even the tough Mac found a few tears squeezing out of his eyes. He looked at his wife and daughter and said, "Kind of hits a person right in the gut, doesn't it. Let the lad stay with us until he is quite well."

The two women got up and stepped the few steps to Mac and put their arms around him. It was at times like this he showed that Aussie's are unequaled for hospitality and caring.

His wife suggested a spot of tea and they each had a half cup. They talked of many things. Mac said, You know, my loves, I work around men all the time. We pass on lots of stories about the Yanks. They claim they don't like to march, they don't like to train. It's claimed they hate being soldiers and prefer to occupy their spare time playing Baseball, Football or golf.

Yet they volunteered by the millions. When they fought they carried that same spirit, energy and innovation. They were amazing fast learners. They would fight to the last man rather than retreat.

> *They amazed the world. Hitler and Tojo had underestimated and misjudged them. They knew they were the last bastion of freedom for a free world. It was an awesome responsibility which they realized and fully lived up to.*

He was almost eloquent in his statements. They knew it was time for bed.

Frank was very tired and had brushed his teeth, washed his face and gone straight to bed.

About 10 minutes later Katie knocked on his open bedroom door and asked him how he was. Then she offered to give him a back rub so he would sleep better.

Frank noticed she had on a cute negligee of a non-revealing nature. Frank had spent so much time in hospitals in his life and he knew even those two minute back rubs were a luxury.   This time Katie had him take off his pajama top and lay on his stomach. Then she spent a full fifteen minutes working slowly using efferflauge and kneading gently with some firmness. She could feel Frank relaxing and midway through her massage she knew Frank was asleep. She thought to herself, "I have always wished there was time in the hospital to give each patient fifteen minutes of massage. It would be so healthy for them."

Katie pulled the sheet over his back so he would stay warm and then continued to look at him as she reflected. "I am beginning to understand why my sister fell for him. If I'm not careful I could do the same."

Then she rose slowly from her position wishing she could look into a Crystal Ball and see if they had any future together.

"I've been struggling to accept the death of my soldier husband just as millions of other women across the world had to. In the case of the Aussie's it had been much worse for us than the American women. Our Aussie men went into the war long before the U.S. and into strange places like Burma and the many British Colonies spread all over the world. At the time of the War it was said there were 120 million people in the U.S. and 6 million sheep. It Australia it was just the opposite. 120 million sheep and 6 million people."

Katie went to her room reluctantly. As she slipped into bed she thought of how nice it would have been to just slip in beside Frank and go to sleep beside him. "I guess I'm very vulnerable, but he's even moreso than I. A man usually is."

———◆———

At breakfast Katie asked, "What did you do after you were shipped back to the U.S.?"

In six months I was back on active duty and they tried to make me an instructor, but I couldn't hack it. I just wasn't up to ordering a lot of men to become gung ho . All I could think of was the pillboxes, the flame throwers, the dead and the wounded. The hospital ship. The Hospital rooms. The men that would never walk again. I couldn't train anyone for that. I was classified as having combat fatigue.

"I was sent to Camp Roberts, California where I was made a barracks non-com. You made certain the men got up. I wasn't in good enough shape to close order drill them. They used to crowd around me at mess time and ask me to tell them how it really was to be in an Infantry Division in the Jungle. I had to lie to them! I couldn't tell them how bad it was!"

"I knew the war was a year older and the supply lines were improved and the equipment was better. But, deep down in my heart I knew the Japanese had another year to build their fortifications, such as on Okinawa where our men were crawling over dead bodies as they continued to fight. And it had been just as bad in Europe where in the Battle of the Bulge men froze to death standing up. For the Navy, the Merchant Marine and the Air Force. **I could not train anyone for that!"**

Katie looked at Frank and said, "You know Frank you probably aren't all that different from most men in combat. When you were in combat your fears were overcome by the need to capture the pill boxes, or the enemy machine gun or mortar emplacement. But when you got back to the States you couldn't urge anyone to kill."

Frank looked at Katie and said, "Thanks, Katie. It was claimed our I Corp Commander, General Eichelberger, who fired our 32nd Division General and took his place leading us, did not want to visit wounded in the hospital. It was alleged he feared it would weaken his resolve to win. He would be afraid to send men to their certain death to take a position. On the other hand I spent months in the hospital and I saw the terribly wounded. Many messed up for life. That's why I couldn't train men to die and lose their arms and legs."

Katie answered quickly, "Frank, let's change the subject. The War is over for us both. Now what would you like to do as soon as you get well?"

"That's a good question, Katie. One I ask myself continuously. I'm imposing on you so have to get myself off your hands very soon."

Katie wished she had not asked the question. Great remorse filled her and she was so disgusted with herself. "Frank, please forgive me for asking. I'd miss you terribly if you were to suddenly leave. Dad volunteered on his own, after you went to bed, to make certain you stayed as long as you needed to."

Suddenly the strangest feeling came over her. She knew what it was. She didn't want Frank to leave. She almost blurted out, "I'd like you to stay with me forever."

Deep down in her heart she knew you should truly get to know a person before you went out on such a limb. You had to see them under all kinds of circumstances. What really was their temperament like. It's not enough to guess. Katie knew that we humans sometimes want companionship so badly we blindly ignore all the warning signals and just say, "Oh, they are such a nice person. We will work it out, but that wasn't looking at life realistically."

She said, "Without love and respect marriage means nothing."

She knew several of her nurse friends were in that predicament. Marriage could be like a minefield---an explosion was possible at any time.

Frank said, "Thank you so much. I'd like to try my hand at running a small business myself. Does that seem strange?"

"Absolutely not, Frank. You are to be complimented to have enough guts to go it on your own. Afterall, nothing could be worse than what you already lived through in the war."

"Katie, that's exactly the way I feel."

Katie had often thought of how nice it would be to have a husband that ran his own business.

CHAPTER 26, THE NEXT MORNING.

The search for The Missing Gambler picks up steam.

At breakfast Katie said, "Frank, One of my best nurse pals in Melbourne is Marge. She is happily married to a severely wounded soldier, and they have two lovely children. I dreamt about her last night. "I'm going to call her right now and see if she remembers that guy that was always shuffling cards."

She called Marge's home first and was excited to find her home. After an initial few minutes of bringing each other up to date, including the fact that she had a former patient of Frances staying with her. Marge asked, "Is Frank the American Soldier that Frances was waiting for?"

Katie just said a simple, "Yes."

Then Marge became panic stricken. "Oh, my God. May heaven help them both!"

Katie quickly brought up the subject of the Missing Gambler.

Marge's response was, "Oh, that sounds so exciting. My Darling husband is an absolute nut on mysteries. You know for the men in the service the War was a real mystery."

"About all I have is that at one time his name was Ray Pearson or Jerry Wasco.

"Well, Katie, we'll give it a go matey. If you can get me any more information and particularly if you can get me a picture it would sure help."

"Thanks, Marge, don't use up a lot of time, but kick the idea around."

Marge's response was, "You know I will. You'd do the same for me!"

The two women rang off both expressing their loyalty and affection for each other.

————◆————

Frank helped Katie with the dishes. He thought to himself, "Katie looks so much more like the Frances I remember. She sure is nice and

I feel so comfortable being around her, but I realize nurses develop a great rapport with their patients. It's part of their way of life.."

An hour later Katie said, "I'm due on the 3 P.M. shift at the hospital today. Would you like a short walk around the neighborhood before I go?"

"That would be great. Tell me when you'd like me to be ready."

As Frank walked back to his room he was very relieved to know he had a place to stay for a couple of weeks and a chance to recover. As they walked they talked. They shared many thoughts and they wondered if they should be chasing the Missing Gambler.

Katie wisely announced, "Frank, I try to approach life one day at a time. If it's meant that the Missing Gambler is to be found maybe we'll be a part of it and maybe not."

They walked hand in hand for thirty minutes before Frank became tired.

Katie said, "Take a nap, Frank I'm going to eat a bite at 2 P.M. Join me if you feel like it."

She walked him to her room, stepped inside with him, gave him a quick kiss.

She exited before he could respond. He was asleep in ten minutes.

———•———

Katie and Frank had dinner before Katie left for her 3 P.M. shift at Sydney General Hospital. At about the same time, many miles South in the beautiful major city of Melbourne, Australia Nurse Marge, Katie's friend, had arrived an hour early to talk to Hazel, the gal on duty in records and they decided it would not be an easy task to go all the way back to War time records, but it could be done.

Marge said, "Would you like to be a part of a secret mission such as finding a girl's father that has been missing for at least ten years?"

Hazel laughed, "Aren't you the sly one. Give me some facts and I'll think about it."

Marge swore her to secrecy and told her what she knew. Hazel and Marge shook hands.

———•———

Hazel was in her fifties and had formerly worked as a secretary in Personnel. She was excited as her meeting with Marge brought memories of those war years flooding into her mind. Time was reducing them, but they were so dramatic they barely lay under the surface of her mind. The hospital had doubled it's bed capacity as wounded were brought in by the plane load. And when a Hospital Ship docked with wounded the staff would all forget about hours. Doctors and nurses worked ten and even twenty hour shifts. **You couldn't let men die because it was 11 P.M. and your shift was over!**

Working in records and personnel Hazel knew of many nooks and crannies where records had been placed temporarily and now years later they were still in temporary. Marge also knew if she found a Jerry Wasco there would be no clue where he might be today.

At first Personnel did not want to be involved and were reluctant to let Hazel snoop. Many a newspaper reporter had made the same requests over the years. Marge persisted and they gave her a minimum of time and the name Jerry Wasco came up perhaps easier because it was unusual and near the end of the alphabet.

Then they found it twice. Once in 1942 and once in 1943. The records showed he had two different doctors and in both cases was rescued at sea. Hazel knew that each Doctor treated hundreds of men a few minutes at a time. Would a Ward Nurse remember him? All they could do was try. From Personnel she got the names of nurses on duty those years who were still on duty with the hospital. With those names Hazel began the laborious task of tracking down the nurses.

"Do you recall a merchant seaman who was injured while being rescued at sea in both 1942 and 1943. Originally his name was Ray Pearson, but our records only show a Jerry Wasco. Maybe he often had a deck of cards in his hands."

Hazel would carefully write down the nurses name and their replies to her questions. . Three days later she called Katie and said, "I'm getting some interesting answers, but have not struck any pay dirt yet. Don't worry, now that I'm into this I'm going to work it through. Keep trying to get me a picture."

A totally unexpected result was that several nurses had guys in their mind that they apparently never forgot and they asked Hazel if there was any way they could locate them. Of course there wasn't and this made Marge think of Katie's sister Frances and how she had wished Frank Beckman had contacted her right after the war. Hazel thought, "Many a heart still pines for a friendship made during those war years."

A couple of them remembered the name Wasco. It was such a strange name. Several nurses said, "Be sure to check with Nell. She was such a flirt. She had so many boy friends she had her own little address book. It was green, but Nell, well, she wasn't green. She got around, but she was nice. She helped many a soldier with a little feminine R & R "

Hazel had entitled Nell as 'The Green Book Nurse.' One of her Hazel's shifts coincided with Nell's and she suggested they have dinner together. She wondered what Nell would say if she started the conversation with, "There was a mighty strong rumor that you approached every good looking man in your Ward for dates just before they got released."

Instead Hazel first gave Nell the background of her problem and the fact she was at a dead end. Hazel etched her face in sorry and said, "Please Nell I need your help."

Nell seemed to give the matter her sincere thought. Finally she said, "I guess you learned I was the number one flirt. Well, it got me quite a few dates and maybe I helped a few lonesome guys at the same time. You know, Hazel, I met so many guys I can't remember their names. Bill, Tom, Henry, Jerry--you know there was a Jerry I really did like."

"What was his last name?

"I'm terrible with names. I found it wiser to not try to remember their last names. You know how men were supposed to have a little black book with all their conquests in it. Well, mine is green. And you've been sweet to me, and haven't mentioned my green book. I'll call you tomorrow if I find a Wasco."

The next day Hazel received a call from Nell. "I found his full name, Jerry Wasco. I remember him now. I should have remembered him because he was in our hospital twice. Once his ship had been sunk by a Jap torpedo and the last time, which was 1943 his Dutch ship was sunk in a storm in the Tasman see. He was rescued by another Dutch boat carrying American Soldiers from Sydney. I remember his playing cards bothered me. That's against my religion."

Hazel was elated, "That green book is a lifesaver."

Nell continued with, "You know he was kind of a strange guy. He just would not talk about his past. I even made a note of that. It kind of worried me. I finally concluded he must be married and didn't want to lie so just clamed up."

"Oh thank you so much. If you think of anything more please let me know."

Nell didn't seem to want to hang up. They talked about the war and in-between Nell seemed to be reliving the war. She mentioned several names of guys she wished she knew where they were now. "Finally, she said, wonder if I could write the War department."

Hazel concluded with, "It's worth a try. "

———◆———

Hazel immediately placed a call to Marge, who in turn placed a call to Katie in Sydney. Katie was at work, but Marge talked to Frank. He listened intently and was profuse in his thanks. They continued to talk and came to the inevitable conclusion that Jerry Wasco most likely was sailing around the South Pacific-unless he was dead--and that was entirely possible. It wasn't only Jap torpedoes that sunk ships. The Japs opened fire only too often when their subs had been sailing on the surface and they sighted a small cargo vessel.

Additionally the ever present Jap Zeros and bombers sank hundreds of cargo vessels. It had been a brutal War for everyone.

Marge promised to keep looking and Frank thanked her again and again. He promised that Katie would also call her.

Frank composed a cable to Barney Lange.

BARNEY LANGE. STOP. JERRY WASCO IN MELBOURNE HOSPITAL MAYBE 1942 AFTER BEING TORPEDOED. STOP. AGAIN IN 1943 WHEN RESCUED FROM DUTCH BOAT IN TASMAN SEA. NO ADDITIONAL WORD. STOP. FRANK BECKMAN C/O McINTYRE BURRIS.

Katie was on duty so Frank just saved the cable. Her folks were out to dinner with friends. They had invited Frank, but he had declined using the excuse he needed to rest. He did, but was wide awake when Katie returned from her late evening shift. Her folks had arrived about an hour earlier and Scott and his wife had gone to bed.

Katie was pleased they had actually located the hospital Wasco had been treated at, but where might he be now. Perhaps Davy Jones had welcomed him to a watery grave as it had so many men.

Katie fixed herself a bite to eat and she and Frank continued talking. Katie said, "Frank, I'll give you a little massage, which will put you to sleep, but could you just rub my shoulders while I sit in this chair."

Frank replied, "If you'd like you could lay down and I'll do it."

Katie laughed, "Wouldn't I like that. I'd be asleep in five minutes. Say, why don't you get into your pajamas and I'll do likewise."

They did just that. Frank massaged Katie's upper back for almost ten minutes. She kept her tops on and he worked slowly and she was barely awake as he finished. He took off his top and she began working on his upper back. Soon she asked, "Do you feel comfortable?"

"Katie, I feel so comfortable and happy I wish this could go on forever!"

Katie knew she should answer, but didn't want to right then. As she reflected she felt Frank fully relaxing and knew he must have fallen asleep. She thought to herself, "If I'm not careful I will talk him into asking me to marry him and I know I couldn't say no."

"It's too soon for us to decide."

As she continued to reflect she wondered, "Who really knows? When will the time be right?"

Katie went to bed saying a prayer, "Please give Frank and I wisdom."

That night she dreamed she was Frank's wife. They lived together in a small apartment and they were deliriously happy. They both knew it was forever.

CHAPTER 27, What should Frank and Katie do next?

It was certainly exciting to know that Jerry Wasco was still alive in 1943, but with two known sinkings he led a perilous life and may not have survived another sinking.

Frank and Katie found their morale was sinking with such thoughts. Katie knew just as Frank had survived the Battle of Buna many a man was still around that fate had not claimed as yet, but she said, "Well, Matey Frank, let's still give it a go."

Marge helped matters by calling and saying that her husband Don wanted to meet Frank. Don had some ideas on checking places in Melbourne.

The clincher for certain came when another cable came from Barney Lange. It read:

> *FRANK BECKMAN. STOP RUTH PEARSON IS BEGGING HER MOTHER STOP GO ALL OUT TO FIND HER DAD. STOP. MABEL IS SENDING YOU $1,000 STOP. SHE HAS FUNDS TO PAY MORE. STOP. DECISION UP TO YOU. STOP BEST WISHES. STOP BARNEY LANGE.*

Katie was home when Frank received the wire. Katie exclaimed, "A thousand dollars. Why that's a lot of money!"

Finally Frank said, "Well, puts a guy on the spot doesn't it. I guess we don't have to answer, but we can afford to take a trip to Melbourne and Ruth and her Mother may hold it against us if I don't go."

Katie quickly responded, "Yes, you should go Frank, but I want to go with you. I know I can get the time off, but wonder what my Dad would say?"

When her Mother returned from shopping Katie decided to start the fishing. She helped her Mother put the groceries away and said kind of off handed," I often call Frank dear. If Dad hears me don't let him be upset. We call most of our patients Dear and Frank is truly a special kind of a guy."

"He is for sure. I would have love to have a son as nice as he is."

Katie thought to herself, "Besides my parents my Sis is looking over my shoulder wondering about Frank and I. And of course wondering what might have happened if he had come to Australia two years earlier. I wonder if she is suffering from regret?"

Then Katie made her bold move, "Frank is receiving $1,000 from the Mother and Ruth is begging her to continue the search. Don thinks Frank should come to Melbourne. May I go with Frank. I feel he still needs someone with him, and I want to be with him."

Her Mother gave Katie a hug and answered, "It will be just fine with me. I must talk to your Dad first before I give my official O.K."

"I am so glad you understand, Mom. Thank you."

It was still morning and Katie and Frank decided they would tackle the Maritime Headquarters. The young Aussie gal on duty was a blond, breezy type who from the way she talked knew her way around the waterfront. She found a Jerry Wasco and they were elated. Then they became somewhat deflated when she informed them he had only substituted for a Winch Operator that had cut his arm and his employment was for only two weeks in 1944.

So now they had one more year under their belts. He was still alive in 1944. The blonde looked like she might spend a lot of time at Bondi, Manley or some other beach. Try as they might they could not get any more information from her.

It was time to eat lunch and as they ate Frank laughed and said, "I'll put this lunch on my expense account."

As they ate they pondered the question of checking with a private detective agency.

Katie had heard of a small Sydney Private Investigation firm. It was Hawes and Dove, Ltd. Mr. Dove was in. He looked to be at least sixty. Tall and lanky--like he might have grown up in the Aussie outback on a remote cattle station. .

Once he started firing questions at Frank his prowess as a private investigator was obvious. Frank and Katie looked at each after each question and found themselves uncertain what to answer. In exasperation Dove said, "Folks, part of being a good Detective is being able to look at people and come to a conclusion. I don't know if you are just unwilling to share or are trying to con me. If you really want to find this man I have to know every possible detail about him!"

He said those last words with such challenge in his voice all Frank and Katie wanted to do was get away from him and in private evaluate what they should do.

Dove correctly sensed the situation. "I can tell you need to talk to each other privately. There won't be any charge for my time, but if you return the next interview will cost you five quid."

Frank and Katie felt relieved when they were outside the building and a cooling breeze from the Harbor stimulated their senses. Frank said, "That's kind of a rotten business to be in."

Katie laughed. "My dear, you are in that business right now!"

It was Frank's turn to laugh. "You sure are right."

Katie and Frank checked various other places without any results. They covered a lot of ground and were tired by the time they headed for her home. Katie thought to herself, "I feel so happy being with Frank and my mind and body seemed to be telling me to throw caution to the wind and get to know Frank a lot better.

When they got home Katie found a note in her Mother's handwriting saying she and Dad were out to dinner and likely wouldn't be back until close to ten P.M.

At first this surprised Katie, but on second thought she wondered if this wasn't her Mother's doing. Perhaps their absence meant they wanted Katie to be alone with Frank and see what developed.

Suddenly she wondered if the guiding hand behind this was her sister Frances and it was she that was acting as the Maestro and wielding the baton while Katie and Frank orchestrated a friendship or a serious relationship. Katie pushed aside her reverie and said to Frank, "My folks won't be back until 10 P.M. I've got an idea. I'll give you a good back massage and if you don't fall sound asleep you can give me one, too!"

Then she added, "I'm thirsty, let's have some Tea."

Frank was pleased to be back, "Both sound wonderful to me."

Katie instructed Frank to relax on the sofa while she fixed the tea. As they sat together sipping the tea Katie felt a wonderful wave of happiness flow over her. She leaned toward Frank and put her right arm around him and he reciprocated by placing his left arm around her. Their heads were only inches apart and they kissed lightly on the lips. That taste of happiness led to a second more serious kiss. Within a few more seconds their kissing was moving to the slightly passionate level.

Katie broke the silence with, "I think we're ready for the massage."

As they moved to Frank's bedroom some apprehension came to the fore. She thought, "There are massages between friends and massages between lovers. Frank and I have just moved beyond just being friends."

CHAPTER 28, Katie and Frank get a lot better acquainted.

Frank's mind was racing. He knew the male-female world could be a mine field, but Frances was gone forever and Katie would not remain available forever.

Once in his room Katie said, "On with the wonderful world of massage, Frank, dear. Take off your shirt and lay down on the sheet. Why don't you put on your pajama bottoms. I need to change to something more suitable."

A few minutes later Katie came back with some massage oil. She was dressed in her pajamas. First she massaged his shoulders. As she did so she also used her thumbs to search for pressure points as she mixed Shiatsu {thumb pressure on acupuncture points) along with kneading his shoulders. Then she began long Effleurage stroking of his back.

Then she went to compression, squeezing and rubbing over his skin and it's underlying structure, lightly at first. Then progressively heavier, invigorating and stimulating to the blood flow and lymph glands. Katie worked on Frank slowly, explaining Friction, Chucking, Rolling, wringing, and percussion, both light and strong. She obviously had some extensive training.

Her light, but firm touch, did it again. He fell sound asleep. She said to herself, "I wonder when he will awake and will he be able to return my massage."

She was about to cover him up with the sheet when suddenly she said to herself, "Take one day at a time, girl"

She stopped, got in bed with him, then pulled the sheet over both of them. She could barely keep her arms away from him, but soon she was asleep, too.

He didn't stir for an hour, but the moment he did she put her arms around him and they kissed as their bodies pressed against each other. "It's time for you to give me my massage."

Katie threw back the sheet and slipped out of the top of her pajamas. Frank saw the beauty of her upper body for a brief few seconds. Her breasts were firm, but not large. To Frank her beauty was classic. She lay down on her stomach as she said, "O.K. my War hero, let's see if you remember the massage I just taught you!"

Those words took some of the romance out of the scene and he struggled to duplicate the massage she had just given him. She teased him saying softly, "You rub my back and knead my back. All you have to be careful about is not to bring any pressure on my spine or the lower part of my back where my kidneys are. There are some other important factors, but I'll tell you to stop if you are making a mistake that might injure me. I've had a lot of massage training so I can guide you. Massage shouldn't be done by the inexperienced to the inexperienced."

When he was finally finished Katie said, "Not bad, Frank. Not bad at all. You have a gentle touch.

Frank didn't know what to say except, "I would always be gentle to you, Katie."

Katie only replied, "I am sure of that,"

She was thrilled by his words. Her thoughts of her deceased husband entered her mind for a few seconds and then her need to be close to a male again. Neither of them had on their pajama tops and Katie said, "Let's get under the sheet and rest for awhile."

Then she added, "Let's take off the bottoms of our pajamas and hold each other close. With the sheet over them they wrapped themselves in each others arms. They were both so tired and the massage had relaxed each of them so much they almost fell asleep, but the warmth of their bodies and lips together pushed sleep out of the scene.

Katie began to caress Frank showing him she was not a reluctant partner.

Several times Frank had dreams about Katie and for a few moments he thought this was another. As Katie's hands moved over him his passion took off like a rocket. Katie was worried that he would not be able to hold back. She reduced her movements for a few minutes, but soon realized she couldn't wait any longer. She pulled him atop her. "I'm ready for you Frank. Oh, Frank, Darling, I am ready. Now! Yes! Now!"

With Frank astride her their movements became rapid and their passion overwhelmed them. Then their world exploded and they sailed into the galaxy that only the more tender reach. It was as if they had left this world and were sailing in a special universe. They had reached the summit of the Mt. Everest of life and nothing else would replace or dim the beauty of these moments.

Their minds knew they never wanted to leave where they were right then. Words of endearment gushed from their hearts and both realized what their lives together could offer them.

Minutes later they lay alongside both frightened at the prospect of not being together again, yet wondering what was the right thing to say at this time. Katie knew she probably should make the first comment. "Frank, that was wonderful. It was unbelievable."

Frank, never having been married, knew he could never want more than he had just experienced, but he had difficulty in expressing his feelings. Finally he replied, "If married life is like this I have sure missed a lot in life."

That put Katie on the spot. She stammered, hardly being to reply. "Married life can be like this Frank, but it takes a dedication that not everyone has. Let's hold each other for awhile and talk seriously a little later."

Ten minutes later they were both sound asleep. An hour later Katie awoke and her stirring woke Frank. Their lips came together again and their bodies were responding. Katie suddenly stopped her movements. "Frank, that was the first time for me since my husband died. Let's just relax for a few minutes and let me get up and fix dinner for us. You stay in bed and rest."

Frank's reply was, "I'll just stay in bed until you have finished using the bathroom. Then I want to get up and enjoy your company while you're fixing dinner."

Katie threw both her arms around Frank and squeezed him tightly. "You don't talk a lot, but you sure know how to say the right things at the right time."

As Katie fixed dinner she laughed, "You know, we Aussie's know a million ways to fix mutton and tonight we're going to have lamb chops and mint jelly. Can you handle that?"

Frank was so thrilled that he and Katie had just shared themselves completely with each other he searched for the right words knowing the new elevation of their relationship.

Frank laughed too. "You know the only bad thing I have ever said about the Aussies is about that bully beef and hardtack. We figured that was why the Aussie soldiers were so tough. If they were raised on that stuff they could handle anything."

———◆———

During dinner Katie brought up the subject of love and dedication. She said to herself, "I need to find out more about Frank's approach to this."

Frank kind of beat around the bush, then suddenly he seemed to want to reply. He said, "I never did agree with the concept that a woman was subservient to a man. While I don't profess any prowess as a biblical scholar there is one part of the bible that covers the subject the way I feel it should be."

Katie was surprised and now she was most curious. "Tell me more, Frank!"

"Where it says that love is feeling as deeply about another's needs as about your own."

Katie got up from her chair, walked over to Frank--stood behind his chair.

She hugged him. "Frank, darling, in one simple sentence you have described what is wrong with the world and particularly marriages and relationships. You amaze me!"

"Katie, you have to add to that what you said about commitment. I'm afraid that so many people can't continue to do anything well, with regularity."

"Yes, Frank, that is what it is all about! Love is being always aware of the other's needs are as important as your own, but again the needs have to be reasonable. A need to gamble, be unfaithful, etc is not legitimate. And being considerate one day, and horrible the next day doesn't work either. I know it's tough to be cheerful and cooperative and loving each day. A nurse hears a thousand stories a year. So many are bad. It makes us sad. And it makes us careful."

Frank answered that with, "I think I could be considerate each day, but again I haven't been married so I don't know for certain."

Then Katie threw all caution to the wind. "Frank, I sure hope someday to find a man that could love me forever, and always be considerate and kind to me."

Frank replied, "Katie, I know I will always wish for you that you find such a man."

For a moment his reply bothered Katie. Then he added, "If I knew I was the right person for you I'm sure life with you would be wonderful."

Katie looked at Frank, "I know how wonderful I feel when I am with you. I've had many hours of sorrow and for the first time I seem to be able to put that in the back of my mind and just enjoy being with you. I'm a little ashamed to have gotten into bed with you so soon. On the other hand the War has stolen so many of our years and we can never get them back."

Then Katie began to cry, softly.

Frank put his arms around Katie. He didn't know what to say as his heart told him to treat this lady tenderly! **They ate dinner slowly. They both knew they must make some decisions very soon.**

With dinner over Frank asked Katie if he could call Marge She went over to the telephone and made the call. Marge was in and was sorry she and husband Don had not come up with anything new. Frank took the phone. Upon hearing how Wasco's daughter Ruth was taking all this Marge suggested they come down and check out Melbourne. She said, "Let me talk to Katie."

She said to Katie, "My husband Don feels the search should continue. We were about to call you and offer our kids room for you to sleep in. You'd each have a room. Our kids can stay with their Grandparents, which they do a lot anyway. You don't want Frank to take off by himself yet, anyway, do you?"

"You're right Marge. Thanks so much for the offer. Let us discuss it for a day or two."

"Don and I would like your company, and I suppose I am very curious to meet Frank. Got to meet the guy that stole Frances heart."

Katie was sensitive when Frances name came up, but she gallantly replied, "He's a very nice guy."

Marge replied, "I know he must be exceptional."

CHAPTER 29, Frank and Katie go to Melbourne.

It was easy to convince her Mother, but not so easy to convince Dad. Even the promise they had separate bedrooms didn't get his consent. Finally his wife had to virtually tell him to put up or shut up. She said, "Frank is not ready to travel alone. Secondly, this is a wonderful opportunity for them to get to know each other better. I like Frank very much and so do you. If you're worried about them sleeping together they can do that in Sydney. They can rent a Hotel room."

Katie talked to her nursing supervisor and was able to get three days off in a row and her Mother and Father agreed to let her go with Frank. Again Katie wondered what part her sister Frances might have played in this, but she had progressed mentally to the point she had put Frances in Frank's past where it belonged. She desperately wanted to go with Frank and share a Holiday with a male. It had been too long. Most of all she didn't want Frank going off by himself.

Frank commented, "Even if we don't find any trace of Wasco it would be nice to see Melbourne. I was in rehabilitation there and longed to see the city. Also I'd like to visit Camp Seymour. The 41st went there and we didn't. I've heard so much about Melbourne and never visited it. So with it all agreed Frank sent Barney the following cable.

BARNEY LANGE. STOP. LEAVING FOR MELBOURNE 36 HOURS. STOP. FOUND OUT WASCO DID WORK TWO WEEKS IN SYDNEY STOP. EARLY 1944 AS WINCH OPERATOR, STOP, SPOKE BRIEFLY SYDNEY AGENCY. STOP. THEY ASKED TOO MANY QUESTIONS. STOP. STAYING WITH NURSE FRIEND OF KATIE'S, STOP. IF NECESSARY WILL GO TO BRISBANE, TOWNSVILLE AND PORT MORESBY. RECEIVED MONEY FROM MABEL. STOP FRANK BECKMAN.

Katie and Frank had a most beautiful ride together on the train to Melbourne. The train was a far cry from the troop trains of 1942, 1943 and 1944. Then the cars had tiny two bench compartments that opened from the outside of the trail. Four men could sit on one seat. The problem was that ten men were assigned to each. One sat on the floor between your feet and one in the luggage rack. The men each had a duffle bag, a back pack, and their 1903 rifles. No toilets and no water. No aisle's to walk up and down on.

At the border of each province you had to unload the entire train which included all your equipment as the size of the rails changed limiting each train to travel to only within that Province. Seven days and nights, sitting upright to reach Rockhampton.[17] You did get to see the countryside and unbelievable Kangaroos often ran alongside the slow train. Barney recalled they could not make one hill. They backed down and tried again.

It was interesting that after the war the Author received a postcard showing Kangaroos on the Golf Course Green. . They were considered sort of like sacred cows and would watch a person putt. No doubt knowing for certain that mankind was crazy.

When Katie and Frank arrived in Melbourne Marge was waiting for them. They transferred to a commuter train that took them to Surrey, where she and Don lived.

It turned out that Don was a frustrated Mystery Story Writer. He complained that he had writers cramp. First by writing his stories--then by writing publishers and getting the usual rejection letters. Don had written out the addresses of all the maritime organizations and facilities that Katie and Frank might consider visiting. Don had made some contacts and those were noted. None had resulted in any leads, but the next day Katie and Frank would continue the search.

---

17 The Author will remember that trip to his dying day. I had become deathly ill a few days before and on the trip our Medical officer wanted to hospitalize me. He had taken one look at my yellow face and he knew I had come down with serious hepatitis. I was panic-stricken to leave my outfit so he let me stay until we reached Rockhampton. I went to a field hospital for two months, where I was told the hepatitis had come from the contaminated blood in my yellow fever shot. When we later went into the Jungle my resistance was low and I easily came down with severe Malaria along with the usual Dysentery, Jungle rot, jungle sores, lack of water, malnutrition from scarcity of food. etc, and etc, but no scarcity of Japanese.

After a pleasant evening of visiting Don and Marge went to bed giving Frank and Katie freedom in using the one bathroom. Don had put the luggage for Katie and Frank in just one bedroom.

The coast was clear and in the bedroom Katie quickly removed her clothes. She stood completely nude and wiggled her hips as she said, "I'm yours all night Frank, darling."

Frank stared in rapture. Her bare shoulders and arms were a tantalizing background for her firm breasts which were pointing at him. Below her breasts was a slim waist that led to sensuous hips which she was moving seductively to tantalize him. Her bare beautiful thighs were almost more than his eyes could handle.

"Katie, you are so beautiful"

Katie bowed, slipped into her bathrobe and headed for the bathroom to take a shower. She was like a nymph moving swiftly and gracefully like the mythical goddess of beauty.

Frank removed his clothes slowly and slipped into his bathrobe. He thought of those days in New Guinea and the years afterwards. For a few moments he thought of Frances and then his mind moved quickly back to Katie. Again he felt like he was dreaming. If so it was at least a pleasant dream and not a nightmare where he was once again in combat in the Jungle.

When Katie returned from the Bathroom she was wearing her nightie. She threw her arms around Frank and kissed him passionately. Then she walked over to the bed and turned back the covers. She slipped off the nightie and quickly lay down without pulling the sheet up.

Then she winked at Frank and said, "I'm ready and waiting, love."

Frank quickly took off for the bathroom. When he had showered she was covered by a sheet. She threw it back so far he once again viewed almost her entire nude body. He slipped in beside her and she drew the sheet over both of them and then she fiercely threw her arms around him. She knew he was not talkative, but she wanted to talk a little before they made love.

She said, "Frank, life is a long journey--when you're a nurse it's not only long for you, but you fret and worry so much about the welfare of others. Sometimes that's good because it get's your mind off your own problems."

Katie knew from her study of psychology that her long journey comments might give Frank an opening to say something. It worked. He said, "Katie, when I was growing up I could hardly wait until I became a man. I guess I became a man at Buna--fighting the Japanese in those concrete pill boxes. Watching my buddies die--almost dying myself. What a lousy way to become a man. Then my folks death. And all the time thinking about Frances, but when I saw you I thought you were my Frances."

Katie could hear Frank choke on those last few words. Than he continued with, "Now, for the very first time since I was drafted I feel truly happy. I'm still a little afraid! I maybe wonder if I'm just not having a wonderful dream.

It was a strange feeling for them both. They were talking so seriously yet they were holding each other so tightly their bodies were reaching out to each other wanting to become one. They had taken the train so they could enjoy the scenery, but it was a long tiring trip.

Now they were going to spend their first night together, like an illegal honeymoon.

Katie said, "I'll lay on my stomach for a few minutes. Please rub my shoulders. They are a little tight from sitting up."

Frank did it so willingly she was thrilled. Then she said, "Now it's your turn."

Frank did as she expected. He was asleep in five minutes.

She knew she would tease him forever. "You went to sleep on our Honeymoon!"

Factually she had no difficulty in joining him asleep. They didn't wake until some of the morning light entered the room. Frank looked at Katie and said, "I wish I could be a part of your life forever. Katie, if I can get a job here will you marry me?"

Katie looked at Frank with a look he would never forget. "Frank, darling, are you sure you are ready to make a firm decision?"

" I know I could truly love you forever for I recognize what a rare and beautiful creature you are."

Katie replied, "I would consider it a privilege to marry you. I know you will find a job. Maybe not the right one at first, but I can keep on working. I will accept your proposal on the basis there are no ifs. Just that we plan to get married! We are intelligent people. We can work out the time."

Frank squeezed Katie so tightly. "I agree. I want you forever, Katie, my true love!"

That moment was one of the rarest times in a persons life. To finally make a commitment!

Then as to officially seal this moment forever they began to caress each other. Their kisses reached a passion they hadn't imagined possible. Katie pulled Frank on top of her. Her hips enveloped his and he felt the slow but powerful movement of her body. Their movements began like the gentle flow of a small stream, but like all true passion soon became a rushing river.

Their hearts and minds raced as if they were reaching out far beyond life itself.

They were paddling madly through the rapids of love. With their final thrusts they burst through the last barrier and floated into the calm waters of the sky--their bodies thrilling with ecstasy as they had reached the pinnacle of perfection in man and woman coming together.

Katie wanted to remain silent, but she could not. "Frank, I'd marry you tomorrow. I don't want to ever be without you for even a single night. Whatever it is I know you are right for me."

He replied, "I'll never leave you Katie, as long as you want me."

Katie began to cry. Katie covered her mouth with part of the sheet so as to not awaken Marge and Don. Finally she quieted down, but the tears continued to stream from her eyes. Frank knew it was not the time for him to ask questions.

After almost fifteen minutes Katie said, "Frank, my Darling, Our making love and your words afterward were the best I could ever dream and hope for. Yes, after the loving I love you even more and I'll love you forever for I know you will always love me and be kind to me."

The mental and physical drama put them both asleep quickly. Finally Marge rapped at the door. Katie was half asleep, but she said, "Come in, Marge."

"Thanks, Marge said. Don has already gone to work. I go on the evening shift."

Then she slyly added, "You kids must have been really tired."

Katie replied, "We had a lot to talk about. We've agreed to get married. No date set."

Marge rushed to the bed and wrapped her arms around both of them. "I told Don last night, "If I've ever seen true love I see it in the eyes and mannerism of Katie and Frank. I wonder when they will get married."

After Marge left the room they paused to reflect on her words. **The both agreed, "What a wonderful confirmation of our decision to get married."**

CHAPTER 30, Frank and Katie search

Katie used the bathroom first and got dressed and went into the kitchen to help Marge. When Frank came in Marge was so happy she gave Frank a hug and said, "I'm honored to have a brave man like you-- who almost gave his life for Australia--to be my guest. My house is your house, Frank."

Frank was on the verge of breaking down and Katie noticed it right away. "Thanks for the kind words Marge. Frank and I appreciate them so very much."

Then Katie said, "How about a little coffee now. Breakfast will be ready soon."

Frank wondered if they would have a steak and eggs breakfast that the Aussie Soldiers were always claiming they ate back in Australia and when he was able to later get out of the hospital for a few hours he had seen that on several restaurant menus.

Instead they had some fruit, two eggs for Frank and as much toast and coffee as he desired. Their activity during the night had made him hungry. Marge discussed several places they might like to take a quick look at--that was in addition to the places Don had suggested. Frank said, "Looks like with all these things to do we'll be too busy to visit Camp Seymour, sixty miles outside of Melbourne where Barney Lange and the 41st Infantry Division went to first."

Marge replied, "Yes, it's 60 miles out of town and better save that for another visit. I'm going to miss seeing you this evening as I work. Katie if you fix dinner tonight I will appreciate it very much and Don will be so interested in learning what you find out today."

———◆———

They made two calls on Maritime Organizations that morning. Lunch was in a picturesque waterfront cafe. They knew they would remember it forever. They could see the harbor and a little of the ocean beyond the harbor.

Frank looked at the view and he was completely overcome. Tears rolled down his cheek. Katie looked at him and said, "What are you thinking of, love."

> Frank replied, "I've talked this point over with other men in the States. We would look at the Pacific Ocean and think of what happened on the other side. Now, in Australia, I am so close to New Guinea, when I look at the Pacific the war seems so much closer. I think of the men that didn't make it back and I feel a little guilty that I did, and have someone as lovely as you."

Katie reached for his hand. "Yes, I understand. The War cost me my husband and it brought me you for a wonderful replacement."

Frank grimly responded, "Replacements, that's what war is all about. So terrible."

Katie wanted to get off the subject. She switched to some History of Melbourne. Then Frank paid the bill and they headed for the third Maritime Organization. They were informed Wasco had not chosen to register with any of them. They suggested Wasco had likely been successful in getting employment and did not want to follow up on inquiries in general.

To Frank and Katie only part of that was correct. He did not want his name floating around as he was some kind of a fugitive. That was the whole problem. He didn't want to be found. Frank took a generous viewpoint, "I guess if your past was something you really didn't know you wouldn't want your name kicked around. Maybe someone would claim you did or didn't do something and how would you prove them wrong?"

Katie agree that could easily be the case.

Don had also come up with the idea of calling on two firms that rented Cranes.

He added, "Maybe it's just a dumb idea, but you know if I worked a Winch on a ship and got into a big city like Melbourne perhaps I might like to look at the granddaddy of all winches--a big Crane. Maybe I might visualize myself as getting away from the sea and settling down and wanting a job on dry land. Operating a Crane might be an alternative. Both of these firms are only a half dozen blocks apart."

At the first firm for a moment they seemed to remember the name Wasco, but in examining their records they could not find his name. So that left O'Dell Heavy Equipment Company and they knew they were going to have to press harder to get these folks to research for Wasco.

When they arrived it was obvious O'Dell was not a big firm. The yard had only a few pieces of equipment in it. Frank commented to Katie, "They are either small with not much equipment or they might have much more and it's all out working some place."

The office was a small one story building whose exterior was sheets of galvanized iron and the roof was the same. They stepped inside. Their initial vision went to a counter and they could see behind the counter a few desks and file cabinets and a woman working at one desk.

There was a hand crank adding machine on a stand, but on the ladies desk was a Rotary Calculator which Frank immediately recognized as a Rotary Monroe. A very fast calculator, made a lot of noise, didn't produce a tape, but was definitely state of the art. The office was dusty and the windows needed cleaning. The lady appeared to be thin. Only her upper body was visible above her desk.

She surprised Katie and Frank by getting up and moving toward the counter. She was tall, blonde and her clothes looked clean and neat.

Frank said with a very friendly voice, "We are looking for an American that might have worked for you. We do need to find him and sure would appreciate your help."

The woman immediately recognized Frank's lack of an Aussie accent.

Katie added with her lovely Aussie accent, "I'm Katie Martin. My maiden name was Burriss. I'm a nurse from Sydney, but took my training in Melbourne. Frank Beckman just came over from the states.

During the War he was seriously wounded in New Guinea saving our nation from a Japanese invasion."

"I'm Molly. Thank you Frank for what you did. My boss Clancy O'Dell was seriously wounded on the Kakoda trail. He's very busy, but he might have time to say hello to another New Guinea Veteran. Now, what was the name of the man you are looking for?"

"It might have been Jerry Wasco. Originally he was Ray Pearson. He worked as a Winch operator and Merchant seaman."

Katie's and Frank's eyes were on triple alert as Frank spoke. Molly waited too long to answer. Katie nudged Frank with her foot. It had been obvious to him too that Molly paused to reflect when she heard the name.

Molly was an honest lady, and right now that was her problem. She replied, "Our owner, Mr. Clancy O'Dell is just back from a fishing trip and has a lot of papers to grade. Sorry, that's a joke we have about paperwork. He's a good man and keeps on top of things.

He handles any questions about men who might have worked here. Please be seated and I will knock on his door and see if I can interrupt him."

Frank whispered to Katie, "Now listen for her knock. I'll bet she has a signal system."

Katie and Barney listened intently for the number of knocks Molly made. They couldn't tell for certain. It sounded like four or five. Then Molly opened the door, stepped inside and shut the door."

Katie said, "Looks like a pow-wow is about to take place."

A few minutes later Molly emerged and shut her bosses door. She walked over to the counter. "Mr. O'Dell will see you in perhaps five minutes. Please sit down."

Both recognized that Molly went back to her desk. Her friendliness had left her.

Katie whispered "Don't get your hopes up too high Frank, Darling. This guy Wasco has done a good job of covering his tracks, but we might be catching up with him."

In exactly five minutes Molly got up, said, "Katie and Frank, I believe Mr. O'Dell will see you now."

They walked around the counter and followed Molly. She opened the door and stepped inside with them. There was a big man seated behind a large battered desk with papers spread over it. "Frank and Katie this is Mr. Clancy O'Dell." He did not get up. "Please be seated."

Hearing those words Molly quickly left the room.

Clancy O'Dell was an overweight kind of broad shouldered gent somewhere around forty. His face was wrinkled from the sun and age. His hair was white and sparse. His shirt was a clean work shirt, not a dress shirt and he did not wear a tie.

His office was what you would expect. Dusty with papers strewn all over. Some on top of a file cabinet--some stacked on several chairs.

He rose rather stiffly from his chair and looked like a big St. Bernard as he lumbered toward them. He did bow to Katie and put out a huge hand to shake with Frank. "Welcome to my humble quarters and I'm glad you survived, Frank. . My thanks to you and your mates. Australia will always be grateful to you. I don't have much time to spare, but my old Mother would kill me if I didn't thank you. I doubt that I can help you."

His words made Katie think of how even a compliment could be cruel. Clancy was joking about his Mother. Frank would give anything to have either of his parents alive.

"Mr. O'Dell, I am from Portland, Oregon and am hoping to settle here in Australia. One of my Portland friends has asked me to look for a Jerry Wasco on behalf of Wasco's family."

That statement obviously startled Clancy. He looked at them and hesitated. "I didn't say I ever heard of a Wasco, but tell me about his family."

Clancy seemed to be weighing their words as they described Wasco's family and the search they were on to find him.

Finally he smiled and said, "Wasco never worked for me, but he and a friend of his came into the office a couple of times. Just offhand I would guess the last time was about two years ago. I have not heard or seen him since nor his friend."

Frank replied, "Can you tell us about his friend?"

"I don't even remember his friend's name. Let me ring for Molly."

Molly entered and Clancy said, "Molly, I need the name and any address of Wasco and his friend. Please check carefully."

Molly replied, "His friend was Bill Stone. I don't have an address for either."

Molly left the room and closed the door. Clancy looked at them, "

He said, "I'm sorry, but that's all I can help you with."

Frank quickly thought to himself. I'd better ask this guy about his New Guinea service and maybe he will be more helpful. So Frank said, "Tell me about your time in New Guinea."

Clancy hesitated, then said, "I was first wounded on the Kakoda trail, through the Owen Stanley mountains. Then I was seriously wounded helping the 32nd Division at Buna. I owe my life to an American medic by the name of Freddy Flarity. After giving me first aid and pulling me out of the line of fire he went back to aid another man in my squad. Flarity was hit by machine gun fire and never made it back alive."

Then suddenly Clancy said, "You know me old brain isn't what it once used to be. Now that I get to thinking about matters when Wasco and Stone were in a couple years ago they were headed for Mexico or South America. They would not discuss their plans."

Katie entered the conversation with, "Would Molly know more about their trip?"

Clancy called Molly back into the room and said, "Molly, I just remembered that Wasco and Stone were headed out of Australia. Did they tell you why or when they would return?"

Molly smiled and said, "I teased them about that, but they would not talk. I know I was busy that day and didn't talk to them for long. I figured one day they would walk in and tell us."

Then Clancy said, "If they came back where would a Sailor go besides a pub."

Molly was thoughtful for awhile and said, "There is always one place a sailor might stop That would be a Yacht sales firm. Sailors often will browse around with the thought that someday they will own maybe a thirty-six footer. Be their own Captain and cruise about a bit."

Clancy came back with, "Good thinking, Molly. Very good thinking. That, however doesn't apply solely to sailors. Even my thoughts have gone that way more than once. Yes, to own a thirty-six footer with a leaded keel to keep her upright and a nifty little auxiliary engine to use when there isn't any wind."

Then he looked at Katie and said, "I'll bet even a lass like you can sail a thirty footer and have hankered more than a few times about sailing around these islands in your own craft."

Katie looked at Clancy, "You're sure right on that. I've seen the Kyema, the big Sydney Yacht that used to win all the races up and down the Australian Coast. I've even met Mr. Carr and got to go on board. **Yes, we Aussie's don't call each other Matey for nothing.**

When they left Molly had kindly made a list and given them a map of the bigger Yacht Sales Firms. Also a couple of boat builders. They showed Molly the picture of Wasco, but it had been taken the summer of 1940. Molly said, "There is some resemblance, but apparently his years as a Sailor has made him more rugged. As to Stone, Molly did her best to describe him and Katie wrote down Molly's impression. "Stone is one rugged looking individual."

Once out the door Katie looked at Frank. You're sales ability sure showed on that one. You don't talk much, but you got Clancy talking by just asking him about his service."

Frank replied, "Let's call on a couple of Yacht Sales Firms. Then send Barney a cable."

They made two calls without any results. Then sent the following cable:

BARNEY LANGE. STOP. LUCK WAS WITH US TODAY. STOP. CALLED ON O'DELL HEAVY EQUIPMENT WASCO AND FRIEND BILL STONE VISITED OWNER STOP CLANCY O'DELL TWO YEARS AGO. STOP. WERE HEADED FOR MEXICO OR SOUTH AMERICA. STOP. NO WORD AND NO ADDRESSES SINCE. STOP HAVE MORE PLACES TO CHECK. STOP LEAVING MELBOURNE FOR SYDNEY TOMORROW. STOP. KATIE AND I PLAN TO GET MARRIED SOON. STOP. WILL TRY TO GET A JOB FIRST. STOP. SHERLOCK HOMES AND FUTURE WIFE KATIE (WATSON) MARTIN. .

They took the train to Surrey and Frank fell asleep enroute.

When they arrived Don was not home from work. Katie insisted Frank take a rest while she prepared dinner for the three of them. It was an exciting evening. Don was so pleased one of his suggestions had born fruit. He also replied, "I know much of this may have to remain confidential, but I'm going to get some kind of a story out of this sooner or later. My work get's a little hum-drum day after day and this is getting me out of my rut. Even my lovely wife Marge has commented I am more cheerful now, but I never would have thought of a sailor out shopping for boats. I go out every year and look at the new cars, but will never have the money to buy one."

Katie laughed, "Don, it's like us women. We go in fancy shops that we know we can never afford to make a purchase at, but it sure is fun looking."

Then Don added, I'll bet that Clancy has lots of connections. He could get you a job or make suggestions as to what kind of a business to go into."

Frank and Katie could see Don had a good mind with some great ideas.

———◆———

Marge wasn't off work until 11:30. Katie and Frank decided to go to bed and get some rest. Of course they had one other thing in mind also. It was almost a repeat performance of the night before. Katie stripped off her clothes in front of Frank, wiggled her hips as she grabbed her bathrobe and headed for the bathroom. He was next and when he returned she flung back the sheets so he could see she was entirely nude. They clasped each other tightly and this time they did not need the conversation of commitment before they started making love. Tonight there seemed to be a special urgency and within a few minutes Katie pulled Frank on top of her with the words, "I'm ready, Frank, Darling. I am ready. I can tell you are too."

CHAPTER 31, Friday, Saturday and Sunday.

Marge knocked at their door at 8:30 and they were sound asleep. Katie woke up and jumped from the bed, opened the door and said, "Frank got pretty tired yesterday. Guess I ran him a close second. Anyhow, we have to get moving. Our plane for Sydney leaves at 3:05. They ate breakfast with Marge and she was so excited about O'Dell, and the suggestion to visit some Yacht sales firms. They left on the train at Surrey by 10:30 and took their luggage with them. Marge hugged them fiercely. "I love you both and know you'll be so happy."

On the short ride to Sydney Frank seemed philosophical. "Everything has worked out so well since I came to Sydney. Maybe, like Sir Arthur Conan Doyle, writer of the Sherlock Holmes stories lectured on, "There is a presence that leads us." Then he added, "But how do we know?"

Both had been checking their watches. As they got off the train they only had four hours time and they should be at the Airport a half hour early. Katie said, 'We'll take Taxi's today."

They only took a half hour luncheon. They knew they were rushing things and wished they had another day. Soon they were out of time, but arrived at the airport on time

Once the DC-3, formerly a C-47 arrived at cruising level Frank said, "This is the trip I have wanted to take, but never expected it would be between Melbourne and Sydney. I thought it would be between something like Portland and San Francisco. More service people rode on C-47's during the service than any other plane. I was one of the very few that didn't."

Then Frank said, ""What are you going to say to your parents?"

Katie replied, "I've been thinking of that constantly."

Frank smiled, "So have I."

Katie then said, "I suppose they would like a long romance, but we're a lot older than they were and we've both been through a lot. However,

Mom and Dad didn't have a lot of dates before they got married. In fact I was shocked how they hardly knew each other."

Then Katie said, "Only one thing bothers me, Frank, Darling. I want to keep sleeping with you and my folks may not agree to that."

Frank looked at Katie, "Not any more than I want to."

Katie replied, "I'll talk to my Mother and if she is for it she'll lower the boom on Dad. She has lots of experience doing that."

Later Katie said, "Guess I'm chicken to bring up sleeping together. I'll slip into your room at night and if we get caught, well, we'll get caught."

Frank and Katie practiced the script they would present to her folks as to their engagement. Why did they decide on marriage when they just barely knew each other? Frank laughed as he said, "If they say you barely know each other I could reply--that is true, we have only slept together without clothes for two nights."

Then they went back to Wasco. Frank said, "It's wonderful that Wasco was alive two years ago, but taking off for Mexico or South America means he may not be back. As for Stone, the same thing applies. I didn't expect to get any leads from any Yacht sales companies in Melbourne. If Wasco or Stone had recently been checking with any they likely would have stopped in and said hello to Clancy."

It turned out that Katie's Dad had gone to bed before they arrived, so they only told Mrs. Burriss about their engagement. She took it so calmly they were surprised. Then she said, "Katie and Frank, this is the happiest news I have heard since Frances married. I know you two were meant for each other!"

With Marge and Don's boost, and now her Mother's Frank and Katie went to bed both beaming with happiness. Katie slipped into bed with Frank, but they were so tired they were both asleep in ten minutes, clasped in each other's arms.

The next morning was Saturday and her Dad had the day off. He was very excited to hear the news about Wasco and Stone, but somewhat dismayed they might not have returned to Australia. He was profound in his offer to help. He would map out all the Yacht dealers. He would check a few pubs on his way home from work and see if he might pick up a tip or two.

Katie helped her Mother with the dishes. Her Mother said, "I feel we must bring up the subject of the engagement right away. You have to be at work at 3:30 today. So let's have an engagement dinner Sunday about 1 P.M. Meanwhile I will first get Mac's agreement and then I feel Frank should ask Mac for your hand in marriage."

Katie was very nervous, but her Mom promised her there would not be any hitches. So Saturday evening while her parents were home with Frank he brought it up before both of them. At the last minute her Mom said, "I'd better be in the room so I'll know what happened. I'll also tell Mac I will kill him if he isn't nice to Frank."

And that's how it all turned out. Frank presented it to both parents and Mac said, "Frank, my lad you might think my three women, my wife, and daughters made me agree to this. That part is likely true, but I always wanted a son. One I could respect. That was very important to me. I respect you and I like you. I made this decision on my own. You may marry Katie."

Frank had expected Mac's reluctance to be obvious and he was taken by surprise. The two men enthusiastically shook hands and Katie's Mom hugged Frank and Katie hugged her Dad. The thought that now he had a family, and it would include Frances to a small extent was overwhelming. A few tears trickled down his cheek.

Mac and his wife noticed and Mac said, "Now that you'll be marrying Katie we'll be expecting you to keep staying with us until you get married. If you need to save money when you first get married you can keep staying with us as long as you both want to."

Katie's Mom joined with her agreement to Mac's offer and Frank replied, "I appreciate your hospitality so much and I will be happy forever to have Katie as my wife. I promise to treat her with respect and kindness. That was how my folks were. I wish they could be here now."

As he said those last words more tears came down his cheek and he asked to be excused to go to the bathroom. In the bathroom he broke down. It didn't seem fair that he couldn't send his folks word. Then he thought, "Maybe, from someplace in the Universe my folks sent me to Katie. When he returned to the living room his face was still red from his crying.

Katie's Mom looked at Frank and said, "We'll try to take a little of that sorrow off your shoulders. You may consider us your Mom and Dad."

Mac looked at Frank. "Lad, my wife is a wise lady. We will do our best for you."

———◆———

Katie had a ride home when her shift ended at 11:30 P.M. and was greeted by Frank and congratulations from her folks. Katie could tell things had worked out well. They had a midnight toast to happiness.

The parents went to bed first and then Frank gave Katie a word for word picture of what had happened, except for his breakdown. Katie was delirious with happiness that things had worked out so well. Frank was not so vocal, but he said again, "Your Dad was so nice."

They headed for bed and Katie slipped into Frank's room when she was ready for bed. Katie said, "Now if Mom catches us in bed together she won't say a word, but I'm not sure about my Dad. Maybe we should go ahead and get married very soon."

Frank's reply was, "Wonder what your folks might think. I'm ready anytime."

Katie was very tired and they went to sleep right away, but at about 5 A.M. she woke up and went to the bathroom. They could not go back to sleep without making love. This time their passion was even greater and their climax more beautiful. All the stars in the sky seemed to welcome them and the life they saw on the horizon was so promising it seemed as if heaven had reached down and taken them in its arms.

After breakfast Katie called Frances and Frances cried she was so happy. Katie knew Frances was crying she was so happy for her sister, but she knew that Frances was also crying tears of happiness for Frank. She said, "Frank was one of those one in a million guys. You are very lucky, Katie."

Then she added, "Katie, you are one of those one in a million ladies and Frank is equally lucky to be engaged to you."

Katie replied, "Oh, Frances, thank you so much. Will you tell Frank that?"

———————

The engagement dinner was beautiful. Even Mac fussed around making certain everything looked great. Frank's parents were not well off. Frank had gotten the family car which he had stored in the old folks garage in Portland. Frank's folks had been killed during the first part of the war and were just getting caught up with their depression debts. His Mother had willed her wedding and engagement rings to Frank. Sunday, with Katie's approval, he gave his Mother's engagement ring to Katie.

He and Katie both cried as he put it on Katie's finger. Her parents eyes did not remain dry. Katie had been slated to work Sunday evening, but she traded for the day shift Monday so after the engagement dinner they went for a walk around the neighborhood. The parents insisted on stopping at several neighbors and proudly introducing their son-in-law to be.

> *The next morning they had a cable from Barney Lange.*
> *SHERLOCK AND WATSON STOP. CONGRATULATIONS ON ENGAGEMENT. STOP WONDERFUL NEWS ON WASCO STOP MAYBE AH WING COULD HELP ON SEARCH. STOP. RUTH IS ECSTATIC. STOP. MABEL SENDING YOU ANOTHER $1,000. STOP. PLEASE GO ALL OUT ON SEARCH. STOP BARNEY LANGE.*

CHAPTER 32, How Bill Stone and Sandra Burke met.

It was slightly over a year ago Sandra Burke had been sitting in her tiny import shop hoping for a customer. It was a basement shop with an outside stairway and just a small sign, 'Sandra's Imports' She hadn't made a sale in two days. It seemed like everything had gone down hill since her husband died.

He never really recovered since he had returned from his volunteer service with the British Forces in North Africa under General Montgomery. He had been in an out of the hospital constantly. First it was in English hospitals, then he had returned to Australia and it was obvious he would never be able to return to work. His broken body helped break his mind as well.

Sandra was known as the nice lady with the limp. Her lack of operating capital prevented her from stocking her store with any quantity or variety of imports. As her stock fell so did her sales. In desperation she sold most of her personal possessions. She offered to close up shop as she hadn't been able to pay her rent for over six months. Her landlord also owned her apartment house and she hadn't paid that rent either. He was a tight fisted old miser to everyone but Sandra. His answer was, "Sandra, I never had a daughter. If I ever had one I would wish she could be just like you."

When Bill Stone walked into her shop he held a small piece of paper in one hand and a container in the other. He introduced himself and asked if she was Sandra Burke. When she replied she was he set his container on her counter. His eyes looked as if they would pierce the night. His hair was cut short, but he had a beard and a mustache. Both were trimmed. His skin was dark and weather-beaten from exposure to the tropical sun. He appeared to be six feet in height and close to two hundred pounds. His voice was clear and he spoke in a soft and gentle manner, "One of my shipmates, a man by the name of Jay, gave me your name and address. He sold you a few carvings a couple of times."

Sandra was thoughtful for a moment and replied, "Yes, I remember Jay."

Now Bill opened his container and took out two carefully wrapped items. He unwrapped the first one. Sandra recognized it in an instant. It had to be from the Sepik River Natives. Sandra picked it up carefully and turned on a light near her counter to examine it more closely.

Her basement shop had no daylight from the outside.

Bill Stone asked, "How much is it worth?"

She replied, "I've only had a few pieces like this to sell. I got them from your friend Jay.

Stone said, "I got this one from Jay. The one I haven't unwrapped yet I got by myself."

Bill had planned to play it tough with Sandra and get a price from her. Now that he had met her he could not treat a fragile lady like her with other than kindness. "Jay owed me $50.00."

Sandra kept looking at it. Finally she said, "I would give you $50.00 for it, but I don't have $50.00. My business is down and I have to sell everything on consignment. I am certain I can sell it. I would promise you I would not sell it unless I could get $50.00 for you."

Now Stone knew this poor lady had her back against the wall. "How much would you try to sell it for?"

"I would try to get $75.00 for it."

Stone did not reply. He turned to his other package and unwrapped it. Then he handed it to Sandra. "Oh, Mr. Stone! It's beautiful! It must be very rare. I could not place a value on it. How did you ever acquire such a thing of beauty?"

"I guess I was in the wrong place at the right time."

Sandra looked baffled. "I guess I don't understand, Mr. Stone."

Stone hesitated and then knew his honesty might be at stake with this gentle soul so he replied, "I came about it honestly. I will tell you if you promise to keep it a secret."

She put out her small delicate hand. He took it gently. It was so soft and small he could have crushed it with just two of his fingers. As he started to talk he stammered a little from the embarrassment. "I happened to finally make a trip up the Sepik River. One of the Native kids wasn't paying attention to the crocodiles. One slipped out of the water and grabbed him."

" The natives got hold of the Croc and couldn't hold him. I looked at his tail for a second. I found a spot I thought I could hold onto and I did. The natives pried open his mouth and released the kid. I was bleeding pretty badly myself. They asked me to stay for a special ritual dinner. I did and at the end of the dinner I was presented with this carved figure."

Sandra asked, "Have you been back."

"No. It took six weeks for my hand to heal. I really don't care to have the reputation of being handy to have around to save their kids from crocodiles."

Sandra eagerly replied, "You must go back! By now you will be famous for the entire 200 miles length of the river. I'm sure they would love to see you again."

Stone smiled, "Actually I was fascinated by their culture. I would like to go back, but being a seaman I go where the Captain decides the ship is going."

Sandra replied, "Please have a seat. May I heat some water and serve you some tea?"

Stone agreed and while they were drinking it he said, "I didn't have much for breakfast. Would you have an early lunch with me?"

Sandra didn't want Stone to leave. She had never met such an unusual man .

She thought Imagine tackling a crocodile with his bare hands. "I could close anytime for an early lunch."

They ate lunch at a little cafe which also was down one level from the street. There were many flowers to brighten it. Stone had a steak and talked Sandra into one. He noted she was hungry as she ate. There was something about this lady that Stone also had never encountered before. He wondered if it just wasn't because she was obviously the neediest truly nice person he had met for some time. Yet she had the guts to try to run a small shop, but it looked like her business was about to fold up.

During lunch Stone asked, "Who would you contact to sell my carvings to?"

"The small one might be sold to a customer. I have a few that might be interested."

"Sometimes when I can't sell them I call an importer and exporter that comes around once in awhile. He would be someone that would likely give you an offer on your larger carving."

"Could we call him right after we finish lunch and try to set up an appointment at your place tomorrow morning?"

"Oh, yes. That would be a very good idea. I don't have a phone, however."

After lunch they made the call and set up an appointment for 10 A.M. the next day.

Stone walked Sandra back to her shop. He noticed she was tired and limping a little. "Are you all right. I notice you are limping a little."

"I guess I am not the normal strong Aussie woman. I had Polio when I was young. Maybe I'm also tired today."

She invited him back in the shop and he asked her many questions about her business and it was two hours later when he left. One of the last subjects they discussed was, "Sandra, when we meet with your Agent tomorrow morning I want to ask you to be sure to let me do all the talking. If he turns to you and asks you any question at all you just look at me and say, "These are Mr. Stone's carvings and I can't speak for him."

Sandra was so relieved, "Thank you, so much. I would have been worried the rest of the day wondering what kind of a salestalk you would want me to give. You know, I'm not a salesperson. I let the people decide what they want."

Stone replied, "I've done lot's of fishing in my day and I know a lot about men. Let me cast the line and make the decisions."

Sandra was so relieved. "Anyone that will tackle a Croc knows what he is doing."

Stone replied with, "There are a lot of folks in this world that are croc's. They will take your arm, leg or gobble you up. Just give them the chance!"

That was an admonition Sandra knew only too well was true.

CHAPTER 33, The next morning. Her life would change forever

She opened her shop at her usual hour of 9 A.M. She had one small sale for ten shillings. Stone arrived at 9:45 and the Agent was there promptly at 10 A.M. Stone didn't waste any time with pleasantries, but he was courteous and smiling as he showed the Agent the two pieces.

The Agent looked at the one Stone had acquired from Jay. "Very nice, yes I can use this one. I usually pay Sandra $75.00 for these."

The Agent looked at the second piece. Stone carefully observed his eyes and mannerisms.

"Why, Sandra, this is very nice. Yes, much better. I can give you $250.00 for this one."

Stone pretended to relax, but now his eyes went on special alert as he observed the Agent and Stone said,. "My bottom price on the first one is $200.00"

The Agent seemed shocked. "Why I would lose money at that price."

Stone calmly replied, "I wouldn't want you to lose money. You don't need to buy it, but I wouldn't want you to make too much money off Sandra. I will bet my last dollar she needs the money fifty times more than you do."

The Agent was panicky with the thought that he might not end up with the second carving. "Well, if it is going to help Sandra a lot I will pay her $200.00 for it."

Sandra's admiration of Stone skyrocketed.

Stone looked at the Agent. "Thank you. We have a deal on the first one."

"Now on the second one it almost cost me my left hand. I saved a Native from a Croc. I won't take less than $2,000.00 for it."

The Agent had observed this man was not only tall and muscular, but he must have a connection with the Septik Natives. He could this guy was a man not meant to try to bargain with. He looked the carving over very carefully. "All right, I will give you $2,000 for it."

"Make out two checks. One to Sandra for $700.00 That is her commission. Make out a second one to Bill Stone for $1,500.00. I wouldn't do it again for any price."

The Agent quickly made out the two checks. He handed one to Sandra and one to Stone.

Stone said, "You hold onto your checks. We'll go to the bank with you and get money orders. We'll bring the carvings with us. Sandra, let's close your shop for fifteen minutes?"

$700.00, why she hadn't seen that much money at once for years. Stone's last words to her the day before were for her to not say a word. So she didn't. The three of them went out the door, Sandra locking it as she left and she changed her 'open' sign to her 'back at" sign.

After Sandra and Stone had the funds they shook hands with the Agent who said, "I guess I will have to raise my prices, but contact me when you have more."

Stone didn't want to lose a contact for Sandra so he was exceedingly careful with his reply. He said, "I don't know if I can get more. Only time will tell, but I thank you and will give you the chance to bid."

The Agent eagerly extended his hand again. They all three shook again.

———◆———

Sandra was in a daze as she walked back to her shop with Stone. It was only a few blocks, but unknown to her Stone was waiting for her to say something. They walked down the steps to her shop, she unlocked the door and they stepped inside.

Once inside she looked up at Stone. "I didn't earn $700.00. You must take most of it back."

Stone was relieved and very pleased with those words. He thought to himself his quick appraisal of her was still correct. She certainly wasn't any Gold Digger. Now he knew he wanted to help her and those unselfish words she had just spoken made his mind move quickly. First he said, "Shush, little lady. You'll never convince me you didn't earn it.

By keeping quiet you really worried him. Secondly, I think the guy has maybe wanted to help you, but was too tight fisted to put some action into his feelings."

"I've read some books on selling. One book I read said, 'If you want a man to sign a contract hand him the contract and then the pen. Don't say anything. The first person that talks loses.' I wonder how high we might have gotten him to go. Maybe $3,000 for the pair."

Sandra was glowing with thanks so much all she wanted to do was praise Stone and not try to figure out what might have been.

She said, "I haven't had $700.00 for years. Now perhaps I can buy some stock."

Stone looked at Sandra. "I'd like to try my hand at being a businessman. Could I offer a suggestion?"

They were both seated and Sandra felt so emotional she could not hold back any more. She reached out with one of her small hands and placed it on Stone's forearm. "Mr. Stone, I know I can learn from you."

"First, call me, Bill. Now my idea is that you take just $350.00 of your money and buy stock. Mark it up 100%. Then I want you to take $500.00 from me and do likewise. On my investment I will take 10% of the gross. A simple example would be you buy an item for $50.00 You mark it up 100% and sell it for $100.00 If it's mine you pay me 10% or $10.00

Then he added, "You know, Sandra, some folks get very mixed up over mark up and percent of profit. You mark up a $50.00 item by 100% and sell it for $100.00. Then when you speak of profit of $50.00 that's actually a profit of 50%. And don't give any discounts. Appear shocked if they ask for one."

Sandra was so surprised she didn't know what to say.

Stone realizing her discomfiture and uncertainty replied, "Why don't we go shopping for stock together. I'd like to visit a few wholesale houses with you. Maybe try a few ideas."

Sandra started to cry and then threw her arms around Stone and sobbed, "Oh, Bill, I must be dreaming! You are being so generous and kind."

As Stone held her fragile shaking body he realized **She had been out of aces for some time.** You had to have money to make money, or else a friend to loan you the money. In a game of cards you could often bluff and win a hand, but when you don't have money to buy stock you will soon be out of business. She was drying her eyes when he said, "I've wanted to be a businessman for so long. Would you like a partner in your business?"

"Bill, do you really mean all of this? I must be dreaming a wonderful dream."

Bill Stone looked at her. "Are we partners?"

Sandra looked at Bill and completely broke down. "Oh, yes, Bill. Oh, yes."

CHAPTER 34, Bill Stone, the not so silent partner

Stone wanted to first visit the major competition and then the Import Wholesalers. By the end of the afternoon Sandra had a lesson in the real Bill Stone. He asked a hundred questions at each wholesaler. He would only deal with the Manager. He requested and got an additional ten per cent discount for cash. He demanded the right to return any of the merchandise that was sold elsewhere for less than Sandra's Imports. It was a banner afternoon and Sandra was worn out watching Stone in action. They had dinner together and some color returned to her face.

Sandra insisted that Stone return to her apartment with her and come in for at least an hour so they could discuss business further. They sat next to each other on her small sofa and she found herself leaning next to him and holding his hand.

Suddenly he picked her up as if she weighed no more than a feather. He placed her on his lap. His sudden action frightened her, but he quickly said, "You're a frightened lovely lady. Don't worry I won't hurt you."

"You may think I don't know how it is to be scared. During the War. I was a winch operator on board ship. We unloaded ammunition, fifty gallon barrels of gasoline, and dynamite.. When the Japanese bombers came over we were all frightened, yes, even myself. I've cradled many a dying man in my arms wondering if the next time it might be me. Sandra, you have nothing to fear from me."

With those words she could not hold back any longer. She moved her arms slowly and placed them around his neck. She kissed him on the cheek and left her cheek against his. She told Stone about her husband and how his War time injuries finally took him from this world."

When she finished she hugged him fiercely. "You're as solid as a brick wall, but you aren't all that tough inside, are you Bill?"

He laughed. Then he said, "Sandra, you need your rest. You have hardly any stock left. Why don't you sleep in until 10 A.M. Give me a key to your shop and I'll be down there at 8 A.M. I want to make a drawing of the inside space and do some thinking.

My ship is going to be in Port undergoing some repairs which will take ten more days so I don't want to lose any time."

Sandra's heart sank as she realized he would soon be gone, but her spirits rose sky high as she suddenly realized she might be spending most of those days with this strong man who had just rescued her business. Just then Bill said, "Time for me to get back to my Hotel room. I'll open at 8 and be sure and get some rest."

With Stone gone she quickly got ready for bed. She was worn out from the excitement of the day. She lay back in bed, "I guess my life is like a sailors. I'm subject to my share of the storms of life and right now my storm has momentarily abated and I'm in a calm port."

Sandra fell asleep dreaming of Bill Stone. When she awoke in the morning she could not help but wonder if a man like Stone could ever become seriously interested in someone like her. The answer seemed obvious. "This was just a lark for him. He was probably a womanizer with a girl in every port he visited in Australia. And perhaps at least a dozen beautiful native women in the Indonesian Islands, where the Dutch ships once again were dominant in shipping circles."

The next five days were days of transformation. Stone had put his entire $1,500 into merchandise, but insisted she save $350.00 of her $700.00 for herself. The stock filled her small store and they arranged and rearranged things. Stone could tell Sandra tired easily so he insisted that he go by himself and once again check all their competition.

They placed a tiny ad in the paper which just said, "See the new Merchandise at Sandra's Imports." At the top of the stairs from her shop she placed a sign with the same words.

Stone enjoyed being in the store himself. He would try a different approach with every prospective customer that came in the door. He would write out his comments and the results he got. He found he did best when he asked them leading questions, and then said nothing until they answered, or else said something. He found he got his best results by just asking, "What might you be looking for today?"

Sometimes when an attractive woman was the one he got a reply that was an open invitation to turn her visit into a friendship. A couple of times a woman that made a purchase would insist he write down her phone number, "In case you want to call me!"

Australia was still a rugged Nation, and many of the women had a beauty that attracted a strong man like him. Stone had only one Sister, who also died from Polio. No brothers. His Mother never really recovered. When Mother died, he had no other female women in his family. Gentle Sandra needed him. He had sailed in many a storm and risked his life to save others. Now it was just a frail Lady, maybe his sister and Mother were calling him to help. Sir Arthur Conan Doyle, who wrote the Sherlock Homes Stories lectured on the Super Natural.

The repairs to the ship Stone sailed on took another five days and in the first six days with the new merchandise the shop had $800.00 in sales.[18]

Sandra knew she had become an entirely new person. She felt she had dropped ten years off her age physically. Mentally, she had been about to crash. Now she had money in the bank and stock and sales she had never dreamed possible.

It was the time she spent with Stone that had turned her almost back into a school girl. Her smile, her enthusiasm and the security of his presence were like a beautiful dream. Behind the heaven on earth she was experiencing was the cloud that soon he would be going back to sea. They ate all their dinners out. Bill had said, "You are too busy to take time to cook."

Often at dinner he would tell her a little about a Boat he was supervising being refitted. So often he was gone during the day for several hours. She recognized he had great responsibility but he was still interested in her telling him about each customer that came into the store when he was not there. Finally one day, he told Sandra about his Mother. Then later about his Sister and lack of any other close family members. In turn Stone seemed very interested in as much as she cared to tell him about her life. She wished they were Bears and could spend the winter in a Cave together. For certain, she was very, very grateful.

---

18 The Author has had extensive experience dealing with Australian Pounds and Dutch Guilders. Exchange rates change so I've converted sales figures into U.S. dollars, making it easier for my readers to understand.

Bill had told her he was now sailing on a small Dutch Boat. There were at least a Thousand Dutch Cargo Boats at the start of the War. They carried almost all the cargo between the hundreds of small and large islands in the Pacific. Now there are only a fraction of that number.
Part of the Crew was Javanese and they are housed at the stern of the vessel.

My meals are served to me in a Teakwood Dining room. I get to eat with the Captain. Often we stop at a dozen Ports on one trip. I am going to ask even the Javanese crew to help me buy things we can sell as imports.

Then it was time for Bill Stone to ship out, on his regular job.

At first Stone's shipmates needled him almost 24 hours a day about the gorgeous female he must have met while their ship was being repaired. Finally Stone said, "Yes, I met a nice lady, but you guys are going to help me help her. He explained how he was trying to rescue her business and now he was her partner. He expected them all to pitch in and buy imports for Sandra that she could quickly sell for a good profit. The crew took up the task with enthusiasm and Bill would check them over and periodically send a shipment to Sandra, along with a letter and instructions. Several times when his ship was in some Port for a few days, and there was a nearby Airport he would fly back to Australia.

———◆———

At the Airport the Driver slid his vehicle to the curb. He jumped out and grabbed the suitcase by the man's feet and tossed it into the back seat of the cab. Then he reached out quickly for the bag in the man's hand.

Just as quickly the man's other hand grabbed the mid-arm of the cabby in a vice-like grip. His arm felt as if a fifty caliber machine gun bullet had shattered it. His hand dropped uselessly to his side. The man said, "Mind your manners. I'll carry my personal bag."

Then with a swift lithe action the man moved quickly into the back seat of the cab. The driver was groggy from the pain, but knew it was his fault. He had not asked the man before he grabbed his hand luggage.

As he pulled away from the curb the cabby thought to himself, "If he had grabbed my right arm I would not be able to shift."

As the Cab pulled away from the curb he looked in the rear view mirror to check traffic. His eyes caught the eyes of his passenger. He thought to himself, "I've seen those eyes before."

As he drove his mind alternated between the severe pain in his left arm and where had he seen those eyes. Suddenly, he thought of the American movie the Australians had been so wild about. The 1943 Movie of the year, 'Casablanca.'

This man was taller and bigger than Bogart, but from his eyes came the same glint of steel. It made you feel like you were looking into a bayonet on the end of a rifle. He wondered if his passenger was a former infantryman who lived from minute to minute in the misery of the Jungle and now looked at the world knowing civilian life was just another Jungle. This time no War perhaps, but guns and bayonets loaded with dishonesty everywhere.

The driver slowed his cab as he approached the address. It was a small three story apartment he had occasionally delivered folks to previously. Most folks that lived there were too poor to use a cab. The building had a brick front, but the driver knew behind that facade was a down at the heels assortment of small lower rental apartments. Yet the neighborhood was very respectable. It's residents were honorable folks who put their best foot forward.

His passenger had carefully observed the meter and handed the cable his fare before he had told him what it would be. The cabby figured this bloke had been there before so he hadn't planned to jack up the fare.

He wanted this guy out of his cab and hoped he would never see him again. Then he thought to himself, "I guess I had better mind my manners in the future."

The man carried his suitcase and bag as easily as if they had been ten pounds. He picked up the receiver outside the main door and rang the bell for Apartment 3-C. When a voice answered at the other end he said, "Bill."

A buzzer sounded and the latch clicked and Bill went upstairs. He walked up two flights of stairs and in the middle of the hall Sandra was waiting for him. The plane had been late and she had squirmed and fussed. But now he was here. Her face radiated with pleasure and relief.

His keen eyes saw her face and he knew how important they were to each other. They had agreed not to embrace in the hall, but it was all both of them could do to not break this pact. He quickly entered. She stepped inside, locked the door and threw her arms around him.

"Oh, Bill, my darling. It's been so long."

He held her closely. She clung to him as if the world was ending and this was their last moments on earth. Then he picked her up as if she were a rag doll and carried her into her small bedroom and sat her on the bed. Then he took off his clothes and stepped into the tiny bathroom to shower. She quickly removed her clothes and slipped into her bed. She had been waiting, day after day for this moment, however not patiently.

She marveled how such a powerful man could be so gentle with her. The only answer she could ever dwell on was that a fragile newborn baby is treated so tenderly because we have that capacity as humans. So why did the War take so many including her husband?

Then he spoke, "Sandra, I live only for this time with you!"

As he slipped into bed with her she hoped his plans had not changed. He had written he planned to be with her for a month to five weeks. She had prayed every since he left the first time that some day she would become his wife. He would never discuss his past. Maybe with so many weeks together he would.

She had often asked herself, "I wonder if I'm better off not knowing his past?"

CHAPTER 35, Frank receives a letter from Barney Lange

Frank said to Katie, "Barney has this Remington #5 portable and apparently he can type a hundred miles an hour on it. Look at the long letter I received from him. I've read it over twice.

Katie looked at Frank and said, "Let me just sit back and rest and you read it to me."

> *Frank read, "Dear Frank, Again my warmest thanks to you and Katie. Looking forward to hearing you are married. I wanted to take the time to let you know the impact your news on Wasco had brought to Mabel and her son and daughter. I called Mabel right away and it was just before she left for work. She asked me to bring the cable over right away. As I drove over to her 4-Plex I thought of how I used to deliver the Oregonian to that same apartment in that 4-Plex my first three years in High School. [19]*
>
> *Mabel called Ruth at her office and Ruth fainted. There was a Doctor down the hall and he revived her and sent her home in a Taxi. There are of course concerned where Wasco is right now. Is he in Mexico, South America, back in Australia or what. At least Ruth knowing her Dad was alive up to two years ago has brought real joy and hope to her. Kevin is away at Oregon State and Mabel is in shock. Hang in there on your search for Wasco. Find Stone and hopefully he will lead us to Wasco.*

19   Now the Red Lion Hotel is located there and it corners on N.E. Multnomah which is the Lloyd Center. My last year in High School I was made a Manager with an office at S.E. 13th and Morrison. That building still stands in 1997. I don't stand as well as it does. Guess I didn't age as well.

I'm going to try to reach Ah Wing and see what connections they might have to help find Wasco. By the way I have asked Mabel to get Wasco's Dental and physical records if he had any. Best wishes. Barney Lange.

Katie looked at Frank. "Darling, I know you want to get started looking for a job, but you are making money and it would be so wonderful to find Wasco. I know you want to go to Brisbane and Townsville and check around the harbor. Shall I put in for a week of my vacation. We may have to go without a vacation or honeymoon, but I'd like to take that trip that trip with you. What do you think, Frank?"

Frank replied, "I have the money to pay for the plane fare. I think it would be wise to go ahead and try. I don't seem to be running into any more clues here in Sydney."

Katie quickly answered, "I'll give it a go tomorrow with the head nurse."

———◆———

Luck was with her and a week later they headed first for Townsville and then would head South to Brisbane and spend the rest of their time with Frances and her husband. In Townsville they ran into a gal in one of the Maritime Offices that remembered both Stone and Wasco, but that was the extent of their good luck. She thought it was at least two years ago. She took their address and phone number in case she remembered more. So they left for Brisbane.

In Brisbane they had similar lack of luck, but Frank was desperate to get any kind of a clue. Katie said to her sister Frances, "I hope Frank doesn't run himself into some kind of nervous depression."

Frances smiled. "The way he looks at you Katie he is too happy to be depressed."

Frances husband Scotty had been trying to help. He checked various places on his own and he and Frank would stop at a pub near the harbor at the end of the day and see if they could pick up any information. It was the description of Stone, not Wasco, that brought a clue. One worker said, "I have a brother in Sydney that is working on a thirty-six footer that he says is being bought by some kind of a surgeon. I think he has to do with teeth. He says he thinks he is going to rent it for a couple of weeks to a Sailor and the Sailor seems to be one tough bird."

They got the name of the boat works where the work was being done and that was all the news they left Brisbane with. As they flew back to Sydney, in a DC-3 Katie said, "That sure worked out well. You and Scott got along so well. He is a nice guy isn't he?"

Frank didn't answer right away. Katie looked at him, **"So you're jealous of the guy. He married your girl friend."**

Now Frank knew he was really on the spot, but he didn't hesitate to answer. "Frances was the nicest lady I had ever met in my life, but I hadn't met you. You're the nicest now, and please don't ever think otherwise, Katie, my Darling."

Katie replied, "Oh, thank you Frank, my dearest. You know just what to say."

Upon arriving back in Sydney there was another letter from Barney. It read:

Dear Frank,

Had a most pleasant meeting with Ah Wing, his assistant Delores Lee, and Mabel, Ruth and Kevin. Kevin came up from Oregon State and the Pearson's were absolutely enthralled to meet with Ah Wing and hear how Wasco had saved his life when The China Queen was sunk by a Japanese torpedo in early 1942. Now Ruth knows for certain her Dad has been a hero and the fact he left his family does not overshadow everything. The death of your parents and the drowning of my brother make both of us feel deeply about Pearson disappearing.

Ah Wing introduced the Pearsons to Dr. Fu and this basically means that any big time search for Wasco must be under Dr. Fu's supervision. Also it likely would be his decision as to whether they even want to assist. I am sure Ah Wing would like to see Wasco again and I hope that means the Chinese will put some wheels in motion.

Only other suggestion is to keep the Javanese in mind. Every Dutch ship I traveled on had separate quarters at the stern of the ship for the Javanese. I suspect those people know a lot about what goes on all over that Pacific Region, moreso of course in Dutch New Guinea and Indionesia.

I did have one more idea that I am following through. Was Ray Pearson, or Wasco, ever fingerprinted? I have gone to my two MP friends, now in the Portland Police Department, and have asked them to really go back in the files and see if they have any fingerprints on him. I suppose my Accounting background is making me check places we may never need, but who knows.

Don't give up the ship, Frank. Reminds me when I was a kid in Portland I had a couple of big time fillings. They didn't use Novocain in those days and when the drilling got pretty awful the Dentist always said, "Remember the Maine."

Mexico and South America are a long ways away, but as you know with the advent of the Airplane people move around easily. Wasco could be back in Australia right now. Best wishes to you and Katie. Barney Lange.

CHAPTER 36, Frank resumes his search in Sydney.

Frank immediately went to the boat works to check on the thirty-six footer. He ran into trouble from the start. They wouldn't give him the time of day. "People we contract to do work for aren't interested in our giving out any information about them. Actually the policy isn't as bad as you might think. Some workman lips off and says the wrong thing and we get a client mad at us. So we hear no evil, see no evil and hope we aren't doing any evil. Sorry, and Good Day."

Katie had the day shift and would be home by 4 P.M. and Frank decided to let the matter simmer in his mind and not go out and make some rash engagements. What he had in mind, however was going back to Hawes & Dove and asking them to do a stakeout.

That evening at dinner both Katie and her parents thought Frank's idea was the way to go. He had added to his thoughts that if Stone showed up the Detective Agency would be able to follow him. On the other hand Frank didn't know the streets, the shortcuts nor did he know how to drive well on the left side of the street. After all he hadn't fully recovered from the car accident he recently experience trying to make a quick U turn from the left lane.

Frank laughed, "You folks are being nice to me and I appreciate it. I don't have a car and I doubt that any car rental agency would rent to me again."

Mac didn't say so, but he knew he didn't want to loan his car to his future son-in-law.

Katie looked at Frank, "Life itself takes strange turns, both good and bad. My husband being wounded so seriously. You being wounded likewise. My husband doesn't recover. You do recover. You take a turn on a street and get into an accident. That results in you and I meeting and falling in love. Now we're try to find Jerry Wasco. Like Shakespeare said, 'The world is a stage and we are but players making our entrances and exits. We don't want you to exit."

Katie got up and walked over to Frank and put her arms around him. "I'm so looking forward to our being husband and wife on the stage of life."

CHAPTER 37, We now return temporarily to Barney Lange in Portland, Oregon.

Everything seemed to be going so well in Australia, but it was a good and bad story. Wasco had been seen as recently as two years ago. The bad side was that if he had taken off for Mexico or South America we were now trying to find him in almost half the world.

Whereas he had been missing for 8 years this had been reduced to 2 years. With my business background this meant a 75% reduction in time he was missing.

As to my social life my Thursday 1 P.M. scenario with Elaine had been canceled because Elaine went to the beach with her friend Marsha.

As to my date with Bobbie to see Phil Harris and Alice Faye at The Golden Canopied Ballroom at Jantzen that was the top of the line place to dance in the Portland area. It was where the big bands played. All major cities had at least one. Big time cities like Los Angeles and Chicago had more than one. The Palladium, The Coconut Grove, The Aragon Ballroom. For returned Servicemen like myself it was even more of a thrill. We had wondered if we would ever see those places again.

Folks would drive from all over Oregon and Southwest Washington. Usually there was only enough room for two thirds of the dancers to dance while the other one third crowded at the front to watch the orchestra and it's performers. Phil Harris was a ham. His wife Alice Faye was both beautiful and an actress who could easily satisfy an audience by just watching her.

In all the big bands many of the band members performed specialty numbers. It was not only music time, but it was show time. Who would ever forget the Kay Keyser band and Ishkabible singing The three little fishies. And they swam and they swam right over the dam.

It took a while to get from Northeast 24th and Handcock to Jantzen Beach for it bordered on the Columbia River. No freeways and lots of traffic. Bobbie chatted like a magpie for the entire time. I wondered if she always talked so much and no wonder Frank didn't talk. She was excited, but she couldn't seem to not mention Frank every now and then.

At one point during the drive she asked me, "What do you think of my Mother?"

Alarm bells rang in my mind on that one. I knew I'd better make it short and not rambling. I thought of a couple of replies and dropped them. Finally Bobbie said, "I won't quote you. Just give me a quick comment or two."

By then I said, "Unaccustomed as I am to describing the Mother of a date--let's see--she is poised, gracious and very attractive. A great role model I would say."

Bobbie came back with, "Say now. Maybe you know my Mother better than I realized, but you know that does describe her to a T. I do think I am envious and perhaps intimidated by her. She's probably no worse than other Mothers in respect to giving me constant advise.

"She helped me work out this date with you so I guess I still need a Mother's help, but in a way perhaps I resent my self for not doing it on my own."

I laughed and said nothing. Then Bobbie laughed also.

———◆———

The band and it's leader Phil Harris and his wife Alice Faye were at their best. It was exciting to be there. We started out dancing several inches apart, but the crowd was pressing us from every direction. By the third dance Bobbie was snuggling her body pretty close to mine. Then I think she got a little embarrassed and said, "This place is so crowded everyone has to dance very close, but I kind of like it. Do you, Barney?"

Questions like that were irritating to me and yet I respected them. A salesman was to ask leading questions and I marveled how women had this ability to do it so well. I wanted to be non-committal with Bobbie as I didn't want the wrath she focused on Frank Beckman to suddenly be aimed at me. So I stupidly replied, "It's nice to be close on Saturday night."

Her reaction was to put her head on my shoulder and move her cheek against mine. Made me wonder what she thought I meant and what her desires were. During the second intermission she made some not so kind remarks about Frank Beckman. I looked at her, "No Frank Beckman tonight, remember you promised."

Bobbie looked sheepish as she said, "I promised you would have a nice date with me tonight and I apologize for bringing up FB."

Then she kissed me on my cheek and by the second dance after intermission Bobbie had her left arm securely wrapped over my shoulder and was stroking my neck. She almost seemed more interested in pressing her body against me than dancing. Fifteen minutes later she said, "Let's move over toward the bandstand and try to find a seat. My shoes are bothering me a little".

The dance started at 9 and ended at 1 A.M., but Bobbie's feet only held out until mid-night. She suggested we leave and I told her I always took a date on the Big Dipper before we left the park. She began protesting, but finally said, "It looks ominous to me, but I have never been on it. I'm game for one ride."

As the roller coaster climbs up for the first drop down your apprehension builds and when it reaches the top and you look down you are certain it is straight down. Every woman screams at the top of her voice and as you ride up the next climb you wonder if the trip down is going to be even worse. I knew one thing for certain. If you had a most romantic evening dancing taking your date on the Roller Coaster would shake herself up so much at least for the next half hour you better not try to kiss her. Romance went out on the first dip.

When we got to Bobbie's Mother's home the house was ours because her Mother was at the beach. I wondered what this might portent. I was soon to find out that Bobbie didn't want me to leave right away and wanted to do some necking on her sofa. Ten minutes later we had gone from our sitting position to laying on the sofa. Her kisses were passionate and perplexed me. I think she got the idea and said, "For tonight let's keep our touching above the belt. If we date a lot we might want to change that."

So that was her road sign for this evening, but we did ourselves proud above the belt. One other thing happened before I left. She asked me to take her out the next Saturday night. I thought to myself, "I think women ought to take over the sales field. They sure are good at it."

I thought to myself, "Oh what the heck."

But I didn't say that. I answered, "It's been a nice evening. Let's go out next Saturday."

Well, that seemed to increase her passion, shall we be business like and say 25% more. I retaliated by letting my left hand stray to her right thigh and she made no comment nor did she move my hand back upstairs. Her short skirt had moved closer to her belt and my hand was on bare flesh as she was wearing a garter belt.

All kinds of thoughts ran through my mind, but I was also getting a little sleepy and tired. In fact five minutes later we were both asleep and didn't wake up for some time.

Our common sense couldn't argue with our wrist watches. It was time for me to leave. Bobbie's parting shot was, "I wish we could go to the beach sometime."

As I drove home lots of thoughts raced around my tired mind, but my tired body shoved them aside. Once home I was in bed and asleep in five minutes. .

CHAPTER 38, Summary of Barney's activities before we return to Australia.

Kevin had come up from Oregon State College and he, his Mother Mabel and sister Ruth and I met with Ah Wing, who was in town. Delores Lee, who I fantasized was the Dragon Lady from the childhood stories I read in the Saturday Evening Post, continued to captivate me.

I was thrilled to watch Mabel, Ruth and Kevin and the rapt attention they paid to Ah Wing. It was unbelievable drama when he told them how Ray Pearson had saved his life when the China Queen was sunk. It was as if Ah Wing brought the Father and husband back to life. It also brought terror to my heart to recall that my brother was dead and buried and no fluke of fate would ever bring him back to life.

Now Mabel and her two children knew Pearson was a brave guy and for the moment his faults seemed to fade away. He had been a hero, not just a run away husband and Father.

Dr. Fu attended the dinner and said very little. I could not read his mind, but his presence sent out an aura of power. I could not fully understand the radiance that seemed to power the entire room. It was a strong presence. There was Ah Wing's pleasure to meet the Pearsons. Dr. Fu, Delores Lee, being in the Chinese Tong. The Pearsons and I were elated, but with my accounting background I knew a lot of Chinese Tea would be served all over the world before we found out what happened to Pearson. The sobering thought hung in my throat making it dry--was he even alive?

I walked the Pearsons to Mabel's car. Just before we left Delores asked me to stay and visit with her for a little while. We adjourned to her small room and she again told me about her husband who had been killed fighting the Japanese in Manchuria. Apparently he had been wounded many times, had come home for a few days when he was recuperating. One day his wounds took him. She again said how she saw the depth of the war in her husband's eyes and in my eyes she saw her husband's

199

eyes. It was an eerie thought and to some extent it frightened me. O n the other hand she was so beautiful that I desperately wanted something about myself to appeal to her. And I let her know I had thought of her often. Just before I left her room she put her arms around me and kissed. She spoke several words in Chinese and I felt if she wanted to tell me what she said she would. But she offered no explanation and just said "Good-bye for now."

I drove my blue coupe back to my run down apartment in a daze.

———◆———

I finally decided I needed to tell Bobbie, before our upcoming Saturday night date that Frank Beckman was going to be married. I took her to lunch at the Barbecue Pit in the Pittock Block built by the early Portland businessman who also built the Pittock Mansion for his private residence. The Barbecue Pit was one of those places that you lined up and they took either a slab or beef or ham out of the brick oven, and carved off the meat you ordered, be it just a sandwich for lunch or a full dinner.

The cole slaw was something I could never pass by. It had some kind of a white sweet sauce on it. The Cole slaw was at the start of the line before you reached the Brick Ovens. At the end of the line was coffee and pie.

I sort of laughed to myself as to the comparison. Taking Bobbie to The Pit as we called it and telling her ex-boyfriend was engaged might drive her further into the pits.

When I met her she was bright and cheery. I gave her the news about mid-lunch. I should of waited until she didn't have food in her mouth. She was so surprised she started to choke. When her coughing subsided she gave me a dirty look and said, "Remember my comment about the stork bringing all those babies to the Australian Gals, by way of their Yank Boy friends. So an Aussie gal captured his heart."

For the next five minutes Bobbie never took another bite of food, but her remarks were very biting as she cussed and snapped at one Frank Beckman. She made no comment as to wishing him well. I wondered how Shakespeare would of said it. Maybe something like, "The damsel wished him, but not well, rather she wished him hell."

I finally said, "You're going to be late for work."

As we walked up the street a few blocks to the Terminal Sales Building Bobbie put her arm in mine and said, "I had a great time with you Saturday night and I'm looking forward to even a greater time with you this Saturday night.'

I looked at her carefully and wondered if maybe she might wink her eyes and wrinkle her lips like her Mother, but she didn't. As long as I was back I rode the elevator up to my office to check on calls. I knew I was going to spend the rest of the week wondering what her interpretation of even a better time Saturday night would mean. Of course those thoughts centered on 'The belt situation.' Would her position Saturday night mean I was welcome below the belt. I thought to myself, " Is it just me or do women always call the shots."

CHAPTER 39, Bill Stone may only be around the corner.

When Katie's Dad, Mac, heard of the consideration of hiring Hawes & Dove to do a stake out he was as adamant against that as he had been about loaning his car to Frank, who had proved he hadn't learned to drive on the left side of the road. Mac said, 'Give me and Frank a couple of days to snoop around. This can't be that hard. Frank, my boy, let's us go to Barnacle Bill's after I get off work tomorrow. Matter of fact why don't you go a half hour early. We'll buy a few pints for some of the men. It's near The King's Boat Works. Bound to be a couple of the lads stop by for a drink.

The first day after work, they found one guy that worked at King's. He told them he stopped at Barnacle Bills every day after work. They decided to treat him to Melbourne Bitter Ale and that loosened his tongue. First he gave out with all kinds of yarns. He claimed he knew everyone in the business. Finally they said, "Aren't you working on the boat Bill Stone is going to take for a test sail."

The workman, one Arnie, did a double take. "Are you pals of Stone?"

"The Stone we know is kind of a tough guy."

"That's him, all right. Not a bad bloke, really, but sure is demanding. By the time he takes her out it'll be purring and will sail itself. If it doesn't we'll catch hell."

"Where's Stone hanging out these days?"

"Don't have the foggiest. Say Matey, maybe with the little lady he brought up here once. Sounded like-yeh, she's taking the trip with him. I remember now-Stone said something about going up the Septik river. That's near Wewak. Something about Imports. That must be it. They might be running some kind of a bloomin Import store. You know Matey's I heard lot's about that river. Ever been up it?"

Mac answered with, "Never been up it. Heard lot's about it."

Arnie continued with, "That bloody Stone is one touch hombre. And fussy, why I never ran into a guy like him before. His lady friend is so small she better not get him up in his cups. He could pick her up with two fingers and twirl her around."

"What's her name."

"Don't have the foggiest."

"Want another pint?"

"You taking off, mates?"

"Frank here got himself engaged. He better show up soon."

"Yeh, I bet. Don't knuckle under too quick, me boy. Keep a little space for yourself. Me wife and I battled for years. Me wife says, "If the pubs didn't close early she'd divorce me. Been trying to figure out a way she'll divorce me anyhow. Knows I need another Sheila."

They paid for another pint for Arnie, shook hands with him, patted him on the back and took off. As they headed for Mac's home he said, "What do you think, son?"

Frank liked the tone and the word. He replied, "Well, with a little luck we may find Stone very soon. If he knows where Wasco is we may have solved the puzzle."

But like many a puzzle. The solution wasn't going to come tomorrow.

———◆———

When Mac and Frank arrived home only his wife Irene was there. Katie had the 3 o'clock shift and would be off at 11 P.M. When Katie's Mom heard the news she was as excited as the two men. Even moreso she was thrilled that her husband and Frank seemed to becoming pals.

She said to herself, "My prayers are being answered."

Frank just had to call Katie. She wasn't available, but called him back within the hour.

Irene had been keeping dinner warm in the oven for the two men and with the two pints each had drank they were hungry. Frank got the telephone book and brought it to the dinner table and he reviewed all the import shops with Mac and Irene.

After dinner Frank copied in longhand all the shops and their addresses and phone numbers. He remarked he wished he had Barney's #5 Remington. When Katie returned from work she said she had a very tiring evening. Frank said, "I have an idea where to start tomorrow morning. Let's discuss it in the morning. Her parents had gone to bed over an hour ago. Katie said, 'Let me take a shower first. I'll be in your bed waiting for you."

She was sound asleep when he slipped in beside her and he didn't waken her. They had been teasing each other that some nights they never woke up and made love, but it was the closeness and the knowledge that they would share each other for life that made everything else take second place. It was the second time around for Katie, but all new for Frank.

Katie wanted to accompany Frank the next morning and agreed with his decision that he would first call some Import Wholesalers and hope for vital information.

On his first call he asked for the Manager and was told he was not in, but how could they help him. Frank replied, "I'm really looking for a slightly built lady that likely has a small import shop. Perhaps she has a friend or a partner who is a rugged type of guy."

The lady speaking said, 'I can tell you are an American. Are they friend's of yours?"

That non-plussed Frank only a bit. He came back with, "I hope they are. His name is Bill Stone."

"You might be looking for Sandra's Imports. She had only a small business for years. We thought she was going to completely fail. Then this man Stone appeared from somewhere. He is in the Merchant Marine I believe and her business has taken off like a rocket. "

CHAPTER 40, Sandra's Imports

Katie and Frank rushed to get ready. It didn't seem possible that in the next hour they might find Stone and he might tell them where Wasco was. Katie tried to ease the tension by saying, "I won't check either of our pulses. Our hearts are likely in Atrial Fibrillation."

Frank laughed, then suddenly said, "Whoa, my love. We forgot something!"

'And what did we forget my love?"

He looked very profoundly at Katie, "We have to have a presentation, like a sales presentation. We can play it by ear, but let's take 15 minutes and outline some kind of an approach. Like our opening remarks. What do I say and what do you say?"

Katie and Frank went down the stairs to Sandra's Imports at 10:05 A.M.

They opened the door and saw a rather frail appearing brown haired lady of perhaps forty look up at them with a very pleasant smile on her face. She was perhaps 5'5" tall. They looked the place over quickly and did not see anyone else. They were disappointed. Perhaps Stone would not even be there today. Katie said, "May we look around?"

Sandra pleasantly replied, "Be sure to do so. Ask any questions you like. We get our shipments in every month or so. Everything we have has been in stock for less than a month."

Then she asked the key question Bill Stone had established as an absolute must, "What kind of Imported things are you looking for?"

She was to not say a word until the visitor replied. Bill had said, "The first one to talk loses. Never say a word until they give you some kind of an answer to that question."

Katie was non-plussed and Frank knew it was up to him. He replied, "We would enjoy looking around, but we also would like to meet a man we understand has some interest in this shop. His name is Bill Stone."

Frank was a Salesman too, and he understood and respected her approach, but now he had turned the table and it was up to Sandra to reply.

Sandra took the question in stride for many a morning he had opened the shop so she could sleep late and rest. So he was a known quantity to some customers. This young couple seemed harmless so their inquiry caused Sandra no alarm or distress.

Sandra answered very pleasantly, "Yes, he is in the back room. He'll be out in a moment."

Bill had also warned her to never leave the store with a customer in it. They might grab something and leave. Bill had also told her to keep the conversation to a minimum. Do not encourage people to talk and tell you their life's story. They would come back every day and talk to you. Keep the place strictly business.

Stone appeared in a few minutes. Katie and Frank stared at him and saw perhaps a slight resemblance to Humphry Bogart. He was taller and brawnier. He looked like a powerful sailor with his skin tanned and wrinkled from constant exposure to the sun. His eyes were clear and he looked directly at you. He had a pleasant smile on his face, but Frank and Katie recognized the toughness this guy personified.

Sandra observed Bill did not seem to recognize them. So she said, "This couple asked to speak to you."

Stone said, "How may I help you?"

Sandra's words verified this must be Stone. Katie and Frank were elated, but shaken. Was the search over? Was it possible Stone would lead them to an alive Jerry Wasco?

Frank's mind went on triple alert. "My name is Frank Beckman and this is Katie Burriss. Katie is a Sydney nurse. Katie and I are engaged."

Stone was not interested in chit chat. He replied, "Congratulations and nice to see you. Have I talked with you before?"

Stone had got down to the facts quickly. On board a ship you didn't bounce around with a lot of silly conversation. You made decisions and gave orders loud and clear.

Frank was on the spot now. He sensed the impatience of this man. Frank replied with, "Not to our knowledge. We are looking for a man who I understand a Bill Stone knows. His name is Jerry Wasco. I have his picture here. This is a very important mission! We hope you are the Bill Stone that knows Jerry Wasco."

For a couple of seconds Katie and Frank thought Stone was ill at ease. Then his composure seemed to come back as he said, "Why are you looking for this man and why did you come to me?"

Frank almost smiled to himself. Stone had not immediately disclaimed any knowledge of Wasco and he had complicated the conversation by asking two questions.

Katie was looking intently at Stone and at Sandra. Afterwards she would say privately to Frank, "I could tell she was just as curious as we were."

Frank knew the best way to get along with Stone was not to challenge him. To be clear and concise and appear to be honest. Frank replied, "The Jerry Wasco we are looking for was originally a Ray Pearson from Portland, Oregon. He had a wife and two children and he disappeared in early 1941. We believe his ship was sunk twice. As to why did we come to you we heard you were a pal of his."

Stone replied, "Please sit down. I'll get a couple of chairs. Sandra is not feeling well and I'm not doing a lot better. Must be some kind of a bug I picked up and passed it on to Sandra. Tell me something about the family your Wasco has.."

Sandra knew Stone well. They had spent many hours in each others arms and she sensed that something in Stone's past had caught up with him. She could tell he was stalling and trying to think. That was uncharacteristic of him and it worried her terribly. She said to herself, "I know Stone is hiding his past and it is entirely possible that he is hiding a Wasco along with his own past."

As she thought about that and tried to observe Katie, Frank and Stone she became very frightened. She began to tremble with fear, 'Was Stone in such trouble that he would leave and that would be the end of their romance and her hope to marry Stone. And what about their trip she was looking forward to. Two whole weeks sailing with Stone.

Katie's powers of observation were honed by the hundreds of patients she had attended. She thought, "This guy may be a Gambler like Wasco, but right now he doesn't know how to bet his cards."

Frank was very businesslike and at the same time his natural sincerely shown through his words. He told more about Mabel and her kids and how Mabel had divorced him. That Ray Pearson had likely left Portland to avoid something involving gambling. Frank was very careful to point out Pearson had not run afoul of the law and there was not even any rumor that he had done anything wrong. One simple fair conjecture could be that he owed money, and someone was demanding he was to do something illegal to pay off the debts. So he left town."

Stone seemed to be digesting or absorbing this information and he didn't seem inclined to ask any more questions. He just seemed to sit there.

On the other hand that one sided conversation was collapsing Sandra. So Stone's pal had left a wife and two kids behind in America. That was exactly what had been worrying Sandra. Had Stone done the same thing? What was there in Stone's past so serious he would never discuss it with her?

Sandra was standing through all this unsettling conversation and she had been having severe dizzy spells in the past couple of days. She had not told Stone fearing he would cancel the trip. She told herself, "I'm going to make this trip with Stone if it kills me."

A wave of dizziness overtook Sandra. Katie had been wondering if Sandra was well. Sandra started to fall and Katie grabbed her and helped her to the chair Katie had been sitting on. Sandra was limp and Katie knew immediately at least she had fainted and at worst----even a heart attack or a stroke. Katie looked at Stone, "Help me stretch her out on the floor and let's hope she has only fainted."

She took her pulse and quickly felt her forehead. "Her pulse is very irregular. She has a very high fever. Mr. Stone, does she have a Doctor?"

"She told me she went to a Doctor once a year, but I don't know the man's name."

Katie went back to taking Sandra's pulse. "I'm not getting any pulse. Oh my God, I think she has stopped breathing. Katie screamed, "Frank and Mr. Stone get an ambulance now."

Katie immediately began CPR. She opened Sandra's airway by the tilt/chin-lift maneuver. Then she looked, listened and felt for breathing for 3-5 seconds and began resuscitation. Stone grabbed the phone book and Frank ran up the stairwell to be on the lookout for an ambulance and perhaps even a policeman.

Just before the ambulance arrived Katie announced, 'I got her breathing again. Oh, this is serious Mr. Stone."

All Stone could say was, "Thank God you were here and that we weren't on our trip to Wewak. Oh Sandra, please get well for me. I need you."

That statement impressed Katie, mightily. Two ambulance attendants came running down the stairs. Katie said, "I'm a registered nurse at Sydney General. Get your stretcher immediately and take her there. This is serious. I did CPR on her and she is breathing again, but I don't know for how long. Her heart was very irregular and she has a high fever. She passed out."

CHAPTER 41, Sydney General Hospital.

Katie was due on the 3 P.M. nurses shift that afternoon. Sandra had been first taken to emergency where she regained consciousness, but was very weak. She was admitted to the hospital and Katie talked to the head nurse at the nurses station near Sandra's room. They were doing many tests, including of course if Sandra might be pregnant.

Katie saw a physician she knew come to the station and heard him say, "Still don't know a lot about Sandra's condition. She didn't have a stroke. She was a Polio Victim at one time in her life. She isn't a strong person with a lot of back up energy so watch her closely. She might lapse back into unconsciousness. She's going to be here for several days."

Frank had been sitting in a nearby rest area and Katie said, "Let's go to the cafeteria and get something to eat. There she explained to Frank the little she knew, but said, "I'll try to look at her chart when I am on duty. Maybe I can get switched to this floor."

Frank wasn't talking much. Finally he said, "We never found out where Wasco is. Stone is in the lounge. Let's go ask him."

The first thing that Stone wanted to know was word on Sandra. Katie gave him what little news she knew. Then she added, "Let me feel your forehead."

At first he declined, but she insisted. "My God, you've got a fever as high as Sandra's. If you're going to be around checking on Sandra we can't have you infecting the hospital staff as well as it's visitors. Stay there for a few minutes. I will be right back."

As soon as Katie left Frank looked at Stone. "O.K. Stone, we're working for Sandra and you. Now it's your turn to work for us. Where is Jerry Wasco?

"O.K. Frank. Guess there is no question I owe it to you. Honestly I have not seen or talked to Wasco for almost two years. He was leaving for Mexico or South America or both and I have been worried. No news can be good or bad. We were good pals. I had no idea he had a family.

It's hard for me to believe he would not of gotten in touch with his family."

"I meant to take some steps to locate him, but always figured one day he would show up. I guess it's the old story one day turns into a week, a month and then maybe two years."

Frank was shocked to hear those words and just then their conversation was interrupted by Katie, "Come this way Mr. Stone. If you infected Sandra it's time we find out what is wrong with you. Don't give us any trouble!"

Stone didn't like being shoved around, but he recognized logic especially when it involved Sandra. "O.K. for Sandra's sake I'll do most anything."

Katie took Stone to a Doctor who after examining him put him in isolation. Then Katie came back and Frank gave her the lack of news of Wasco. She was stunned. Then it seemed to hit Frank and Katie at the same time. Frank said, "I waited 6 years before I came back to Australia to try and see Frances. We humans just put off things don't we."

It was almost noon and Frank and Katie went to the hospital cafeteria. They hashed and rehashed things even touching on the fact that it didn't look like Sandra and Stone would be taking a trip on the 36 footer in less than two weeks.

Frank reluctantly said, "Guess I'd better get a cable off to Barney Lange. Frank took paper and pen and with Katie's help wrote:
BARNEY LANGE. STOP. LOCATED BILL STONE TODAY. STOP. HE HASN'T SEEN WASCO FOR TWO YEARS. STOP. STONE'S GIRL FRIEND AND STONE ARE BOTH IN SYDNEY GENERAL STOP WITH UNDIAGNOSED FEVERS STOP. RATHER INVOLVED SO WILL POST AIR MAIL TO YOU TODAY. STOP. FRANK BECKMAN.

Frank and Katie headed for the Cable office and as they walked Frank suddenly said, "Holy Cats, did I ever goof off."

"Frank, dear, it can't be as bad as you sound. At least I hope it isn't"

"I was so sure Stone would know where Wasco was that was all I could think of, but I should of been asking him if he knew anyone that went with Stone."

"Well, Frank, Sandra was an emergency and Stone has been put in isolation, so don't kick yourself too hard. Let's hold off on the cable and go back to the hospital. Maybe we can get some word to Stone. I don't think they will let either you or I see him."

"Oh, Damn it."

"First time I ever heard you use that word. I say it once in awhile myself so you're off the hook as long as I don't hear it too frequently and it's not used to describe my failures."

Frank looked at Katie, "Yes, Ma'am, I'll be careful on that one."

So it was back to Sydney General and they went to the nurses station on Stone's floor.

They were right. They could not see him, but they could talk to his nurse. They explained the problem at length and she was sympathetic. Frank wrote out several specific questions and after looking at them she said, "Oh, I can do that without violating any hospital rules."

She went to Stone's room and came back. "He's asleep."

Katie asked, "Any additional word on him or on Sandra?"

"Sandra's problems are possibly related to her general health being below par. Stone has picked up something or maybe he has had something wrong with him that has just become a bigger problem. We don't think he has Dengue or Blackwater fever or he would have gotten very ill before now. Can I just call you when he is awake. Remember you can't see him."

Frank replied, "I understand. I needed to send a cable to the States so I'll hold off. We'll go back to Katie's folks home."

Katie replied, "I'm on duty this evening. If Stone doesn't wake up until after you go off shift let me know and I'd like to talk to the nurse that takes over.'

———◆———

Katie went on duty at 3 P.M. and called Frank at 8 P.M. Stone was still asleep and maybe Frank wanted to go ahead and send his cable. Katie could tell Frank was not happy with himself, but as any nurse knew only too well that things often did not go too well. Afterall that was what hospitals were all about--to treat those with problems.

Mid-morning, the next day, Frank and Katie went to the hospital. They checked on Sandra first and found she needed all kinds of attention. Low blood count, possible thyroid condition and irregular heart beat. She should of been taking digitalis for possible years. She was run-down and maybe she didn't have whatever Stone had. They were, however, not permitted to go into her room, but were permitted to talk to her over the telephone.

When Sandra found it was Katie she was profound in her thanks. "I am so disappointed that Bill and I may not be able to take that trip, but so grateful that you folks came by. Do you have any good news on Bill?"

Katie had to admit she didn't. Sandra then said, "I want to help you find Wasco if I can without causing any problem between Bill and I."

After the two ladies rang off Katie looked at Frank. She could see his disappointment. She knew they were at a dead end right now, but when Stone awoke maybe there would be news. Instead Stone's condition became worse and he was either unconscious or semi-conscious for the next several days.

CHAPTER 42, Henry Lee

Out of the blue came an unexpected phone call for Frank. The man identified himself as Henry Lee, a local restaurant owner, and said he wanted to meet Frank and Katie, but mostly he wanted to meet Stone. Frank immediately said, "Why do you want to meet Stone?"

Henry replied, "One of my peers in my Chinese World has asked me to do whatever I can to find Jerry Wasco. I have been given to understand you also would like this matter brought to a successful conclusion as soon as possible."

Frank answered, "I would like to be out looking for a job as I plan to get married soon. It would be a wonderful send-off to find Wasco alive and well."

Henry made arrangements to meet Frank for dinner at 5 P.M. at his restaurant and as Katie was not working that evening she was invited, too.

Henry was kind of a non-descript looking Chinese. Short, thin, clean cut, intelligent looking, polite and without any facial characteristics that made him stand out. Even his age was kind of in the middle. He wasn't young and he wasn't old--afterwards Frank and Katie guessed mid-forties, but that was an un-educated guess at best.

Frank explained his relationship with Barney Lange and Henry was grateful to be brought up to date on that. Mid-meal Frank said, "Barney mentioned the Javanese crews on these Dutch Vessels and they might be a great source of information."

Henry replied, "The very same thought has been going through my mind. The actual ship-owners are usually reluctant to reveal names of their crews. Give me a description of Stone." Frank also showed Henry the picture he had of Wasco, but that was nine years old. Then Frank said, "I would like to share my mistake with you. I neglected to ask Stone if Wasco took off with anyone."

Katie cut in with, "Frank feels terrible about that, but we had two sick people on our hands so our minds got off Wasco."

Henry replied, 'Very understandable."

Frank continued, 'We left instructions with one nurse, but apparently he has been either unconscious or semi-unconscious and not able to be answer questions."

Henry did not reply, but it was obvious he was weighing the facts and was interested in listening to Frank and Katie.

Henry then said, 'I must get back to minding my staff. You may order anything else you may desire. There will be no bill and please do not leave any tip. We Chinese have kind of a barter system we use. Some folks call it chits. We do a favor for Chinese in America or someplace else and they do us a favor when we need it."

Henry got up and bowed and did a fast about face and was gone.

Frank looked at Katie. "You know, love, whenever anyone turns 180 degrees like that it will forever remind me of 'to the rear march in basic training in close order drilling.' It is kind of interesting when hundreds of men are walking in one direction and all of them turn and move in the direct opposite direction."

Katie replied, "So when you got in the Battle of Buna you forgot all of that. "

Frank laughed, "You have that right. What a mess that was. Men attacking the Japanese concrete pill boxes. Men falling right and left. Men going in all directions for ammunition and to help someone else. Dragging the wounded out of the line of fire. Wishing we had the artillery fire the high mucky-muck officers thought wasn't necessary. It didn't take us long to find out how wrong they were."

"Let's get off that subject. Reminds me one Monday morning at coffee at Riggs Pharmacy Barney Lange said the Saturday night dance lesson at the Uptown Ballroom was the Cha-Cha. They were taught "The Chase." and that dance step, also used in Round Dancing is the exact duplicate of 'To The Rear March' in close order drill. Except for one slight difference."

"What is that Frank? I've never danced the Cha-Cha."

"I took that lesson before Barney did. In the Army the drill Sergeant yells, 'The the rear march, step, turn. In The Cha-Cha no one yells at you and you do a Cha-Cha step which counts out to 1,2, Cha-Cha-Cha, not one, two, three and four as in close order drill."

CHAPTER 43, The S.S. Van Heemskirk

Frank Beckman was getting to know the hospital like the back of his hand. He checked around for Dental Surgeons and found there were several. He left a message with each Doctor's receptionist that he was looking for someone buying a boat that was involved with Bill Stone.

Barney said to Katie, "I've had a dozen call backs so far wondering who Bill Stone is. Looks like a lot of Dental Surgeons own Yachts."

Katie replied, "I think you'll find Doctor's of all types own a lot of boats. It takes money and they have it."

In time Frank got a call from the receptionist of Dr. Roger Gray. She put the Doctor on the line and he was distressed to find Stone was in the hospital. He asked his Doctor's name and was going to immediately follow up. He was told Stone was in isolation so he couldn't visit.

Sandra was slowly gaining strength, but Stone was no longer the strong man he had been. Word was that he had lost 15 pounds and continued to be in an out of consciousness.

Finally one day there was a call from Henry Lee. A Javanese cook reported Jerry Wasco had a friend by the name of Wilhelm Schule and he had last served as 3rd Officer on the Dutch ship Van Heemskirk."[20]

Frank had learned much about those Dutch ships from his letters from Barney, from Katie's Dad and from the boat works men that hung out at the pub. Also the fact that Wasco had barely survived the sinking of one in the Tasman Sea.

---

20 Actually the Dutch Ship Van Heemskirk, was sunk by Japanese Bombers in April 1943 in Milne Bay, New Guinea. In 90 fathoms of water. On board were men from A Battery, 205th Field Artillery, with their 105 mm guns, ammunition, gas, telephone and radio equipment, etc. My apologies for using this name, but my intent is to insert a small tribute to the men. Two days later Tokyo Rose, from Japan reported over the radio it was sunk and the loss of part of the 205th artillery The obvious question is how did she get such detailed information in only two days. The sinking of the ship was one thing, but the Artillery outfit on board is the obvious question.

In the past couple of days Frank had been going into a funk as there were no clues except Wasco might be in Mexico, South America or even back in Australia, or perhaps some other place. Henry sensed this and said, "Frank, we won't have any trouble locating The Van Heemskirk. Maybe he's once again serving on it."

Frank knew he had to keep Barney Lange up to date. So he cabled:

> *BARNEY LANGE STOP. HENRY LEE WITH HELP OF JAVANESE STOP FOUND WILHELM SCHULE WAS PAL OF WASCO. STOP. FEEL ONLY MATTER OF DAYS STOP UNTIL THEY CONTACT THE VAN HEEMSKIRK. STOP. STONE HAS BEEN IN A COMA AND ISOLATION STOP. SO CAN'T DISCUSS WITH HIM. STOP. FRANK BECKMAN.*

Henry Lee went full steam ahead and was able to make radio contact with the ship, but the news was not good. Wilhelm Schule was not on board and hadn't served on The Van Heemskirk for nigh onto two years."

Frank Beckman cabled Barney Lange in Portland, once again.

> *BARNEY LANGE. STOP. HENRY LEE MADE RADIO CONTACT. STOP. WILHELM SCHULE NOT ON BOARD. STOP. LAST ON BOARD TWO YEARS AGO. STOP. TIME IS SUCH HE COULD have LEFT WITH WASCO. STOP. FRANK BECKMAN.*

Two days later Henry Lee called again. He said, 'Barney Lange's idea of contacting the Javanese is working. Schule has been sighted, but has a new name and will not answer to his old name. He now goes by Adolph Schultz. Additional word that he was an arrogant cuss and a Nazi sympathizer. Confusing thing is why would Wasco be consorting with a Nazi sympathizer? Was Wasco involved with the Nazi's?"

Frank Beckman hoped not and sent Barney Lange another cable.

BARNEY LANGE. STOP. HENRY LEE DOING ALL THE WORK. STOP. AGAIN THE JAVANESE COME THROUGH STOP. REPORTEDLY NOW GOING UNDER NAME OF ADOLPH SCHULTZ STOP AND IS NAZI SYMPATHIZER. STOP BARNEY LANGE.

24 hours later Frank Beckman received a cable from Barney Lange.

FRANK BECKMAN STOP. TALKED TO DELORES LEE IN SAN FRANCISCO STOP. CHINESE PUTTING OUT FEELERS FOR SCHULTZ. STOP. MABEL, RUTH AND KEVIN SO ANXIOUS STOP. THEY WILL GO ANYWHERE, ANYTIME IF YOU LOCATE WASCO. STOP BARNEY LANGE.

CHAPTER 44, News from Henry Lee.

Frank Beckman said to Katie, "I can sure tell I would never be suited to be a private eye or a policeman. You take on the emotions of the family and it's beginning to press on me."

Katie replied, "I know it is Frank, Darling, but you know that is what we nurses go through every day. Accidents and illnesses. Will the patient survive? If they survive what kind of condition are they going to be in the rest of their lives. Will they be wheelchair bound or what other handicap must they spend the rest of their life under. And when they die there is so much sadness. Everyone tries to handle it, but losing a patient is a tragedy for us too. One day they give us a hopeful smile and the next day is their last, and they never smile again."

Frank thought that over carefully and told himself he would never again complain to Katie about being under stress in this search for Wasco.

Right now it was a search for Schultz and the Chinese must have been working overtime. Frank got a call from Henry Lee. Meet me at my restaurant. I do not wish to talk about this over the phone."

Frank immediately took off for Henry Lee's Chinese Restaurant where they met in his small office. As soon as they sat down an attendant brought in some hors d'oeuvres and tea. After some few minutes of chit-chat Henry said, "We have located Schultz."

Frank replied quickly, "Where is he?"

Henry looked at Frank. He talked very slowly. "I cannot tell you. You must promise me that you will not discuss Wilhelm Schule or Adolph Schultz with anyone"

Frank looked at Henry with obvious surprise. "I give you my word, Henry. There must be more to this than just Wasco."

Henry looked at Frank and smiled. "Yes, Schultz is a Nazi sympathizer and may have been involved in some very serious activities. Now you understand the need for absolute secrecy."

Henry continued, 'You may feel compelled to tell Katie. I will agree to that provided you are absolutely certain she will not discuss it with anyone. I know she lives with her parents and neither of you can discuss this with them, as well as anyone else."

Frank thanked Henry and walked back to the hospital where Katie was on daytime duty. He found Sandra could receive visitors and he took it upon himself to leave her with the same request Stone's nurses had. "Who did Wasco leave Australia with and has he had any contact with that person. This would not be a violation of Henry's instructions. If Stone knew Wasco left with Wilhelm Schule that might even help Henry Lee."

Then Frank received additional good news. Stone was finally responding to treatment. He wasn't getting any worse, but he wasn't really getting any better. Maybe Sandra might find a moment he would be lucid enough to discuss Wasco's departure.

Frank was desperately searching for positive news to let him rise above his funk. The news that Schultz was likely a rotten character didn't mean Wasco was alive. Frank didn't even want to try to guess what Schultz had done."

CHAPTER 45, Wilhelm Schule, alias Adolph Schultz

Adolph Schultz, was a swaggering six food blonde, blue eyed well built male of German birth. He had gone to sea at an early age and felt his experience made him superior to almost everyone else. When Adolph Hitler came to power he expected a high commission in the German Navy, but on his first interview he was classed as 'Not inclined to obey orders.'

He was already serving on German freighters so he was serving in a necessary position. As the German U-boat manpower pool fell he was finally accepted for submarine duty. His sub was sunk in the Pacific. He reached land with only a pair of pants and his knowledge of English allowed him to get by with his claim he was a Dutch seaman.

He conned his way into getting a berth on a Dutch Ship where he was able to handle his crew assignments easily, but he was not always cooperative. He was approached by another German Agent to serve as one. His desire for adventure and his loyalty to the German Military made him jump at the chance.

He continued after the war and one of his missions was to approach American and English Agencies, thusly becoming a double agent.

His name change came about after the war when he was exposed and fled. There were tens of thousands of Nazis in many areas all over the world. The last thing they wanted to do was to go back to Germany at this time. They also took the role of maintaining the old order in the hope eventually Nazi power in many countries would be established and Germany would again become a dominating world power. For centuries there had always been Crusaders.

Schultz was now serving on a former Liberty ship operating as a tramp freighter, calling at the larger ports in the Pacific. He was due to arrive in Townsville, Australia where he always radioed in advance to stay at a favorite hotel.

This Hotel served a double purpose for him. There was a German Madam that ran a very discrete escort service which particularly catered to Germans. Secondly, the hotel was patronized by certain German elements as well as private citizens that were still dedicated to German Power.

Schultz, in his mid-thirties, was in his best swagger, when he checked into the Hotel. At one time it was called the Alt Heim, but during the war it changed it's name to Vista Hotel. The bell hop carried Schultz's baggage, made certain the bed was made and the room had the necessary towels, glasses and had not been accidentally already assigned to someone else.

As the bell hop shut the door Schultz made certain it was locked, extracted a pocket notebook from his coat and sat down by the telephone. He turned to the page he was seeking when a closet door opened and he heard a voice say, "Turn around slowly with your hands up."

His first impulse was that it was a joke being played by one of his friends. As he complied he saw himself looking at a .38 caliber being held by a steely eyed determined male. The door from an adjoining room opened and two more men entered. In a matter of moments Schultz was bound and gagged. A laundry cart appeared from the room next door. It was half full of sheets which were quickly removed and Schultz was placed inside and the sheets were placed on top of him. The cart went into the room next door, out the door and down the hall to the service elevator. There the cart was wheeled outside. Schultz was placed in the trunk of a waiting car.

One man took the cart back inside, and went back to the room. Schultz and the other two men left with the two men already in the car. Back upstairs the returning man went into Schultz's room, took his luggage to his own room and methodically went through it. He removed several items. One of the other men had taken the notebook Schultz had left by the telephone. Schultz's remaining luggage was returned to his room. The searcher wore gloves and poured water into one of the glasses, dampened a wash cloth and one of the towels and hung up the suit and some shirts that Schultz had brought with him to indicate the room was being used. .

Then he returned to his room. His telephone rang and the caller only said, "You may stop by at your convenience."

That was the signal all had gone well and he replied, "I have time to leave now."

That was the signal things had gone well for him too.

———◆———

Schultz was now in the basement of a non-descript house that was more or less isolated at the end of the street. Much foliage covered the yard and the driveway led to the rear of the house where it could no longer be seen from the street. A stairway led directly to a concrete basement whose meager furnishings included a large cage. It had been originally built to house several large monkeys. This was necessary at night, or when the owner was absent. Otherwise they would have totally destructed his furniture, drapes and dishes.

Schultz was inside the cage. Each of his arms locked to opposite sides. There was enough slack in both chains that he could feed himself. Schultz was in total shock. Instead of three days of wine, women and fine food he knew he was in deep trouble, but he wasn't certain which of his deeds had caught up with him.

He was heavily blindfolded in a manner there was no chance he could see. Nevertheless his interrogators wore hoods to make certain. First they asked him to describe his activities for the past 8 years. He came up with a story that he had an Uncle that served in the Dutch Navy who helped him escape from Germany and got him a position in the Pacific on a Dutch Ship, He had difficulty remembering the name of the ship, but finally admitted it was The Van Heemskirk.

The men let him talk for an hour, prodding him frequently to continue. Schultz knew he was in a trap. If he strayed too far from the truth it would catch up with him, but he had no option except to lie and not reveal the truth about himself.

At the end of an hour he was begging for a drink of water. One man said, "We'll give you a glass of water when you tell us in detail about Jerry Wasco."

Schultz thought to himself, "That was the biggest mistake of my life, but how was I to know that raid was going to be made a day earlier. That was what tripped me up. Now what do I say to these men. I can't admit the truth, but do they know the truth anyhow. That's why I changed my name. Now at least some of what has caught up with me."

Finally Schultz spoke. "Gentlemen there is no use beating around the bush. You know Wasco and I left Australia. What information in particular do you desire from me."

One of the men replied, "As we just asked you. Tell us in full detail about your trip with Wasco. Don't lie to us. We know who has all the details and they won't be happy if you lie to us."

Schultz knew he was boxed in, but he was not prepared to tell the whole truth. He tried to get his mind to move swiftly and come up with an answer, but the real answer was obvious. If he ever told the true story of Wasco and himself he would be signing his death warrant. If they knew three-quarters of the facts he was a dead man. So there was only one answer. That was to stall them and hope they were just leading him on--not to tell them the facts. Then he thought of some interrogation facts he had learned. Ask them a question or tell them something to lead them away from their question.

So finally he replied, "I hope Wasco is alive and well. Is he?"

Schultz did not know the men were wearing masks. They sat close together and he knew the men were altering their voices so he didn't really know how many were asking him questions.

One man did reply to his question. He said, "We're asking the questions. Give him water and one slice of bread three times a day, until he decides to tell us the truth."

CHAPTER 46, Is Wasco Alive?

That was the question that was hounding Frank and Katie night and day. They knew it was the same question that Barney Lange, Mabel, Ruth and Kevin were being ground to pieces by. Frank was calling Henry Lee each day and asking to stop by.

Sandra was being released from the hospital the next day, but Stone's condition was still in question. The time for two week trip he and Sandra were to take had already started, but the yacht was still sitting in the boat yard. The work had been completed, but the Dental Surgeon didn't have the time or anyone else to take the trial run with.

Then two calls reached Frank Beckman that took him completely by surprise. One was from Marge who had received a call from Nurse Nell and one was from Clancy. Nurse Nell had received an unsigned letter. All it said was, "I was a patient of yours and remember you well. I am returning to Australia and will need some physical therapy. I will call you to see if you can recommend anyone. Please keep this letter confidential. It was signed with a W."

Then Frank asked, "Where was it mailed from?"

Nell replied, "I looked at that first. It was mailed from Los Angeles."

Clancy's call was very similar. He received a letter which simply said, "I expect to arrive in Melbourne soon. I haven't seen you for two years. I'll need to locate at least a studio apartment near a bus line. Still needing some physical therapy and won't be getting a car. Please keep this letter confidential. It was also signed with a W."

His letter was also postmarked from Los Angeles.

Frank Beckman knew he had to talk to Henry Lee before sending any cable to Barney. He called Henry and said it was urgent he speak with him. Henry seemed a little more relaxed than when Frank had talked to him several days before. Henry said, "I can tell the urgency in your voice and seeing you will be my pleasure."

Frank Beckman was more than a little surprised with that sentence, but the two men met in the late afternoon. When Frank told Henry about the letters Nell and Clancy had received, both postmarked from Los Angeles, his eyes almost popped out. He sat upright and was obviously in intense contemplation. Then he got up and walked around his tiny office. "Please tell me once again those phone conversations you had with Nell and Clancy."

Frank repeated what he had told Henry pretty much word for word. Henry finally said, "There is nothing you and I can do except I must notify Dr. Fu who will notify Ah Wing. Perhaps it is just a coincidence. Another person with the initial W, but why so secretive?"

Henry rubbed his chin and said, "Can I tell you something you must repeat to absolutely no one, not even to your Fiancee Katie."

Frank looked at Henry, "Yes, I will hear it on that basis."

Henry Lee's expression changed from one of concern to one of pride. As if something of great note-worthiness had been accomplished. He said, "Wilhelm Schule alias Adolph Schultz has been located. He is in custody, but I cannot reveal who has him and where."

Frank Beckman looked at Henry and knew it would be stupid to come up with the usual remark, "Are you certain?"

Instead Frank said, "Whoever you are working with packs a wallop."

Henry looked at Frank, "I am not absolutely certain of the meaning of many American slang words, but I have heard that one before. You maybe hit the nail on the head."

Frank said nothing. Henry was rubbing his chin again, obviously thinking intensely. Then he spoke, "You must call Nurse Nell and Clancy O'Dell and try to make them promise they will not discuss with anyone the letters they received, except to check into therapists and a small apartment. Tell them that message comes from me and to call me collect at any time if they get even the slightest additional information."

"Henry, you can count on me to follow your instructions promptly.

Frank wanted to also wire Barney Lange. Finally he decided he could say;

BARNEY LANGE. STOP. AS YOU ARE AWARE SOME WHEELS ARE TURNING. STOP. DID YOU EVER FIND ANY FINGERPRINTS FOR PEARSON. STOP. WONDER IF THEY WOULD MATCH ANY THE FBI, CIA, TREASURER AGENT OR GOVERNMENT HOSPITAL HAS STOP OR IF THEY KNOW OF A WASCO. STOP. FRANK BECKMAN.

CHAPTER 47, Now back to Barney Lange in Portland, Oregon.

I was trying to keep swimming, but was in the dark. Ah Wing and Dr. Fu were in San Francisco and I would occasionally get a call from Delores Lee. A couple of times she mentioned she was looking forward to seeing me again. She mentioned my eyes again and I didn't know if returning to her past was something that was therapeutic for her or if she was just being friendly.

Then I received the cable from Frank regarding the fingerprints. I had spent considerable time convincing the Portland Police they should take the time to look them up.

The police found back in 1940 they had booked Ray Pearson twice for gambling involving some kind of an after hours situation I didn't really understand. So the prints were on record. I decided I'd better call Delores Lee and let them put the pressure on the police department to send out the prints, unless Dr. Fu wasn't ready for that yet. Delores was very cordial to me and didn't discuss my eyes, but she did say she was looking forward to seeing me again. She would deliver my message and let me know any results.

She called me back the next day and said, "Dr. Fu was taking steps to get the fingerprints sent to several appropriate designations."

Then she added, "There have been many important developments. I hope to be able to get back to you within three days."

———◆———

I was getting daily phone calls from Ruth and her Mother. I guessed their whole life was in upheaval and besides their going nuts I was also. Mabel and Ruth had me over for dinner several times and they were treating me like their family. One Friday night we went to a show and one night Ruth asked me to take her to the dance at the Uptown. I told her I usually didn't take anyone on a date to the Uptown, but would take her to some other dance.

It didn't take her but a second to say, "How about Jantzen Beach?"

Well, Kay Keyser was going to play there and in my second year in College in my speech class I was assigned doing a 15 minute show on the State Radio Station. I decided to make it a quiz show sort of like Kay Keyser's College of Musical Knowledge. Apparently my professor liked it and increased the time to 30 minutes. I had to write it, direct it and MC it. After about six sessions of that I told him I would flunk out of school if I continued. It was taking most of my time. Anyhow Kay Keyser would always be a favorite of mine."[21]

Bobbie was pretty steamed up when I told her I was taking Ruth to Jantzen Beach, but I was finding that I liked Ruth a lot more than Bobbie. Also if I went out regularly with Bobbie for any length of time and then discontinued I would be the subject of her wrath as Frank Beckman was. As to Elaine, Bobbie's cuddly Mother, I had scheduled one more two hour lunch with her. It turned out to be three hours and got pretty steamy, but I realized Elaine was just having fun and her description of fun fit any man's including mine.

Elaine was still mentioning the subject of going to the Beach with me for a weekend, but her friends Beach home had not been available so far. Elaine assured me it would be soon.

---

21 True story of my second year at the University of Oregon. What was the Professors name. Was it Hargis?

CHAPTER 48, Wasco is alive

I never knew if it was Sir Arthur Conan Doyle's belief that we got messages from outside this world, or if it was some premonition of my own, or merely a strong hope on my part because it meant so much to Ruth. Or was it that Ruth had an outside power that she had reached that was guiding so many people into the search for her Father?

To me the remarkable thing was that I was late for work, bumped into Bobbie in the hall of the Terminal Sales Building and that is how it all started.

Then great sadness would overtake me as I would recall how my brother on July 4th had gone to a Church Picnic with our neighbors and drowned. Of course the war loomed above all. So many millions killed, and for what? Except that man was hell bent to prove he was inhuman.

The fingerprints apparently kicked around wherever they were sent and were likely still sitting most places waiting for someone to follow up. Then one day I received a cable.

BARNEY LANGE. STOP. STONE IS NOT AS STONED AS HE WAS STOP. HE IS RECOVERING STOP. STILL NOT CERTAIN WHAT HE IS RECOVERING FROM. STOP.
SANDRA HAS BEEN WORKING OVERTIME STOP QUIZZING HIM ABOUT WASCO.
STOP. MAYBE WASCO WAS GOVERNMENT AGENT STOP COULD HE BE CIA STOP WAS HE INVESTIGATING SCHULE STOP. STILL NEED ANOTHER CONNECTING LINK. STOP FRANK BECKMAN.

I went ahead and called Delores Lee. She seemed very interested in Frank's cable and I wondered if maybe Frank was out making statements that Dr. Fu wasn't ready to have go out over the wire. I asked Delores if she had any news she cared to pass on to me.

She replied, "Barney, the way you put that I will say I would like to pass some news on to you, but for the moment I cannot."

I was fantasizing more and more about Delores and I wasn't going to take any chances and spoil my small contact with her. I said to myself, "If I ever had the opportunity to take her to a dance at Jantzen I would probably be so nervous I could not dance. Maybe I would have a heart attack, but I would be willing to take the chance."

As Delores and I rang off I could not help but lean back and try to be a little philosophical. I concluded with, "Life is having good and bad surprises come suddenly.."

———————

My first word came from Sergeant Fizz at the Portland Police Department. "Barney Lange, you old dogface, keep this up and they will give you a direct appointment to the Detective Staff in the Portland Police Department. Hold out for second Lieutenant and don't start as a private as you did in the Army."

I could tell Fizz was holding back. "So what happened, Sir"

> *"Don't use that Sir stuff on me. I'll tell you what I know. The word came through just an hour ago that the Missing Gambler, one Ray Pearson, was in fact a CIA agent, badly wounded in Mexico. He spent a year in a military hospital in Maryland. He was finally discharged. The CIA has someone out to lunch, or on vacation, or their system is broken down for they claim they don't even know where he is right now, but, give them time. They will track him down."*

I was not able to answer. My throat closed and I felt my chest jerk as I struggled to keep my composure. I knew somewhere in the heavens someone had looked over Wasco and Mabel and her kids were about to find out there was a Santa Claus. Finally I was able to speak. "Fizz, imagine what this is going to do for Mabel and her kids!"

Fizz paused for a second and sounded philosophical as he replied, "Yes, I understand. The few that find their missing relatives are lucky. People missing, killed, wounded. Family fights--what a mess. I'd quit, but someone has to do it."

I said, "You're a real pal for calling me, Fizz."

"Barney, this was an unofficial call. Don't mention I told you."

So Fizz and I rang off and I immediately called San Francisco. Delores was out and would not return until late afternoon. I didn't feel like leaving any details so I just asked them to tell Delores, "Great news, call when you have time. Barney Lange."

———◆———

The next question was if I should call Mabel at work. I knew I must. In fact I decided to drop everything and go to her office. Mabel had her own small private office and I was soon seated in it. I could see the apprehension in her face and I didn't beat around the bush. I gave it to her in as few words as possible. "Wasco was discharged from a Military Hospital, possibly in the past year and it appears he was with the CIA."

Mabel looked at me and burst into tears. Did she ever cry. I felt like going over to her and putting my arm around her, but maybe they were tears of happiness and she didn't need any arm around her. I sat there wondering. Finally she was able to stammer, "Barney Lange, I don't know how you ever did it, but you accomplished a miracle."

I looked at Mabel. "I may have got it started, but it took a lot of other people."

She then said, "Thank God, he turned out O.K. I always thought he was a nice guy, or I wouldn't have married him. Then darn it, I divorced him. So what do we do now?"

"Mabel, I think the Chinese are carrying the ball on this one. I have already called San Francisco, but Delores Lee was out. Likely they already know."

Mabel continued with, "I have spent a lot of daytime hours and a lot of sleepless nights wondering how we would approach him if he was found alive. It is going to be traumatic."

I replied, "Mabel, should I stay and talk to Ruth. Do you want her over here?"

"She works only four blocks from here. Let me call her."

Mabel just said, "Ruth dear. Important good news. Can you come over?"

Ruth arrived ten minutes later. When she arrived I repeated my story and Ruth outdid her Mother in crying. She became hysterical. Finally her Mother picked up the phone and made a call. It sounded like she was talking to a nurse. Then she looked at me. "Ruth and I are going to our Doctor's Office. I don't know who needs a sedative more, Ruth or I."

A few minutes later I was walking them to the Taxi. Before stepping inside they both gave me a big hug and a big kiss. Mabel said, "I'll call you this evening."

I drove to the cable office and sent Frank Beckman the following:

FRANK BECKMAN. STOP. FINGERPRINTS DID IT. STOP. RECEIVED CALL TODAY WASCO WAS CIA. STOP. BADLY INJURED STOP. NOW OUT OF HOSPITAL STOP. NO WORD WHERE HE IS. STOP. DELORES LEE WAS OUT STOP. TALKED TO MABEL AND RUTH. STOP. THEY ARE HYSTERICAL AND ON WAY TO MEDICAL OFFICE STOP. I THINK I WILL CABLE HOMER AND BILLY. STOP BARNEY LANGE.

I sent the following cable to Homer and Billy:

> *H & H BARNES. C/O SS MONTE. STOP. WASCO WAS CIA STOP. SERIOUSLY INJURED RELEASED FROM HOSPITAL. STOP. DON'T HAVE CURRENT ADDRESS STOP. WHAT PART OF THE WORLD ARE YOU IN. STOP BARNEY LANGE.*

24 hours later I received a cable from Homer and Billy.

> *SUPER SLEUTH BARNEY LANGE. STOP. FANTASTIC JOB. STOP. WE ALL STILL FLOATING AROUND STOP IN THIS PALACE OF LUXURY. STOP. BILLY ALMOST GOT MARRIED. STOP. I ALMOST GOT MARRIED STOP. HOW ABOUT YOU STOP. FINDING ANY GIRLS TO CHASE STOP. BE CAREFUL. STOP. HOMER AND BILLY BARNES. STOP. C/0 S.S. MONTE.*

I laughed as I thought this is what I should do. Get a job on a luxury liner and cruise the world, but I would have to be something like an Accountant and would be locked in an office during the day. However, each day had an evening and a night.

CHAPTER 49, Where is Wasco and how was he injured?

Mabel called me about 6 P.M. I had just gotten home and hadn't started fixing my usual dinner of mixed vegetables, fish, two oatmeal cookies and coffee. My Dad had attended health lectures in Portland as I was growing up. Yes, that's what they called them. Some well known nutritionist would give a free lecture Sunday evening and try to convince those in attendance that unless they attend his evening lectures for the next 4 or 5 evenings they would not be able to lead a healthy life and they would be dogged by all kinds of illnesses and death would come to them at a very early and untimely age.[22]

> *In those days if you attended health lectures you were not termed any kind of an evangelist, but rather some kind of a nut. The really strange part of it was my Dad didn't quite make it to age 96, and in good health, whereas one of his brothers, who teased him for his devotion to good nutrition made it to age 97.*

Mabel informed me, spurred on by her daughter Ruth, she wasn't going to wait around until the CIA decided if they wanted to take her into their confidence. She told her boss, "I will work in-between phone calls, or I will stay home for the next week."

Her boss, who besides supposedly running his business spent part of his time chasing Mabel didn't have a choice. Mabel had become so indispensable to his business, and his customers liked her better than they liked him, knew his hands were tied.

---

22 Just because I tried to put some humor in this does not mean it was not true. It was absolutely true.

Mabel tried burning up the wires to the CIA, but she finally succumbed and realized that the CIA were particularly effective in giving excuses and never answering a question. At first they even denied they had heard of Jerry Wasco. Then they tried saying, 'Well, if he was one of our employees he isn't now."

Several days later they claimed, "He's retired and we don't know where he is."

Mabel, not being anyone's fool replied, "You send him a pension don't you."

Well, that was kind of a word that everyone that was loafing expected to be their final reward for loafing and so that even brought a tiny bit of enthusiasm into their normal dull voices.

"Yes, that could be the case."

"Well, transfer me to your office that sends out the pension checks. My kids want to know where their Father is."

The dull voice seemed to not know where that department was. Finally they said, "That information is private. You may call back at a later date and see if the policy has been changed."

———◆———

By the end of the third day Mabel decided to turn to our Senators and Congressmen. She received both interest and curiosity. She reasoned, "They have to come up for election every two years and right now there is only one year before election."

Then she decided to keep hounding the Senators as well for they might have more clout. Mabel decided the pension issue might ring more bells, and certainly even the most stupid could more than likely grasp the significance a pension would have to a disabled employee.

Her angry persistence paid off. The CIA called, **"Jerry Wasco had retired to Covina, California where his address was N. Prospero Drive."**[23]

---

23 I picked this address because by the time I was 40 I was running 42 Sales Offices, across the United States in the Office Machines and Business Systems Field, out of offices in San Gabriel, across from the Old Mission, the oldest building in the Los Angeles area. I lived at N. Prospero Drive, Covina. Remington moved my job to #1 Park Avenue, but I declined to move. It was a difficult decision to make.

The telephone company didn't have any Jerry Wasco at that address and claimed they never did have. Mabel was really mad, but her firm had many business friends in Los Angeles area and she called one of them. He volunteered to drive out to Covina immediately. He called back within two hours. "There had been a Hank Weidler at that address, and he recently moved out without any forwarding address."

Frank had forwarded me the information from Melbourne General Hospital that apparently from the sinking in the Tasman Sea Wasco had lost his memory, which accounted for the fact he could not remember his family. Because he had been in the same hospital a year earlier he was told his name was Jerry Wasco,

But, what about now! Then Mabel laughed. Sure, Weidler was just a couple blocks North of Wasco Street in Portland. Had part of his memory returned. Or had the CIA suggested he change his name. So now Mabel went back to the CIA and talked to several people giving each of them a piece of her anger--a large portion to each.

Their excuse was a world wide organization. She snapped back with, "Were you the ones that were responsible for the disaster at Pearl Harbor. Was it your lack of intelligence that let the Japs bomb the hell out of our men and our ships and aircraft?"

That accusation let them know they were not dealing with a woman that would accept their stock excuses. Finally Mabel concluded, "Oh, to hell with you. I'm going back to my Senator and Congressman. I've got all your names down, and I think I have enough material to write a book. I think I'll call it the WIA-Without Intelligence Agency."

Mabel decided to send cables directly to Frank Beckman. After the third cable Frank asked Henry Lee if he could let Mabel know about the letters that Nurse Nell and Clancy O'Dell had received. Henry said, "Give me 48 more hours."

Frank asked Henry if they were checking on Hank Weidler and a possible ticket of some kind to Sydney or Melbourne. Henry said, "We have just started to do so."

I was biting my finger nails like everyone else. But, I had asked myself many times if I had been sick and was recovering and had been sailing the Pacific for nigh onto 8 years would I go back to Australia.

Well, considering Wasco, maybe now Weidler, could not remember any life in the U.S. I would return to Australia. And how would I go? Well, that was even easier. If I had sailed as a crew member, but now I was recovering, how about a nice long voyage on a Tramp Freighter. You ate with the officers and got a cabin. Big point was it was the cheapest way to go.

And no one would expect you to dress up and eat fancy meals. The cook on the freighter would give you a little special consideration. At least the food would be satisfactory. So I concluded if Wasco was headed for Australia he was on board a freighter.

As to a passport he didn't need one to get out of the U.S. The CIA likely had doctored his passport with the name Weidler and no immigration officers would take a second look at him.

So I called Delores Lee on this point and she said, 'Good chance this is correct. At least we must check. Only problem is no tramp freighter is going to post their passenger list anyplace. So it will be like looking for a needle in a Haystack."

I thought in the shipping news or whatever paper announced the sailings they would announce the ports they would sail from. The size and comfort of the ship would be a factor to Weidler, but he could go from San Francisco down the Coast to San Diego to sail from. That would not be of consequence to him. Maybe it would be easier to find him by going the other way. What about sending word to Frank and let them check into incoming freighters from the U.S. Well, Delores and I hashed that over and we decided, "Why not work from both ends."

I liked that and sent Frank Beckman the following wire.

FRANK BECKMAN. STOP. THINK WASCO IS NOW HANK WEIDLER. STOP. LIVED IN COVINA, CALIF. STOP. LEFT WITHOUT FORWARDING ADDRESS. STOP. CHECK INCOMING TRAMP FREIGHTERS. STOP. MAY BE ON ONE OF THEM. STOP. NO WAY WE CAN CHECK PASSENGER LISTS. STOP. APPARENTLY WEIDLER VERY SERIOUSLY INJURED. STOP. ON CIA PENSION. STOP. COULD BE THE

"W" THAT NEEDS PHYSICAL THERAPY. STOP. MABEL IS PLENTY MAD AT CIA. STOP. BELIEVE MABEL MIGHT FLY TO AUSTRALIA IF WASCO SHOWS UP. STOP. I WOULD SURE LIKE TO SPEND A MONTH IN AUSTRALIA. STOP. I'D GO TO CAMP SEYMOUR, MELBOURNE, SYDNEY, BRISBANE, ROCKHAMPTON, YEPPOON AND OH YES, BONDI AND MANLEY BEACH. STOP. CAN'T STOP A GUY FROM DREAMING. STOP. BARNEY LANGE.

Well, that cable cost me a few bucks, but I felt like celebrating. Hope I wasn't doing it too soon. Figure at the outset we'll know in 2 weeks. It took us 16 days to go from San Francisco to Sydney and we zigged and zagged every six miles so supposedly the Japanese subs could not get a direct bearing on us for a torpedo shot. Sounded scary to me.

Mabel went along with the idea of Weidler going on a freighter. Of course she went all out. That gal was a whiz. She contacted Pan-American in case Weidler had gone on a Clipper. She contacted all the Luxury Liners which prompted me to send Homer and Billy a cable.

H & B BARNES. C/O S.S. MONTE. BELIEVE WE HAVE LOCATED WASCO. STOP. WAS CIA AND INJURED BADLY STOP. LEFT MILITARY HOSPITAL AFTER LONG STAY STOP. LIVED COVINA, CALIF. STOP. LEFT NO FORWARDING ADDRESS STOP. POSSIBLY SENT WORD HE IS ARRIVING IN AUSTRALIA. STOP. THINKING HE MAY BE TRAVELING VIA TRAMP FREIGHTER STOP. IN CASE HE IS ON ONE OF YOUR SHIPS. STOP. BEWARE HE WAS A GAMBLER. STOP. MIGHT TAKE YOUR JOB AND ALL YOUR MONEY STOP. MAYBE EVEN YOUR GIRL FRIENDS. STOP. BARNEY LANGE.

I got two cables the next day. The first from Frank Beckman.

> *BARNEY LANGE. STOP. GREAT NEWS. STOP. WILL FOLLOW UP. STOP. SURE HOPE IT'S WASCO. STOP. WE'VE BEEN GOING NUTS HERE TOO. STOP. OUR BEST TO MABEL, RUTH AND KEVIN. STOP. MUST REALLY BE TOUGH ON THEM. STOP. TRUST IT WILL BE JOYFUL SOON. STOP. IF THEY COME OVER HITCH A RIDE WITH THEM. STOP. DON'T YOU HAVE A COLLEGE BUDDY THAT IS A PAN-AM PILOT. STOP MAYBE YOU CAN BE A STEWARD. STOP. FRANK BECKMAN.*

The second from Homer and Billy.

> *BARNEY LANGE. STOP. GREAT NEWS. STOP HAVING OUR SAN FRANCISCO OFFICE CALL YOU STOP. GIVE THEM MABEL'S PHONE NUMBER STOP. THEY WILL WORK WITH HER STOP. MIGHT HAVE SOME GOOD IDEAS STOP MAYBE WE WOULD NOT have THOUGHT OF STOP. HOMER AND BILLY.*

CHAPTER 50, Ray Pearson, alias Jerry Wasco, alias Hank Weidler is located.

It was like a three-ring circus. Maybe it was closer to Charles Lindbergh's flight when all kinds of flyers were trying to be the first to cross the Atlantic. Our Senators and Congressmen were into the act of harassing the CIA. Mabel was doing a brilliant job on that too.

Ring one was Frank Beckman in Australia who was trying to locate the ship we hoped Weidler was on. Ring two were the Chinese who weren't saying much, but more than likely had at least a dozen folks working on finding Wasco.

Ring three were all of us in Portland, with Mabel leading the way, trying to find out if Wasco was on his way to Australia and if he wasn't for heavens sake what was he doing? Maybe he was reclining on the deck of a ship sailing the blue Pacific, living a life we would all envy.

Meanwhile his ex-wife and non-ex kids were frantically trying to find him. Wasn't that the way life was. If we could eliminate wars and dishonesty we wouldn't need Armies and Navies and Police Departments. They could be raising fruits and vegetables and building houses for the needy. Well, I wasn't much of a philosopher for I was too busy trying to make a living, but for right now I was doing philosophizing.

Elaine suggested we spend another two hour lunch together and Bobbie was suggesting we go out to Jantzen. I was cutting down my coffee time at Riggs pharmacy to one cup.

It was truly fitting that Mabel, working like a combination of a beaver and a terrier, got the word. Bless her heart. With the help of a half dozen other women she had contacted with various shipping companies. One Hank Weidler was soaking up the sunshine and living the life of Reilly, on a tramp steamer with the almost incredible name of Doerffler. Apparently some bird with either that name or a weird sense of humor had inflicted that name on a ship. To make it even more weird there was an unrecognizable bird painted above the name.

> *The S.S. Doerffler was going directly to Melbourne and was*
> *expected to arrive in three more days.*

When Mabel heard that news she fainted. When Ruth got the news from her Mother she was not only shaken, but shook her Mother up even more. Kevin was called and it was lucky he had just finished his last final exam for spring term at Oregon State and he felt he passed the exam. He was just as shaken, but added, "Thanks, Dad, for holding out until I finished exams."

Well, I thought that was a pretty decent and intelligent thing for a 20 year old young man to say. I never would have thought there was an appropriate time for a Father to go into hiding, but I was just proven otherwise.

It only took Ruth someplace between one second and five seconds to tell her Mother, "Call Pan-American and order tickets for all of us and include Barney."

Mabel told me she held out for maybe even a whole five minutes before Ruth handed her the phone and said, 'Now, Mother, Dearest."

Mabel told me afterwards the first two words didn't do it, but the third word, 'Dearest,' did it."

I called my Boss and said I was leaving and that he could contact Frank Beckman for where I was staying. His response was threatening and while he did not come right out and say it he inferred I would be fired. I replied, "For a free trip to Australia in luxury and not on a troop transport this job comes in second place. I might even commit murder for such a trip."

I hoped he might think I was threatening him if he fired me. Next call I made was to Delores. Was she ever pleased. She said, "Chinese may not be too happy we did not find Wasco first, but if a nice lady found him first, well, we women don't mind that."

That evening I called a couple of my fellow salesmen and suggested they buy tickets and come along. That would give fuel to the fire that burned each morning with the delicious coffee at Riggs Pharmacy.

There were several people unhappy that I was leaving. The only ones that mattered to me were my parents. They did not seem to understand that the world had changed and people went everyplace with the drop of a hat. Running a close second to my parents was Bobbie Day.

She said in no uncertain language, "I see no reason for you to go!"

Then I replied with, 'I see no reason for me not to go. I spent five years in the bloody Army living a life you would never understand. Now I'm going back to the Pacific first class. A bed, sheets, deluxe meals. I'd be crazy to not go. I may never get another chance."

That seemed to non-plus her, but she came back with, "Don't say hello to Frank Beckman for me. I'm still mad at that dirty rat. At least you called me first before you left.."

Then I asked if her Mother was home and she was so I explained things to Elaine and she seemed to understand. Then she asked me, "Do you like Ruth real well?"

Well, I didn't want to reply directly to that and suddenly the answer came to me. "I don't really know her very well, but I suppose I will know her a lot better taking this trip with her."

Then Elaine came back with, "Wish Frank Beckman well for me and a happy marriage. I don't think Bobbie would have been too good for him. Bobbie has lived the good life all her life. She is going to need to marry someone with a very good job and some money."

Elaine rang off. I made all my necessary calls and now I needed to finalize my packing. Shirts, a couple of ties, shorts, an extra pair of good trousers and one knock about pair. I would wear a sport coat and take a jacket I could fold up. I took a hat and a crushable cap.

This was going to be a different trip than I took in March 1942. Then I was on a three hour alert to go overseas. 18 men in one room. 6 tiers of bunks, 3 high. My pack, helmet and rifle and a duffle bag would be my only possessions for almost 3 years. Three days after we left San Francisco I had walked to the stern of the ship and saw them burying a man at sea.

He had only lasted 3 days. How long would I last.[24]

---

24   . True story. I was one of about 10,000 men on that ship. It was it's maiden voyage as a troop ship.

This time I would go first class. Maybe that would stop some of my nightmares. Worry wart that I was I started worrying about how the meeting would go between Mabel and her kids and her ex-husband, but I was ecstatic that they would be reunited.

I paused and gave thanks. I had made it through the depths of the depression in Portland, then through the war and now I was going in style to see Australia again. It would be wonderful.

I might get rid of those War time nightmares after all. Then I kind of went into shock. How could I be so lucky. Maybe it was my deceased brother working with Sir Arthur Conan Doyle who had given the O.K. for all of this to happen.

CHAPTER 51, We Leave for Australia

As we assembled at the Portland Airport I could tell Mabel was wound up as tight as a human could and still be standing. She was excited for her kids, nervous to be face to face again with her ex-husband. Overpowering that was her anger with the CIA. "I asked them how they could claim to be an Intelligence Agency. I screamed at them I was so angry."

"I yelled at them, 'I found out where Weidler was and you didn't. Now you folks have passports ready for the four of us when we get to San Francisco. I want you to designate someone and have them call me back in an hour.'"

Then Mabel called our Senators and Congressmen and gave them the same message. We hoped the passports would be ready when we arrived in San Francisco.

The takeoff was fifteen minutes late. We took off on a DC-3 (in the Military it was called a C-47, and did not have plush seats. Just a bare interior with aluminum fold down shelves for troops of all varieties)[25]

Ruth and Kevin had never been on a plane before. I sat with Ruth and Mabel sat with Kevin. The flight was uneventful except they dropped

---

25 . My first trip in a C-47, was from a Jungle Grass Strip, at Doboduro to Port Moresby for food. We were only 10 minutes into the pass in those 13,000 foot mountains when the Radio Operator Stepped between us to look through the bubble at the top of the fuselage.

He calmly stated, "Say Goodbye Men. Jap Zero overhead. It's the end of the line." I looked at Sgt. Lew Garbutt who had assigned me as his helper, and I said, "Goodbye, Lew, we're at the wrong Place at the Wrong time." I expected the Jap Zero's machine gun bullets to tear me Apart in the next minute or two. But I survived. Now retired it still haunts me each day.

My Six University of Oregon Pals, who became Air Force Pilots. All died in Combat. I can still tell you the first and last names of each. I spent almost 3 years in the Pacific.

Often not expecting to last through the day, or through the night.

fairly fast as they reached San Francisco and my ears felt like I had been stabbed.

The Passports were there delivered by a CIA Agent who helped walk us through the paperwork. We took off an hour later. We got the usual, but new to us, welcome in Hawaii. Beautiful sun tanned girls in grass skirts greeting us with smiles and song and dance. Lei's were placed around our necks and we felt like celebrities. The Dining Room was a class act, the food was great and our rooms were top-notch. I was ready to live like this the rest of my life.

The next day we left early and it was a long flight. The Accommodations were nice, but not like Hawaii. The rest of the trip was uneventful, for which we were thankful. The long hours of flying over wide expanses of water found us thinking of Amelia Earhardt and her failure to make land. Factually there was no comparison for our ship was in constant radio contact and had pontoons in the event of a forced landing.

Every couple of hours we switched seats. Ruth would start the flight each day with me and then Kevin would take her place. Once each day Mabel would sit with me and Ruth and Kevin would sit together. Ruth's questions were getting more personal each day and she would not only hold my hand on takeoff and landings, but if any turbulence occurred she held my hand.

Overnight Kevin and I shared one room and Mabel and Ruth another. Mabel and Ruth would each give me a good night kiss and I noticed that each night the kisses were getting more friendly. We would take a walk after dinner and Ruth would try to get me away from Kevin and her Mother. One night she suggested we sit on the beach by ourselves while Mabel and Kevin went back to their rooms, but her Mother decided we would all sit on the beach and watch the waves and the stars. I kept comparing it with being in the South Pacific in an Infantry Division and I was grateful my life had changed so much.

Overriding our thoughts both night and day was Ray Pearson. As I sat with Ruth she talked continually about her Dad. Would he recognize them? If he didn't what would they do?

Pan-Am had promised us we would have overnight accommodations in Sydney and then the next morning we would head for Melbourne. I not only felt grateful for Mabel taking me along, but I made special effort continually to respect the mental trauma they were going through. My brother's untimely death made me feel close to Mabel and her kids.

When I sat with Mabel she explained the many reasons for my being their escort. First, Mabel didn't want to enter a strange country without a male that knew a little about the place. Next I knew Frank Beckman. Third, I had started this action and I must be there to see it brought to whatever conclusion it came to. I was their backup, and they might need me to counsel them. Mabel had taken my hand and said, "You give us confidence, Barney. We need you!"

I guess no one wants to feel the world is depending on them, so I was nervous. I tried not to let Mabel know it, but I knew she was too smart a lady not to read me like a book. That was something I kind of resented in one way. Why did women have to understand me so well? Finally one lady told me, "Barney, that's what we women look for. Someone we can read accurately so we don't get talked into something we shouldn't be doing."

I said, "That's what I need so I don't again marry someone that will be unfaithful to me."

The last leg found us getting into some rain squalls fed with some winds that created lots of turbulence. Then the Pilot announced, "We'll be coming out of the rain very soon and you'll see land-Beautiful Sydney, Australia."

We cheered and clapped and joyful was an understatement. We were almost there. I couldn't see my face, but hoped I looked as happy as Mabel, Ruth and Kevin did.

The pilot made a beautiful landing. If he was showing off to the Australians that was O.K. by us. At the Terminal I spotted Frank and he had a grin a mile wide. I had never seen the guy look so happy. Then I saw the beautiful lady by his side and I quit looking at Frank. Was this his wife to be? If so I would be grinning too.

It was and there was a Chinese man with them, one Henry Lee. Last we were introduced to a Dale Hill. He joked he was the friendly CIA man. Apparently Mabel's reputation had arrived in Sydney before she did and the CIA was taking no chances.

We didn't have to go through customs. Dale Hill remarked courtesy of the CIA. As we walked to our transportation I was so relieved to have arrived on time and in good condition I was a little giddy. I looked at Hill and said, "You remind me of basic training at Camp Roberts."

He seemed surprised, but said nothing. I figured the CIA was more adept at asking questions than answering them. I said, "Over hill, over dale, as you hit the dusty trail."

He smiled, "So you took basic in the Field Artillery."

He added, "We don't need to wait for the luggage. I'm having it delivered to the Hotel."

Before Dale started the engine in his car he turned around partially and said, "Wasco arrived in Melbourne two days ago. He had been wounded in a CIA raid in Mexico, that got bungled. He has spent months in a military hospital in Maryland. The good news none of his vital organs were touched. His rehabilitation is coming along fine. Physical Therapy, lifting light weights and so on is his treatment at this time. He will never fully recover, but he won't look and act like a cripple."

Then Dale turned his attention to his car and started the engine.

We all relaxed. We all said thanks while tears came to our eyes.

We didn't need to check into the Hotel. There were no bags yet so accompanied by the Bell Hop we went to our rooms. It was a deluxe suite with two bedrooms opening off a sitting room with a tiny kitchen, a two burner table top range and refrigerator. Dale said, "There are soft drinks in the refrigerator. Can I get you anything."

Mabel laughed, 'Not until I use the bathroom."

So the four of us on the flight took a few minutes to use the single bathroom. As we exited we checked the refrigerator and each made a choice. I looked at Dale, "No Sarsaparilla?"

He replied, "You know I never tried that stuff. The name always frightened me."

I asked, "What about Melbourne Bitter Ale?"

He answered, "That doesn't frighten me. If I drink too much I frighten others."

Finally the eight of us were seated more or less comfortably in the sitting room using the kitchen chairs and one from a bedroom. Mabel said, "Let's drink a toast of thanks and each of us give our own prayer of thanks."

Then Dale said, "As I said I met Wasco or Weidler two days ago as he got off his ship. Clancy and Nurse Nell accompanied me. Clancy had secured a place for him to stay, but I asked him to come to my Hotel first. There we explained to him that it appeared he was really Ray Pearson and his wife Mabel had divorced him, remarried and soon afterwards divorced again. That in addition to an ex-wife he had two children. Ruth about 22 and Kevin about 20.

I went on to say that Ruth worked in an office and had her own apartment and that Kevin just finished his second year at Oregon State and lived with his Mother in the summer.

Then Dale looked at us. Each of us wanted to scream, 'What did he say?"

Instead none of us said anything. Dale looked at us. "His reaction was of course one of complete surprise. He asked for more details and I sensed that way back in his mind he thought he had a family. I informed him we checked his fingerprints when he was booked for after hours gambling in Portland. They checked with our CIA prints. He laughed and said, 'Guess I did one thing right--I got fingerprinted in Portland. What a remarkable coincidence!'"

"I could tell he was overwhelmed. I continued with, 'Your daughter Ruth and son Kevin have been driving their Mother crazy and Mabel is driving the CIA crazy along with some aid from her local Senators and Congressman. You'd think it was Pearl Harbor all over again.'"

Dale continued, 'That pleased him no end as it would any man. He said, '"Ruth, Ruthy, I think I once knew a little girl by the name of Ruthy. And Kevin. Yes, I knew a Kevin once. Now you say my ex-wife's name is Mabel and my name was Ray Pearson. Sure I knew a Mabel Pearson, but right now I don't remember where.'"

Right then and there was when there suddenly were 7 people and one CIA agent in tears.

> *Then came the happiest surprise of all. "Yesterday I was able to talk him into coming to Sydney. I told him it was something he had to go over before taking any residence in Melbourne. Ray is one intelligent guy. He understood what had to be done. When would you like to see him. He's in the next room and that door to our left opens into his room."*

Ruth jumped up like I knew she would and ran to the door. Then she stopped. Afraid to open it and looked at Dale. He had anticipated this and had moved toward the door. He said, "Let me just dial his room and make certain he isn't asleep or using the bathroom."

Mabel was 100% unnerved. She said, "I don't want to be rude, but could just the four of us go to see him first. Perhaps it will be easier to judge his reaction with a smaller number and it will be easier on us as well."

Dale replied, "Makes good sense. I'll dial his room.'

Dale did and a few moments later he said, 'He said he's as ready as he ever will be."

Dale opened the door to the adjoining room and we stepped through.

CHAPTER 52, The Joyous Reunion--Santa Claus delivers.

All four of us looked at Ray. For certain he was a most handsome man. He was close to six feet tall. A lot of gray was in his hair. His eyes were ones that saw everything. His face was tanned. His body showed the ruggedness of a Sailor.

Mabel spoke first. "Hello Ray. You're looking great. Here is Ruth and Kevin and this is Barney Lange, a Soldier from the South Pacific who initiated the search for you."

Ruth looked at her Dad in bewilderment. She didn't know what to do. Her feet were stuck in their tracks, but she looked like she wanted to run to him.

Ray just stared and stared at Ruth. Finally something seemed to snap in him. He threw out his arms and said, "Ruthy, my little girl."

She was no longer stuck in her tracks. She threw herself into his arms and cried like a six year old child. He held her closely and the tears rolled down his eyes. Then he looked at Kevin and Mabel and took one arm away from Ruth and I could see he held it rather feebly. He said, "Kevin and Mabel."

They ran to him and I turned, opened the door, walked through it, shut the door behind me and looked at the four others we had left out. I said, "He either suddenly has remembered them or he likes them so much he's going to adopt them."

Then I explained what had happened. By the time I finished all our faces were tear stained. Katie was the first to respond. She was bawling as she said, "Barney and Frank. I'm so proud of you both." Then she looked at Henry, "I know you have been working on this night and day." Then she looked at Dale. "Looks like you did good too."

Then I lipped off again. I said, "It wasn't just a dusty trail. It was a rusty trail, but those Caissons kept rolling along."

Henry Lee looked at Frank and said, "Is he the kind of a guy that makes up Confucius stories and claims they are genuine?"

Frank laughed. "Deep down he's a good man, but at times it's hard to see."

Katie came over and sat by me. "If you don't have a girl friend I have a nice single girl friend I'd like you to meet."

I looked at Frank. 'I didn't have a girl friend until Frank left town. Then I've had to hold his girl friend's hand and she almost attacked me once."

Now it was Frank's turn to squirm. Katie laughed pleasantly, "Frank, my Darling, and soon husband to be. You never told me you left a girl friend behind."

Frank looked at me. "You mean you have been dating, Bobbie? You never told me that."

I hoped Frank wasn't going to get in trouble with Katie. I grew reckless and said, "Actually I'd like to marry someone like her Mother. Frank, I think you were dating the wrong lady."

Katie looked at me. "This sounds interesting. Barney, you and I need to have a talk."

I looked at Katie. "I'm just kidding Frank."

I didn't say I was kidding about Bobbie's Mother.

Katie replied, "I know Frank came over to see my sister Frances and not me. Now he left a girl in Portland. Frank, were you really in the Army, or were you really in the Navy and had a girl in every port?"

By now Frank was ready to retaliate. He looked at Katie and me and said, "If there was a girl in every port as beautiful and sweet as you are maybe I wouldn't of made it to Australia."

Henry Lee looked at me, "Maybe time you tell Confucius Story."

We were all happy, but very nervous. Then the door opened and Mabel moved slowly through it, then shutting it. "Oh, was I ever dumb when I divorced him. He sure is one ruggedly handsome man and he sounds like a great guy.'

Then she slapped her thigh, "And to make it worse I added 20 Pounds. Guess it's soup and salad for me from now on. When I get back to Portland I'll go to Johnny Johnson's near 28th and Broadway and get in ship shape again."

Then she added, "As long as I gave him the boot I figured he should spend a little more time with Ruth and Kevin."

Mabel came over and sat with us and said, "I have never seen Ruth and Kevin so happy. I lay claim to being able to finally judge a man. I'd say Ray is very happy right now."

Katie looked intense, but not at anyone in particular. "It's a natural instinct in all of us. We want someone to share our life with us be it marriage, kids or whatever."

Frank entered the conversation with, "I've been alone since my parents died and I know that feeling. You need someone to need you."

Katie moved back to where Frank was and put her arm around him and lay her head on his shoulder. "I really don't care how many girl friends you had before. If no one wanted you then I would be worried."

We continued to talk and Dale said, "The four of you and Ray must be very tired, and you know Henry and I haven't had much rest lately either. The Dining room is reserving a table in one alcove for us. We can eat and then get some rest. Any suggestions, Mabel?"

"I know I'm tired, and happy. Let's see what Ray and the kids want to do. I'm sure curious about Ray and the CIA and how he got injured."

Dale replied, "Give him a little time. I think Ruth and Kevin will lead him into that subject very soon."

———◆———

As we entered the dining room there was not the usual banter among us that you would expect at a big time celebration. In one sense it was like going to a joyous funeral. Maybe that was what it was. In these few short hours we had been burying the past miserable eight years of sorrow. Maybe this dinner was the official wake for that occasion.

The table was round and a perfect fit for eight. Ruth and Kevin sat on either side of their Dad. I sat next to Ruth and Mabel next to Kevin. Frank sat next to me, Katie next to him and Dale sat next to Mabel. That left Henry next to Dale and Katie.

They began serving us food as soon as we sat down. Dale said, "Henry and I worked out a combination Chinese-Australian menu. Some Chinese food. Then I saw the lamb chops. I made a smart alec remark, "We got Aussie bully beef in the jungle. That's ten grades below lamb."

For the three of them it was their first restaurant meal in Australia. .

For me, small time operator that I was, I had five days in Sydney half dozen years ago, two overnight passes to Melbourne. Oh yes, I once got to fly to Townsville for supplies, from Finchhaven, New Guinea and stayed overnight in Townsville.

Ruth was nuzzling her Dad like a girl should after his absence of eight years. If he had any question of his kids missing him they were dispelled. He was properly apologetic and was very nervous. Finally he said, "I guess I'm really on the spot. Why did I leave Portland? Did I confide that with anyone? Can anyone help me on that?"

I had that meeting with Mabel, Ruth and Kevin and Ah Wing and Delores. However, I held back and finally Kevin stepped to bat, "Ah Wing said you owed some gambling debts and you were threatened with death if you didn't participate in something. It must have been terrible!"

Ruth added, "We know you had to leave. If you had been caught you would have been put in Jail and embarrassed us all. This way you turned out to be a big hero. You did the right thing."

I wanted to hug both of those kids for being so tactful. Their Dad looked at them both and said, "Thank you for your forgiveness, but I wasn't a hero. The heroes are those that gave their lives in World War II and in other wars and other just causes. I only worked on Dutch ships hauling men and supplies. Sometimes under combat conditions."

Ray spoke very slowly, "I seem to be recalling a few things. I seemed to know a lot about cards, but don't remember right now being seriously involved in gambling. So I messed up your lives and skipped town. What a terrible guy I turned out to be."

"Toward the end of the War I was recruited by the CIA with the idea that many Nazi's would try to relocate. Particularly merchant seamen and men on German Military vessels and Merchant Mariners. I was to observe, feed information and obey instructions. It turned out that many had gone to Mexico and South America."

"Escaping Nazi's was not the main thing the Allies were worried about. They felt the Nazi's would set up powerful organizations all over the world and once again try to dominate. I could understand that and knew I had an obligation to serve America and it's Allies."

"Two years ago I was to team with a German by the name of Schule who was a CIA agent. I told my superior I did not trust Schule and tried to get them to take on Bill Stone, whom I trusted implicitly. Schule got the nod because he spoke German well. We went to South America for a short period of time and then received a call we were to immediately go to Mexico. There were Nazi's all over the place."

"I would plan a raid and when we got there the Nazi's were gone. Obviously they had been tipped off. By whom? Even the American movie industry, including one prominent Australian Actor, were prominent in Mexican Nazi circles.[26]

I became certain it was Schule. Either he was a double agent or his Nazi sympathies were so strong he was just doing it on his own. I reported my suspicions, but to no avail. Then I hit upon my own plan. I told him the raid was going to take place at 5 P.M. on one day and then sprung the raid one day early."

"When we broke down the door we were shocked to find Schule having a meeting with prominent ex-Nazi Naval Officers. Schule was able to duck out, but seconds later fire power came from another room. Schule could have been part of that firepower. The Nazi's all escaped and I was severely injured. At one time my left arm was scheduled to be amputated."

"Schule claimed he had left to get back-up. A couple days later Schule disappeared. He was removed as an Agent and the CIA claimed they did not have the manpower to do an investigation. They made only a half-hearted attempt to find him."

Mabel came in with, "The CIA didn't even know where you were."

Ray laughed, "I'm not surprised. Anyhow Schule is still out there someplace. I am certain he has changed his name. Maybe he is back in Germany."

Then Ray looked at Henry, "The Chinese are important agents for the CIA. They didn't take kindly to his double-cross. Maybe they took him out."

With that comment Dale Hill said, "There is a reward for catching Schule, dead or alive. You know we haven't got the time or money to prosecute all these guys."

Henry Lee looked at Dale, "How much is the reward?"

---

26   Read the Biography of Errol Flynn.

"At least $100,000."

Henry Lee seemed to smile. Then he said, "You pay in cash, check or American Express? You prefer him dead or alive?"

Up until those last few words Dale had been writing on a piece of paper. Now he looked at Henry. "Henry, we'll talk on that when I drive you back to your Restaurant."

Then Dale handed the note to Mabel. It read.

> *OREGON SENATORS AND CONGRESSMEN. STOP. MABEL, RUTH AND KEVIN RE-UNITED WITH WEIDLER. STOP. VERY SATISFIED WITH ALL ARRANGEMENTS. STOP. MABEL PEARSON JENSEN, RUTH AND KEVIN.*

Mabel looked at Dale and laughed. "I guess this would take the CIA off the hook. Once you guys get cranked up you do good."

Dale smiled, 'For your signature we will cover your expenses here for another full week and will offer you and Ray free Military transportation back to Portland if you desire. This is not to pressure you. If you have any other complaints let me know in the next couple of days."

Mabel took out her pen and signed it with a flourish. Dale said, 'Thank you so much!"

———◆———

The next day Ray went to visit his old pal Bill Stone who was almost recovered. Stone had finally asked Sandra to marry him and she immediately accepted. Stone suggested Ray take the Yacht for a week's trip with Mabel, Ruth and Kevin and cruise the nearby islands..

Ray and his newly re-united family decided to take a rail tour of Australia in short hops always staying over night in Hotels. It was obvious Ray and Mabel still had a mutual charm for each other. I thought that was wonderful. So did Katie and Frank Beckman.

As for me Katie introduced me to a girl friend of hers, but I wanted to travel at my own pace to retrace some old steps of my past. Entertaining a female would be too complicated so I only had a couple of dates with Katie's friend. She was charming, however!

I asked over hill, over dale, legally known as Dale Hill, CIA, to write my boss a letter saying I was on important business and he hoped he would not fire me. Dale obliged.

Henry Lee threatened me with death before he confided in me, rather proudly I might add, that one Wilhelm Schule, alias Adolph Schultz was found dead of starvation in a former Monkey cage in an abandoned house. I asked him if the Chinese had used the cage to send out a message to not Monkey around with them? Henry just smiled.

I did ask Henry who got the reward money and he said the Chinese Benevolent Society. I didn't ask any more questions. I knew if I did I wouldn't get any more answers.

I timed my tour with a return to coincide with the departure of Ray, Mabel, Ruth and Kevin. I found out Frank was dickering to buy a two-bit equipment rental shop in the outskirts of Sydney and that Bill Stone and Clancy O'Dell wanted to be partners with him.

So Frank and Katie decided to get married right away and take a short honeymoon. I was wanted as best man, and her sister Frances would be Matron of Honor.

Ray had actually become anxious to return to Portland. Winter was just starting in Australia and Summer was almost there in Portland, Oregon so the timing was excellent.

Ruth would get rid of her room mate and her Dad and Kevin would live with her for the summer. Mabel didn't live but five blocks away and I could tell she had already started to slim down and there was a really neat sparkle in her eyes. I kept looking, but she didn't wink or wrinkle her lips at ex-husband Ray. I was doing a lot of thinking about Elaine

Dale Hill claimed I was not a member of the family so I could not fly on Military Transportation back to Portland. By a rare coincidence Homer and Billy's ship the S.S. Monte would be arriving in Sydney soon and was going directly back to the United States except for stops at fantastic places like Tahiti and Hawaii.

I could go back with them on the basis that I would work in Accounting in the Purser's Office daily for 4 hours and another 4 hours each evening dancing with the older unattached ladies on the cruise.

I knew none of them could be like Elaine--but then I thought maybe one might. It sure was an intriguing thought. A gorgeous older lady that wasn't living with a daughter like Bobbie. Maybe I wasn't meant to be a Salesman of Business Systems.

So I accepted eagerly. Ray and his family took off, and I ended up being an usher at the wedding of Bill Stone and Sandra Martin. You never saw a happier gal in your life than Sandra. Well, now then, Katie was just as happy. Well, Ruth was something else! Without question Ruth really was the happiest of all.

Yes, for pure joy---Ruth led the world!

Thank you, dear readers. May your years ahead be joyous too!

PS. As to what happened to me. I left Standard Register the next year in August. I went to work for a firm in the office machines field at SW 14th and Taylor Less than ten years later I headed all their offices in the United States. 42 Sales Offices from New York to Los Angeles and I lived at N. Prospero Dr. Covina, Calif.. (as per footnote Page 244)[27]

---

27 Standard Register is still a large firm and they along with Ping sponsor the big Ladies Golf Tournament. Jantzen Knitting Mills is still in the same location on Sandy Boulevard. Hyster and Willamette Iron and Steel moved. Johnny Johnson is still near 28th, but has another name. Piggly-Wiggly at the corner of 28th and Broadway is gone. Across the street lived B.P. John, the other Furniture Tycoon and his factory on S.W. Macadam is now an upscale area called. Johns Landing. Doernbecker Furniture, the big one, just four blocks from my house on Wasco Street, left $50,000 to establish a crippled children's hospital. Today that hospital is a mammoth part of the U of Oregon Medical Center. (OHSU)

Albina Fuel is still at the corner of 33rd & Broadway. Yaw's, the Tik-Tok, Mundens, Honey Dew Ice Cream and the big shoe are gone, but not forgotten. Helen Bernard's Cakes & Cookies is still there. Mosler's Bakery was taken out by the Urban Renewal in Southwest Downtown Portland. If I could bring one little store back it would be Mosler's. That Pumpernickel bread--please, could I have just one more slice. Please!

15046267R00150

Made in the USA
Charleston, SC
14 October 2012